ALMOST PARADISE

Almost Paradise

Bryan Timothy Mitchell

DESCENDANT
PUBLISHING

Descendant Publishing, LLC
PO Box 29
Byron Center, MI 49315

Book Cover by Damonza
Edited By Dawn Carter
Map Illustration by Chaim Holtjer

Library of Congress Control Number: 2023949880
ISBN 979-8-9869878-9-7 (Paperback)
ISBN 978-1-7344584-7-3 (Hardcover)
ISBN 979-8-9869878-5-9 (Ebook)

Printed in the United States of America
First Edition October 2023

10 9 8 7 6 5 4 3 2 1

DESCENDANT
PUBLISHING

www.descendantpublishing.com

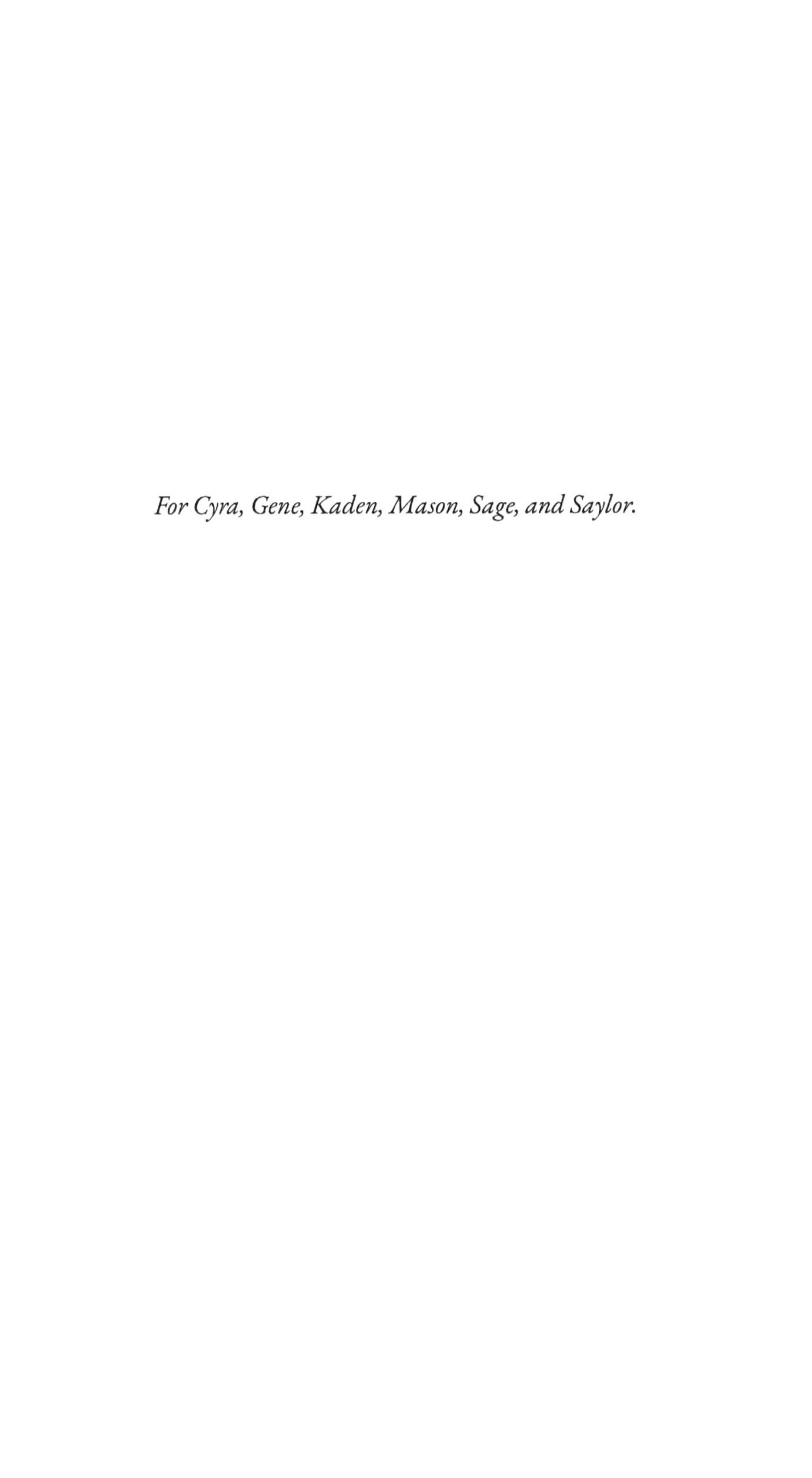

For Cyra, Gene, Kaden, Mason, Sage, and Saylor.

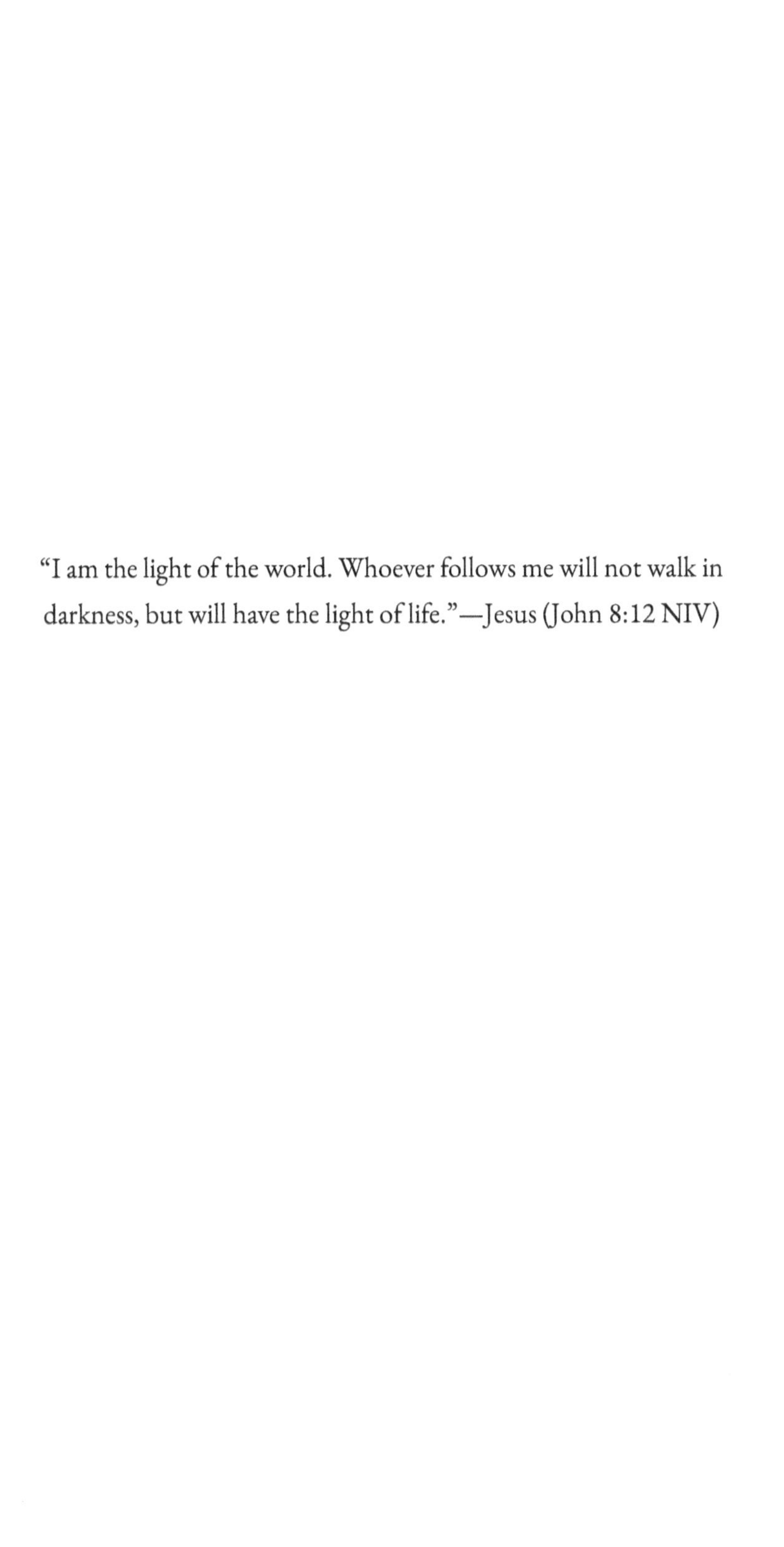

"I am the light of the world. Whoever follows me will not walk in darkness, but will have the light of life."—Jesus (John 8:12 NIV)

CONTENTS

Grand Father Mountain
Boone
NORTH CAROLINA
Blue Ridge mountains
Lust
Limgo
SOUTH CAROLINA
Eastman
Georgia

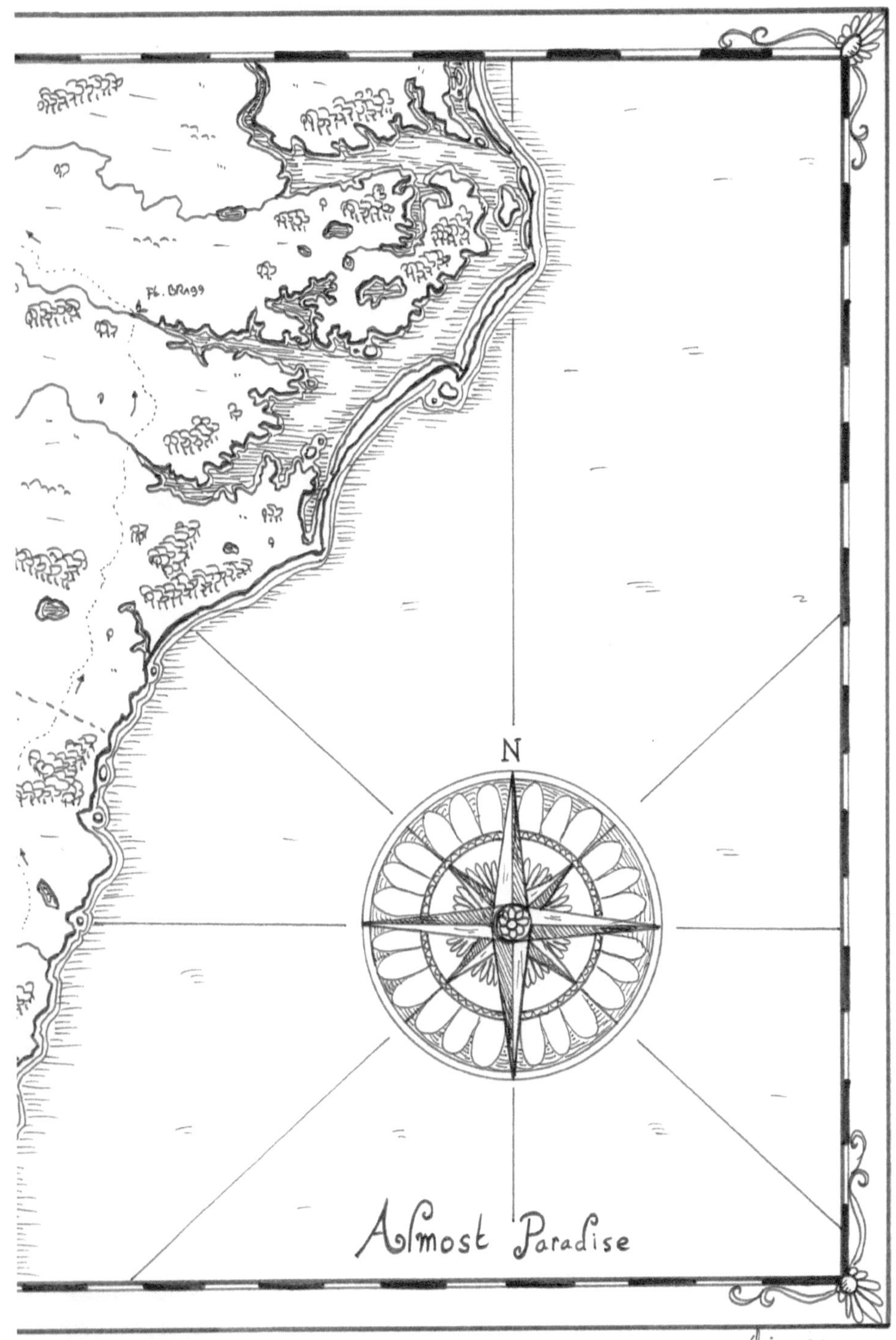

Ft. Bragg
N
Almost Paradise

PROLOGUE

YESTERDAY AND TOMORROW

"Why didn't you help sooner?" Beau asked, standing on the outskirts of Grayton. The rain drenched him and Chance. The stench wasn't as thick as it was on the mountain, but it still tainted every inhalation.

It was a fair question. Beau didn't know that Chance had protected him, Daniel, and Charles as they traveled through the nine levels of Hell.

"Well, now." Chance pushed his hat up higher on his head. "What makes you think I didn't?" He turned from Beau and started toward the mountain, where demons were trying to burrow their way back to Earth. "Don't miss the bus!"

For whatever reason, most people passed on the opportunity to leave this place for Heaven, but Chance doubted Beau would, considering he was the only shadow-man in history to leave the spirit world and enter Hell. Eternal suffering was far worse than living in the shadows sending souls on to Paradise or damnation, but Beau didn't do it for himself; he wanted to save Daniel, who found his keystone—a small special stone that sent the dead to where they were more inclined—to God, or unfortunately, to the Devil.

Chance wished the people here in Grayton were more like Beau and would take a leap of faith. Charles did, but not in a good way. Charles had tricked Daniel, who was and (thankfully) is still alive, into going so deep into Hell that he couldn't turn around and walk out; even made him think the angel who came to save him was there to kill him. But his gambit paid off in the end. Daniel made it home. Beau was heading to Heaven. And Charles had gone up to the Spirit world with one of Satan's generals to do something other than harvest dead souls or suffer hellfire.

Chance slowed his pace, thinking about Charles. Something about Charles's time with Daniel and Beau had changed him. Yesterday, Charles thought he was a demon who hated every soul that entered Hell but discovered he was actually a man who hated himself. Still, even after coming to terms with that, he gave his heart to Satan. Pretty doggone foolish, but maybe Charles thought he had no choice in the matter. Maybe he thought Satan would give him more power. Little did he know, only God could grant such power. He did so for Daniel, who would soon discover the power of spiritual discernment.

God didn't do this willy-nilly, of course. Daniel needed this gift because Satan wasn't finished with him. Demons were already set for an attack, but as soon as they did, Daniel's eyes would be opened to the spirit world. With Satan having a number of his forces focused on burrowing their way out of Hell back to Earth, they'd be hard pressed to cause any harm to Daniel, especially if he went home to his parents, which was his plan.

But Chance was still troubled. What if Satan succeeded? Maybe his revenge on Daniel was a ploy to take their attention away from the escape plan. Chance shrugged off the disturbing thoughts because God was in charge. Always.

Chapter One

In the Plains of Limbo

Chance lumbered from Grayton toward the desert. The fiery peaks of the Purging Mountains tore through smoke that drifted into the cracks of the stone sky. Cold night air cut through the unforgiving plains of Limbo, healing the wounds of the damned with the finesse of an angry butcher. If not for the stench of sulfur, Chance would've appreciated the headlong winds that pressed against his face, for he was not damned, but the lead missionary in Hell.

It was from those mountains that Daniel had fallen into Hell. The avalanche that had followed him down scarred the surface. Boulders riddled the valley and had smothered the fires at the foot of the mountain, emboldening those confined in this sad world.

Demons and damned souls had cut a hole wide enough for legions from Satan's army to march into the side of the mountain, ten columns wide. The sound of iron chipping at rock echoed from deep within the cave. Faint firelight shimmered from the entrance, warding off the cold and allowing them to continue cutting through the night, trying to dig their way out.

Off to the right, his small team of missionaries sat around a fire. They didn't need to worry about spies, at least at night. Those confined to Hell feared the cold. Although it could heal them, it was a painful process that would freeze them in place until daybreak.

Chance sighed at the sight of his teammates' faces. This was the closest thing to home any of them had in Hell. Heaven seemed so far away down here. So much so that most missionaries stayed for no more than a year and rarely ever returned. Chance was the exception. He had remained here for one-hundred and twenty-seven years and would keep at it until his brother, Harrison, got on the bus bound for Heaven.

Miguel spotted Chance and came to his feet. Jethro and Marlin turned and stood with him. Their eyes gleamed with fear. Such looks were common among the damned, but seeing it in the expressions of his fellow angels unnerved Chance.

Having entered Hell eleven months ago, they had worked as faithfully as any other team who volunteered for this sad work and were due to leave at any time. They were weary and oftentimes complained. While complaints were common at their stage, Chance couldn't recall any other team who complained nearly as much as this one. Every night, they'd shared their burdens and prayed for strength. Sometimes it helped. They'd feel resolved and ready to carry on, but eventually, it would wane. With their extraction imminent, their worries would soon be over. *So why the fear?*

Miguel's voice trembled. "You all right, boss?" His eyes darted about the darkened plain.

Chance hadn't been all right in a long time but never said so. He patted Miguel on the shoulder and nodded to Jethro and Marlin. "Good to see y'all. All is well." He lunged past Miguel and sat on an unoccupied log. His crew continued to stare out into the darkness. "Yesterday's business is done. Anything new on the excavation?"

"Nothing we didn't already know, but Azrael stopped by moments ago." Miguel rubbed the back of his neck. "He told us we're to head home at first light."

"Really now?" Chance clapped his hands and chuckled. "Why so glum, then? Within hours, you boys will be in Paradise." Although Chance wouldn't be leaving with them, he looked forward to meeting his new team. Whoever it was, he hoped they'd have stronger spirits than these three.

Jethro glanced at Chance and then back at the fire. "Why do you always ask for extensions? This mission is hopeless. We haven't helped anybody."

Beside him, Marlin gazed overhead at the sky of stone. It glowed a deep purple, signaling the dawn of another day in Hell.

"We help more than you think, Jethro," Chance adjusted his hat, "and don't worry 'bout me, fellas. The Good Lord knows I ain't finished yet. If I overstay my welcome, He'll pull me out."

"You didn't answer his question." Miguel glared at Chance. "Why? There's no good reason for you to stay."

They sounded sour about his staying. *Were they thinking that he'd turn against God?* Chance kept his secrets for many reasons. One was to protect them. The other was to protect his little brother. He rested his elbows on his knees and intertwined his fingers. "I have my reasons for stayin'. As far as why—well, that's between God and me alone." He bowed his head and listened to the fire. It provided little comfort under the unwarranted glares of his brothers. "For goodness' sake, take a seat already. You're making me nervous."

The three men sat. Sad silence lingered about them as the sky slowly reddened. A thin wisp of warm air brushed over Chance's back. The sky groaned and pieces of rock fell from its deep, black cracks.

Miguel spoke first. "I'm gonna miss you."

Chance's three comrades were hunched with forlorn faces. A strange cloud of shame seemed to linger over them. Chance didn't want that.

Not on the day they were to return to Heaven. "You've all done well with your time here. This work isn't for everybody, and each of you has shown your worth by staying faithful to the cause. Don't be upset. Stop worryin' about me. If you want to worry, worry for those who have fallen here."

"There's something else." Jethro poked a stick at the fire. His beard lined his round face. He seemed reluctant to speak. "You have to give up your hat."

"What?" Chance pushed his hat down onto his head and righted his posture. "Azrael told you this?"

"He did." Miguel's eyes met Chance's. Tears leaked down his cheeks. "He said you rely on it too much."

"Goodness." Chance rubbed his eyes. He couldn't believe what he was hearing. Azrael hadn't mentioned this, and they had been working together not even an hour ago. It would take away his ability to travel at the speed of light. He'd be less elusive; therefore, easier to catch. "That doesn't make sense. Are you sure?"

"It's true." Marlin barely moved. His silvery eyes glowed in the reddish light.

Chance remained steady, but his insides squirmed. How could this be part of God's plan? But if it was God's will, then he would comply. "Things change every day, friends." He removed his hat and sent a hand through his long black curls. "I've grown too accustomed to this ol' thing anyhow. Might be the reason why the Lord wants me to part with it. I won't be the same without it, though." Chance came to his feet and tossed it over the fire to Marlin. "You boys get on to the bus stop. I'll miss you and will pray for you and your kin until the last days."

No one moved. They focused on the ground, wrapping their arms around their bellies and leaning over as if they were trying to smother a rising sickness. A heavy weight seemed to descend over Chance, but he refused to sit. His friends acted strangely. The sound of footsteps pressing and grinding into the harsh desert sand approached from behind.

"What is this?" Chance asked.

"You know very well what this is," a voice growled.

Chance knew this voice. It belonged to a powerful demon called Azazel.

A crowd of demons emerged from behind him and wrapped around the perimeter of their small camp. Their leathery red skin and small black horns told Chance that they had come from the first chamber of Violence. Azazel edged up next to Marlin. The seven-foot demon drew smoke from a cigar, igniting the tip. He nudged the side of Marlin's head. "Give it here, Twig."

Marlin couldn't lift his gaze but handed Chance's hat to the ancient demon, who took it and shoved it into the chest of a demon beside him. "Get to work." The demon darted toward the cave with it in hand. *He'll have a hard time wearing it with those horns*, Chance thought.

Chance closed his eyes and inhaled through his nose. Never did he expect his team to betray him, to betray God, but what was done was done. He would not plead for mercy. It wouldn't be granted even if he did.

"What next?" Chance asked. "My boots?"

Azazel's smile revealed rotted teeth filed to fangs. Veins on his forehead formed a "V" that glowed hot pink. He pulled a sawed-off shotgun from his belt and fired a shot at Chance's chest. The force of the blast sent him off his feet, and he smacked past the demons behind him and hit the ground. Although he couldn't die, it hurt worse than anything he'd felt in a long time.

"My hanky then?" he asked, brushing metallic debris off his chest.

"You thought you could take your baby brother from Lust without consequence." Azazel puffed on his cigar. "Now *you* can drift in those fly-infested winds in his place. Who knows? Maybe one day you'll have a family reunion." He pointed at the traitors. "You three, go and find Harrison Barnes. He's somewhere in Grayton. Bring him here. Do that, and you'll get what was promised."

Chance's team got up slowly, avoiding his gaze. Red taloned feet crunched and scraped along the ground as demons surrounded him. They forced him to a prone position and bound his hands behind his back. He called after his friends as they moped their way toward the city of Grayton to search for his brother. "Hold on to what you're feeling now, fellas. That's the only thing that's gonna keep you tethered to God. We're here because we believe in redemption. Like you, I've been tempted. I know it's hard to resist. Never lose hope, gentlemen."

A demon tied a rag around Chance's mouth and cinched it tight behind his head.

Miguel turned and said, "You may see us as traitors, but you betrayed God when you pulled your brother out of Lust. You were never told to do that." Marlin took him by the shoulder and they walked on.

Chance wasn't sure how they knew this, but it was true. He did pull his brother out of Lust without orders. That was more than a hundred years ago. He didn't expect them to understand. They did the bare minimum, while he tried to save everybody he could. As far as his hardheaded brother was concerned, he had no regrets. He'd steal him from Lust a thousand more times if necessary.

Azazel turned to another demon. "I want you to take a party over to the bus stop in town. No one is to leave again. If they want out, they need to march their tails down here and earn it like the rest of us." He turned to Chance. "Time for you to go."

Demons pulled him to his feet. Static prickled at his skin. A buzzing noise crackled overhead. Long bolts of lightning shot down. Before he could blink, he was flying across a tan sky in a whirl of dust, bodies, and flies.

Chapter Two

A Whole New World

Charles stood beside a dumpster at the edge of a packed parking lot. The stench of garbage mingled with a breeze that whirled from every direction. Music struggled to escape the brick walls of a tavern that sat in the far-left corner of a small shopping center. Occasional hoots and bursts of laughter pierced through the muffled noise.

The world had changed a lot since the first time he'd died. His years spent in Hell had tripled his years alive. The stars were all that remained of the world he once knew, and they still dazzled him.

Across the street atop a three-story building, the Nothingness King spoke with the overseers, who were in charge of all earthly demons in and around the surrounding area. The Nothingness King had told Charles to stand here like some imbecile, and he had to comply, since Satan had placed him under the direction of this so-called king.

From where he stood, he saw the overseers issuing him shifty sideways glares. Their eyes were black with malice. Charles tipped his bowler hat and smiled with rotten delight. He basked in their anger. The demons who roamed the land of the living thought too highly of themselves and squandered the privileges afforded them out of fear or sloth.

Five young ladies in low-cut minidresses walked by, giggling their way to the nightclub. They peeked over their shoulders at a group of vociferous men with puffed out chests and well-groomed beards. The scent of perfume nearly pulled him along in their wake. Their flaunting movements, devious smiles, and leering eyes filled him with a wanting he had never experienced before. He never knew what it was to love a woman or be loved by a woman other than his grandmother. After she had died, he was shipped off to an orphanage where he learned how to steal and cheat. Love and tenderness weren't a part of the curriculum that led to his imprisonment and eventual death.

Charles pulled his pocket watch from his vest and depressed the crown. It behaved differently since leaving Hell. The hands moved counterclockwise at a rapid pace. The gears worked so hard that the watch vibrated. Why it did this was a mystery to him. Potentially, it acted this way because it was in a world beyond its making. Whatever the case, it fascinated him. He snapped it shut and rolled it in his fingers. Nice and smooth. Its weight felt right.

Another flurry of young women strutted past Charles and small, shadowy demons scampered after them like an army of two-legged hairless Chihuahuas. Considering the nonchalant behavior of the women, these creatures were invisible to them, just as he was. They snarled and bared their teeth at each other, yipping along the way. One noticed Charles watching them and sniffed at his polished shoes.

"Go sniff elsewhere, you ugly little heathen." Charles nudged it away with his foot.

It hissed, as did its companions. They seemed ready to attack, but a wail of laughter from the club drew their attention. The women were gone. The door to the club closed. Squeaking and squealing, the evil little critters rushed to the tavern and leaped through the solid door as if it were fog.

Charles adjusted his bowler hat and tightened his necktie. Maybe he could do the same thing. He eyed an empty beer bottle that lay next to the garbage bin and kicked at it. His foot passed right through the glass.

A slight thickness crawled around his foot when he did it, as if he had dipped his toes into stagnant water. He planted his hands on his hips and eyed the garbage bin.

"I wonder…" he said. Cautiously, he leaned his head closer to the stinking bin. He felt rather silly about it, but pressed on until his head passed through the grimy metal wall, where he experienced pure darkness and an even thicker stench that rivaled what he had endured in Hell. The pressure around his neck was quite severe. He doubted he'd need to visit a doctor's office for a checkup, though, considering he was dead, having died several times.

"How interesting." His voice reverberated. The music from the tavern sounded more muddled in this stinking chamber. He came upright, and the world opened up to him again. Naturally, the air was fresher and cooler.

He was so proud of himself, having learned so much in such a short amount of time on Earth. Although he could perceive things in the living world, he couldn't interact with any of it. In a way, it was torture. He could look, but touching was out of the question. It did hurt him slightly. He had secretly hoped for medium-rare steak, mashed potatoes with gravy, and a nightcap, but nooooo—that hope had disappeared, much like the ugly little demons through the door.

"Still, better than Limbo," he muttered.

He peered down at his pocket watch. His reflection looked cartoonish on its golden surface. A long nose stretched down his long yet oddly wide face. His green eyes, however, still looked like his mother's. He'd expected them to revert back to that of a reptile's when he had left Daniel behind with Satan. It wasn't an issue though, since the Nothingness King didn't seem troubled by it; however, he knew better than anyone that he had been forever changed by his journey through Hell. Maybe not for the better, but yesterday, he was in Limbo harvesting dead souls. Today, he stood beside a garbage bin, experiencing the world he had once called his own.

Charles looked at the rooftop. *What is the holdup?* Existing in the spirit world outside of Hell would grant him amenities he'd never dreamed of, but the Nothingness King stated he must prove his worth or be sent back to Hell without demonic privileges. Seemed simple enough until the Nothingness King said that Charles's first task would be to destroy Daniel's life. A day ago, such a task would've been miniscule, but much had changed since yesterday. Charles wasn't sure he could do it and was already thinking of ways to get around it.

The Nothingness King shouted, "Heartless Charles!"

Charles's feet came off the ground. Kicking and waving, he lost control of his body and soared higher into the sky, over the road, and onto the rooftop. He stumbled and fell forward. The overseers snickered. It took him far longer than he wished to gather his wits, retrieve his hat, and return to his feet. He righted his jacket and pretended it never happened.

"Yes, sir." Charles bowed.

The Nothingness King was a short, shriveled old man with a stringy gray mullet. His skinny frame reminded Charles of the poor souls who soared in the winds of Lust. He wore a ridiculous magician's outfit. A black cape with red lining flapped behind him, but what annoyed Charles most about this *king's* lack of fashion was his top hat and cane, which he waved around like an arrhythmic, talentless conductor of music. With a perpetual scowl, he spoke through his long, rotted teeth. "Each night, you are to report here to the overseers."

Charles looked at the three demons. Two were older women who looked like twins. They dressed like the younger ones across the street but were far less enticing. They had leathery skin and bulging bellies that rippled as if they had swallowed a bucketful of agitated eels. Their frizzy hair was a mix of black and white. Beside them, the third demon was a man who wore overalls and black leather boots. Skinny and disheveled, he had a rough face, receding hairline, and a red beard. He didn't portray much intelligence, but with glaring eyes, bared teeth, and trembling hands, he looked as if he could explode on command.

Charles tightened his necktie and turned to the Nothingness King. "Is there a particular time I should arrive, your majesty?"

The little man jabbed his cane at him. "Watch your tone."

He must've picked up on Charles's derisive feelings toward him. Oh well, he did tend to wear his heart on his sleeve—oh, he forgot, he didn't have one since he gave it to Satan and replaced it with a lump of coal. "I apologize, sir."

"Get here early. Before dusk." The male overseer spat. His spittle took the shape of a frog and hopped several times before fizzling out.

Charles wasn't impressed, but the sight unsettled him. He had never liked frogs, especially those made of spit. He folded his arms. "What if you're not here?"

"Then wait. Wait 'til dawn if you have to." The man pulled a cucumber-sized cigar from his bib pocket and stuffed one end into the side of his mouth.

"That wouldn't be a very efficient use of my time," Charles said.

"It's what we require." The man lit his cigar using the palm of his hand.

"Fine, but what am I supposed to do?" Charles asked.

"Ruin your friend Daniel," the Nothingness King said, stabbing the roof with his cane. "Do it anyway you like. Report everything: What he does, who he talks to... It's very simple, but if you can't handle it, there is a particular trench waiting for you in the Malebolge. Malecoda is itching to see you again."

The thought of returning to the Malebolge with Malecoda breathing down his neck for eternity was high on his list of things he'd rather not experience, especially since the high-ranking demon wouldn't have forgotten the incident that happened mere hours ago. Charles shuddered. Leading Daniel to ruin was a better alternative. Still, he doubted he could ruin his friend, even if he wanted to. Good thing he was a crafty liar. "Leave it to me."

Winds picked up. Silent lightning flashed through the sky. A hole fluttering with red light opened a hundred feet overhead. Hot air blasted from it. Charles concealed his face. There was a massive bang and the winds stilled. The coolness of the night returned.

Charles peeked. The "king" was gone, along with the hole in the sky. A pungent, electric scent lingered. He was happy to have finally departed from the weird little man. It wasn't only his sense of fashion that vexed Charles. His very presence made him feel queasy—the sight of spiders affected him in the same way. He shivered at the thought.

The three overseers stared at him. The lone male whose misaligned, reddened face bent with rage stepped toward him. His cigar was inches away. Charles breathed in its harsh smoke and sighed.

The man seemed surprised that Charles appreciated the smoke. His eyes widened and he took a step back. "Your host lives in Building 3, Apartment 8 of the Mountain Brook Apartment Complex. It's two miles northeast of here. You best not delay. We want results, and we want them fast." He walked away, and upon nearing the ledge of the roof, he blurred and vanished.

The two older ladies eyed Charles like wolves stalking prey. "You intend to stand against us, don't you?" one said.

Charles winced. Could they read his thoughts? "I'd never go against someone as lovely as you," he looked to the other, "or you. Are you sisters? Twins, perhaps? Because between the two of you, I think," he placed his hand over his chest and wondered why he chose to go this far with his words, "I may be in love." He masked his disgust the best he could.

One of the two ladies groaned. Whatever was within her stomach curled wildly. Her companion grinned a harsh toothless smile at Charles, apparently satisfied by his repulsed reaction.

The other woman's belly jumped and sloshed. She widened her stance and a dark, airy substance leaked from her exposed belly button and onto the roof, forming a small group of shadowy demons which ran to the ledge of the building, leaped down, and scampered across the road toward the bar.

"Well, now." Charles coughed and cleared his throat. "So, that's where those little—things come from, huh?"

The women yawned, craning their necks. Long, green columns of fog billowed from their stretched mouths. Their bodies thinned until nothing was left. Within seconds, Charles was alone.

"Nasty." He shuddered and looked about the rooftop, fearing the ugly, witch-looking women may have heard him. Relieved, he walked to the ledge and watched the cars traveling along the road. "Building 3. Apartment 8. Mountain Brook Apartments. Two miles northeast." Charles took out his watch, clicked it open, and flipped it shut. "Where's north?" he asked, looking at the sky. The stars didn't give him the slightest clue.

Two miles wouldn't be a terribly long walk if he knew where he was going. He figured he'd handle the first thing first, which would be getting off this building. Climbing was out of the question. He could simply fall, but he imagined it would be painful. He tried jumping to see if he could drop through the roof to the floor below, but nothing happened. Maybe there was a door or hatch he could pass through instead.

"This is going to take forever." He sighed and closed his eyes. "Mountain Brook Apartments. Building 3. Apartment 8."

A strange sensation rose in his gut. He opened his eyes. The periphery of his vision bent inward. The world looked like it was at the far end of a blurred tunnel. He shot through it toward the opposite end and crashed face-first in a parking lot. His bowler hat rolled several feet away—again. On a patch of grass, a sign read: Mountain Brook Apartments.

"That's convenient," he said.

He crawled to his feet and took his hat. Bright lights rolled over his skin. A hushing noise intensified. He turned, and a truck passed through him. It felt more like mud than water. Not pleasant. The smell of gasoline, oil and mold clung to his clothes. Something about that smell and the sudden jump from one place to another caused him to feel sick. He staggered toward the sign and held on to it until the dizziness wore off. Six apartment buildings were to his left. All of them had two floors and eight doors. He spotted Building 3 and marched to it and up a flight of stairs. The first door he came to was Apartment 8. He hesitated. The thought of walking through it troubled him. He still felt quite bad due to the smelly truck.

"Get over it," he said to himself. "It's only a door."

He took a breath and started to enter when a young man and woman came out of the neighboring apartment. They walked off laughing like children. Charles expected to see more tiny demons following them, but instead, a young woman with long blonde hair in a yellow blouse and denim jeans stepped through the shut door after them. The couple shuffled past him and headed downstairs, but the blonde came to him.

"Hello handsome," she said, running a finger up the lapel of his jacket and to his neck. Her intense blue eyes seemed to glow in the night. It affected him. He forgot about something important. What was he doing here? "Wanna take a ride?" she asked.

"A ride?" Charles looked at the couple, who were walking to the far side of the parking lot toward a lonely red sedan. "With them?"

"And me." She raised her eyebrows and came closer. Her bright smile revealed how red her lips were. "There's room for one more."

"Who are you?"

"You have a lot to learn." She looked at the couple as they hopped into the car. "I can teach you. Give you a crash course." She loosened his necktie and ran her hand down his chest and took his hand, interlocking her fingers with his.

Charles looked at Daniel's apartment door and remembered why he was there. "But I have things to do."

She brought her mouth beside his ear and whispered. "I won't keep you too long, dear."

The warmth of her breath caressed his neck. Never had he felt this before. Was this what love felt like? It couldn't be, of course. Charles didn't know this woman, but that didn't matter to him now. He wanted more. "What can you teach me?" he asked.

"For starters," she whispered, "I'll teach you how to travel without landing on your face."

"You saw me fall?" Charles looked at the red sedan. The engine started and the headlights brightened.

"Let's go." She blew him a kiss, and her breath sent him off his feet. He drifted over the parking lot toward the car. He shut his eyes, expecting to crash through it. The air changed and smelled like—pine? When he opened his eyes, he was sitting in the backseat of the car with the blonde next to him.

Her eyes seemed to shine. She said, "You are so uptight."

"No, I'm not." Charles checked that his watch and hat were still with him. "It's just that every time that's happened to me, I've ended up on my face, as I'm sure you've noted."

"About that. When you jump, try to visualize how you want to be positioned when you get to wherever you're going. In time, you'll get the hang of it."

Charles folded his arms and looked at the digitized numbers on the console of the car. It read 9:10. He figured he had plenty of time. "To get back to the apartments, all I have to do is close my eyes and say the address?"

She squinted in thought. "Yes, but all you need to do is set your mind on being there and it'll happen." She crossed her legs and leaned her head on his shoulder.

Who did this lady think she was, using him as a pillow? Charles thought about nudging her off, but she seemed so at peace, and it didn't feel bad. He looked out the window. Trees and buildings passed by rapidly. Lights from the lamp posts caused grains in the sidewalk and asphalt to sparkle. Music and the two chattering in the front blended in such a way that he couldn't understand anything that was said. His hat left his head. He turned.

The blonde wore it low over her eyes. It was a smidge too big but suited her, nonetheless. So mischievous. Who was this woman? "How do I look?" she asked.

No one had ever taken his hat before. If it had been anyone else, he might've reacted violently. Although he didn't trust her, he wanted to, which might not be the best thing for him. He hid his emotions and looked back out the window, tightening his tie.

"Well," she said. "How do I look?"

Charles turned to her, and as blandly as he could manage, said, "Stunning."

"Aww, thanks." She returned his hat, propping it farther back on his head than he liked. He righted it. "You never told me your name?" she asked.

"Charles. And yours?"

"I can't believe they didn't tell you." She snickered. "Lesson two. Don't give your name to just anybody. Whoever knows it can cause you a lot of trouble."

"Oh." Charles swallowed. He looked out the window and cringed.

"Don't worry," she said. "I won't take advantage of you. Not yet anyway."

Charles turned. She shrugged as if to say, *Yeah, I said it.* "It's only my name," he said. "What could you possibly do with it?"

She walked her fingers up his necktie, loosened the knot again. "I can call on you whenever I want to."

"So what? Call on me all you want." Charles tightened his tie again. "It makes no difference to me."

"Oh, but it does." She leaned her head back. "If I call on you and you don't show, my voice will bounce around in your head until you do. It won't stop until you show up."

"But what if I don't know where you are?"

"You can jump to people like you do places," she said.

"That's good to know." Charles looked out the window.

The car slowed and turned into another apartment parking lot, where they parked. The couple hopped out, and the blonde started to follow them, but Charles took her hand. "What do you know of the overseers?"

Her carefree expression turned serious. "The man has a talent for all sins, particularly wrath and violence. The women are more powerful than him though, they specialize in gluttony and lust."

"What are those little things that come out of their bellies?"

She looked at him incredulously and said, "They're demons. And don't ask anyone else about the overseers. If word gets back to them that you have, they'll have you banished." She looked out the window. The couple was twenty yards away now. "Have you figured out how to drink and eat yet?"

"We can do that?"

"Come on." She stepped through the car door. "I'll show you."

Charles needed to get back to Daniel, but the possibility of steak was back on the table. He took a breath and stepped out of the car.

Chapter Three
At the Bus Stop

Deafening rain pounded the ruined streets of Grayton. Piles of garbage disintegrated into streams of sewage that ran into storm drains. Light from nearby streetlamps diffused in the steam that rose from the surface like ghostly flames. Brick buildings with busted windows stretched skyward and pierced the dark cloud looming overhead. Within those structures, countless souls who had fallen short of Heaven's glory undoubtedly took shelter. Just shy of eternal peace, they walked this city each day with no other purpose than to suffer a dull and miserable existence unless they took the bus out of town, of course.

The rain stung Beau's skin. He shivered despite the burning. The longer he sat at the bus stop, the more he doubted a bus would come, especially one bound for Heaven. The thought of leaving this place for Paradise seemed impossible. He'd seriously considered giving up and taking shelter, but he longed to reunite with the child he had lost ages ago. The child he barely remembered. Yes, he'd wait there in the slogging rain, even for an eternity, if it meant he'd have a chance to see his daughter again.

All he could clearly remember of her was her name. Angela. The image of her face was just out of reach. Memories of the day she had died, the day she had screamed until the dreaded silence, were scattered in his mind like shattered glass. He picked at the fragments, unable to piece them together.

Tears came. His jaw trembled. He tucked his hands under his arms and stared at puddles of muddy, trash-ridden water. The downpour distorted his reflection.

A voice spoke from behind him. "Might want to pass on the bus."

Beau rose from the bench and turned. A man in a drab olive raincoat was hunched with his hands in his pockets. Like all others in Limbo, he looked deathly ill with gray and warty skin. His face hung and sank into the hollow spaces of his skull.

"Why is that?" Beau asked.

"It's an impossible journey," the man scratched his chest, "and demons are coming to shut it down. They'll find it soon enough, and it's best you're not around when they do."

The man stood a little taller than him. Darkness obscured his eyes, but his posture was relaxed and nonthreatening. Beau was still skeptical of him, like he was everyone else down here. "Got something in your pockets?"

"Trying to keep the rain off is all." The man pulled his hands out and showed wrinkled and swollen fingers. "You were here before, weren't you?" The man returned his hands to his pockets. "With Heartless Charles and that man with the shine still in 'im."

Beau narrowed his eyes. "You saw us?"

"I was here." The man nodded. "Thought I'd take the golden ride, but it didn't work out. A better opportunity came along, anyway. You might want in on it while the gettin' is good."

Hearing this relieved Beau. "So, the bus is real?"

"It is." The man stepped closer. "And it'll take you to Heaven, but you have to go through Hell to get there."

Beau ran his hand through his beard and gripped it. "When does it run?"

"Whenever it wants, but like I said, demons are coming to shut it down." The man groaned and clutched at his upper left shoulder. "Even if that weren't the case, it's not worth the trouble. It's nothing but a guilt trip. You keep no secrets on that ride. No matter what sins you buried, however deep they are, it all comes out. Uglier than ever." He winced and rolled his shoulder. "Feels like the second death is rolling up on me."

Beau nodded. Knowing that those damned here had to relive their original death endlessly never sat well with him. "Sorry to hear that."

"Well, if things work out, I won't have to deal with it much longer." The man nodded down the street. "Back on the mountain, we're digging our way out. Azazel said that once we reach the surface, there'll be no more death." He cleared his throat and spat. "We're making good progress too, but we need more men. I can get you a cush job, but you have to come now."

"Are you saying that you're digging your way out of Hell?" Beau asked.

"Yeah, we figure it won't take too much longer now that we have the cowboy's hat."

"What?" Beau didn't know what he meant by that but waved off his question. "Thanks for the offer, but I'm waiting on the bus."

The man's expression changed. His smile went dark, twisting into something with sinister intentions. "How long do you think you can endure this rain?"

"However long it takes," Beau growled.

The man leaned a little to his right and stretched his neck awkwardly. "Those demons will find this place sooner than you think, and that bus don't run all that often. You're better off coming with me."

Beau wasn't sure why this man wanted him to come along so badly, but he wasn't going anywhere without a bus. "I'll take my chances." He'd had a few run-ins with demons and could hold his own against a number of them if they tried to take him away.

The man raised his chin. "Find out the hard way, then." He started down the street and shouted, "Hey! The bus stop's over here. This way, over here."

Beau huffed. *What a strange man,* he thought. He sat down and rubbed his hands together. The rain picked up and stole oxygen from the air. The water. The stinging. The humidity. It was maddening. He bounced his knees with anticipation. His heels splatted against the ground. The darkness receded ever so slightly, but the rain did not. Seconds seemed like hours. The man continued to call for demons as he slowly walked away.

"The bus stop's over here." He pointed toward Beau. "This guy refuses to help us. He may be a spy for the cowboy."

Nine demons emerged from an alley down the road. None of them were armed, and they had horns hammered into their heads, which meant they weren't truly demons. They were men who only thought they were—much like Charles had. Beau wasn't sure if he could hold all of them off, not without a weapon.

The man spoke to them while pointing at the bus stop. They shoved the man aside and rushed toward Beau.

The man slapped his hands together and smiled mischievously. "You're in for it now."

"Hello, sir." Behind him, a large cardboard box floated down the street with a man inside it. Neither appeared to be wet. "Sorry for the holdup," he said cheerfully. The box twisted and stopped beside him. "Ready to come aboard the Cardboard Express?"

The man was clean shaven with dry brown hair parted at the side. He wore a buttoned-up shirt, a blue blazer, and seemed utterly joyful to be in this horrible place. So much so that it was a bit off-putting, especially with demons sprinting at them.

Beau looked into the box. It wasn't the slightest bit wet inside. "You're the bus driver?"

"Sometimes." The man patted the side of the box. "Tonight, however, I'm driving this beauty."

The demons were less than fifty yards away. Beau turned to them and took a fighting stance.

"Are you all right?" The bus driver followed Beau's gaze. "Oh, I see." He stepped over the lip of the box and waved his hands toward the demons as if he were shooing them away. Waves of light flashed over the demons and their horns fell off. Their red skin turned pale gray. They looked at each other, speaking words that Beau didn't understand. "You're welcome to join us if you want," the bus driver said, gesturing to the box. "I've got plenty of room."

The men gathered their horns from the ground and fled back the way they had come. The driver turned back to Beau. "Can't win 'em all, I guess." He took Beau's hand, shaking it furiously. "I must say, it is a true pleasure to meet you, sir. You showed a lot of bravery when you came down here to save Daniel. It has us all talking upstairs. No one thought it would work out the way it did. Except your lovely daughter. She is so proud. While that can cause the best of us to stumble, she can't help it. And I don't blame her."

Beau was flummoxed. He wanted to ask about his daughter and hop into the cardboard box, but reality set in. This could all be a sick trap set by Satan. What if it was?

"It's not a trap, Beau," the bus driver said, "but if you're worried about it, ask yourself if you really have anything to lose."

"You heard my thoughts?"

"No," the bus driver said, "but you showed them all over your face."

Beau wrung the water from his beard. "I've heard it's not an easy ride."

The driver's smile shrank, but his face still shone with an air of hope. "Strays are skittish and oftentimes full of misgivings. Some grow to prefer the shades. Others, like you, leave the shadows and step into the fire. The journey to the bottom of Hell may have been difficult, Beau." The driver stepped back into the cardboard box with a grunt. "To many, it's harder to fly than to fall." He pointed at Beau's chest. "It depends on you."

"I don't remember anything from my life. I don't know how horrible a person I was. Maybe I belong in this world."

The driver smiled a little wider and patted him on the shoulder. "What you have forgotten, Mr. Beau Buford, will be revealed."

Hearing his name caused Beau's heart to punch his ribs. He stepped back, holding his hand to his chest. "That was my name."

"It still is." The driver squinted up into the cloud. "Not trying to rush you, but would you like to come in out of the rain?"

"I need to tell you. They're trying to dig their way back to Earth through the mountain." Beau looked back where he thought the mountains were, but they couldn't be seen from here. "And they said something about a cowboy. They got his hat and maybe captured him, too."

The driver pursed his lips and nodded. "Then we should get moving, don't you think?"

Beau looked back into the box, where the rain splattered and vanished. He wasn't worried that this was a trick anymore. What worried him was the things he had forgotten. What horrible things did he do to fall out of favor with God? How did he end up as a shadow-man and not another lost soul in Hell? *Only one way to find out.* "Let's get to it."

The driver helped Beau over the lip of the box. When Beau's second foot touched the cardboard floor, the rain ceased, and the City of Grayton disappeared. He was inside a peculiar bus. Eight large windows lined the sides. The colors of a rainbow zipped and twisted on the outside. At the far end, colors splattered against the windshield. They blended, shifted, and curled in a messy display. There was a door to the right and an unoccupied driver's seat to the left. The steering wheel seemed to make slight corrections on its own. The ceiling was ornamented with tiny stars. He reached for them, but they proved to be higher than he thought.

The bus shifted slightly. Beau held out his hands and took hold of a nearby seat. The floor was carpeted with a white canvas that glowed in the light of the colors that streamed along the windows.

He and his clothes were clean and dry. Brown leather sandals and a pair of tan pants. His red flannel shirt had black stripes. Everything was like new.

Rubbing the back of his head, he found his hair shorter and well-groomed. His beard was only an inch thick. The changes were significant, but oddly enough, this seemed more natural to him.

"Thirsty?" The driver was behind him with two tinkling glasses filled with what looked like lemonade. "It's your favorite."

Beau took one. Looking about the bus again, he asked, "How did this happen?"

"Well, you stepped into the box." The driver took a seat on one of the nearby lounge chairs and took a sip of his drink. "Excellent choice, by the way. We're off to a great start."

"I mean," Beau raised his hand and gestured to the room, "this isn't a box. I doubt it's even a bus."

The driver looked about, as if discerning this for the first time. "I guess it depends on how you look at it, Beau." He sat back and crossed his legs. "Try your drink. I want to know if it's the way you like it."

Beau frowned at his cold glass.

The driver chuckled. "Do you really think that I'd put something in it?"

Beau looked at streaks of oscillating colors outside the window and took a tentative sip. Energy surged along his jaw and swirled around his temples. His ears popped, and he sat in the chair next to the driver, placing his glass on the table.

"Too tart?" the driver asked. He looked concerned.

Beau blinked away tears. "It woke me up, that's for sure. Where are we exactly?"

The driver sipped from his glass. "Well, it's hard to say. Obviously, we're on the bus heading to Paradise, but the route we're taking is set by you."

"Me?" Beau looked at the empty driver's seat. "I don't know how to get to wherever it is we're going."

The driver leaned over and patted Beau's knee. "Don't worry. I'll help you. It's kind of what I do, you know."

Beau watched the colors splatter onto the windshield, where they curled and whirled about. "Who's driving?"

The bus driver looked at him, confused, then at the front of the bus. "Do you see anyone up there?"

"No."

"Good." The bus driver shrank back into his seat. "I was worried you were seeing things for a moment."

Beau scoffed. "So, no one is driving?"

The bus driver waved off the question. "Don't worry. We aren't going to crash or anything like that, but are you ready to begin?"

Beau wasn't sure. Revisiting the past, seeing his downfall. If he couldn't change anything, why would it matter? "I honestly don't know."

"You'll be fine." The bus driver stood and downed the rest of his lemonade.

"You're an angel, aren't you?"

He smiled and nodded. "Ralph's the name." He pointed at Beau's glass. "Are you finished with yours?"

Beau's glass was half full. "I believe so." He handed it to Ralph, who took it to the back of the bus where there was a sink, a fridge, and a few cabinets. From there, he turned and headed to the front.

"Come on along." He had a playfulness about him that Beau wasn't sure about. Not that he thought the angel would hurt him or that he was simple-minded. It was that he hadn't been around someone this kind in so long.

Ralph sat in the driver's seat. Beau took the seat behind him and asked, "Where are we going exactly?"

Ralph rubbed his hands together. "We'll find out soon enough." He nodded at the windshield and took the wheel. "Tell me. What do you see?"

Beau shrugged. "A bunch of different colors rolling around."

Ralph turned the wheel to the left and then straightened it. The colors stretched out in straight lines toward the edges of the windshield. "How's this?"

"It changed. The colors straightened out."

"All right. Tell me when they look perfectly straight." Ralph turned the wheel slightly to the left.

"Now," Beau said.

"Perfect. See? This isn't so bad. But here's my favorite part. Hold on." The engine revved. The colorful lines on the windshield thinned. More and more dots of color struck and streaked outward. At the center of the windshield, a bright white spot spread out as they accelerated. Beau shielded his eyes. The spot expanded until it covered the entire windshield. The light dimmed and foggy images came into view.

"Here we are," Ralph said. The engine died down.

They were driving through the sky over a pasture toward a small cabin. Two empty rocking chairs sat on the front porch. A stack of wood sat near the front door. Dawn breached the eastern sky over the forest. A few fleeting stars remained.

"I can't believe it," Beau said.

The bus reached the ground with little impact. It jostled a little as it slowed to a stop a few yards from the porch.

"Recognize this place?" Ralph asked.

"This was my home."

Chapter Four

The Disease

Daniel clutched his pillow. The stench of sulfur hung in his nose. Distant screams echoed in the chambers of his mind. Horrible images oozed from the darkness, cascading through his mind's eye. Chained heretics burned in fiery graves. Dazed, worn-out souls crawled through sludgy slop. Then there was Satan.

He would never forget, because it wasn't a dream. He shifted in his bed and a horrible thought occurred. *Did I really escape?* Hell clung to him like a contagious disease. The horrors came home with him, and his loved ones would suffer from the things lurking within.

He'd drifted toward the sweet void of sleep, but a sense of impending doom jerked him awake. In the dark of his bedroom, the presence of a cunning, invisible madman waited patiently in the shadows for Daniel to drop his guard. Its malicious smile hid in the blackness. It wanted to get into his head. Infect him somehow.

The alarm clock on the nightstand read 1:07. Had he slept at all? Laying there with all these horrible thoughts running nonstop did him no favors. He sat up and flicked on the lamp beside his bed. Its faint light did little to diminish the presence lingering around him. The vents rattled. The curtains swayed. Shadows grew and shrank, taunting him.

Maybe a change of scenery, the living room perhaps, would help him sleep. He needed it since he was leaving Boone, North Carolina, for Eastman, Georgia, in the morning. Driving without adequate rest could prove fatal. If Kristine came along, she could drive, but she had planned to work over spring break. No matter what, he was going. He'd put off seeing his parents for too long.

He went to the bathroom and washed his face. The slight taste of salt reminded him of the tears he had drunk in Hell. He sighed at the mirror and patted his short brown hair. There was something off about his blue eyes. His irises flashed red. They seemed to swirl. He leaned closer. The lightbulbs flickered off.

He backed away. His reflection was not his own. A silhouette wearing a top hat stared back. Black eyes glared at him with palpable malevolence.

No rest for the wicked, Daniel.

The ambient light behind him waxed and waned in intensity. Electricity buzzed like irritated flies. It crawled over his skin like cockroaches fleeing the light. "This isn't happening," Daniel muttered.

You came to us. Therefore, we are with you, always.

Daniel tripped over the threshold and fell back into the hallway.

Stop cowering. Let us in.

The lamp in his room went out with a sickening pop. In the pitch black, something thudded on the floor near his bed. It let out a raspy groan that sounded angry and full of longing. Inhuman. Its smell was beyond this world, beyond death. Pure evil. It called out like a dying friend. "Daniel." A ragged squall ripped from its throat. "Why did you leave me?"

Too afraid to walk, heart pounding, Daniel crawled to the kitchen. Why was it so hard to breathe? Why did he feel so weak?

"Daniel." The voice was closer. Hands slapped onto the carpet. Something sharp cut and tore at the fabric. "I need you."

Daniel managed to get to his feet and flipped the nearest switch. Relief washed over him when the kitchen lights turned on. He backed into the counter. Fumes and wisps of smoke edged out of his darkened bedroom doorway. A hand with long fingers and needle-like nails emerged. A head with a skinny, pointed nose and chin, sharp cheekbones and empty eye sockets inched into view. Its body emerged, covered in tar, dripping to the floor and puffing to smoke. It shivered, baring blood-red teeth. "You abandoned me!"

Its garbled voice sounded familiar. Daniel understood its rage and could almost empathize. This thing, he knew well, like a family member or close friend. Lightheaded and clumsy, he used the countertop to keep his legs under him.

Its face sagged with sadness. "We were good together," it sobbed, glaring at Daniel. It took a heaving, inward breath, and its rage returned. "But you ruined everything."

"What are you?" Daniel forced the words out. Keeping his eyes on this thing, he felt along the counter and found the small stone that got him through Hell. Its smooth texture and considerable weight comforted him. He squeezed, but nothing happened. It didn't warm his hand. It didn't glow. The demon crawling across his floor didn't shrink away. But he wasn't in Hell anymore. Still, there must be power in this stone; Daniel felt it surge up his arm, begging to be unleashed.

The thing on the floor was three feet away when it stopped and came to its knees. Grimacing, it said. "It's so cold out here. LET ME BACK IN!"

This thing looked familiar. It had the same build as him. Its face—was like his. It was a hideous version of himself. Daniel inhaled through his nose. The stench of sulfur burned his sinuses. "What are you?"

"No time for questions." Its voice broke, sounding desperate and short of breath. "Let me in. I'm dying out here."

Daniel took a step back, tightening his grasp on the stone. "Go away."

The thing chuckled itself to a cough. "If I were with you," it spat black goo that fizzled to smoke, "you would've thrown it already. Without me, you're a disgrace."

An overwhelming sense of calm poured over Daniel. He looked down at the spirit with pity. "I'm not the one on my knees."

It raised its hands. "Wait."

Daniel slung the stone. It zipped through the demon's chest, ricocheted off the floor, and smashed into the bathroom mirror. Smoke spewed from the demon's wound and sank through the floor. The hideous thing wept and looked at Daniel. It wanted to speak but collapsed to the floor and dissipated into nothingness.

All was still and quiet. Daniel dropped to his knees, panting. Hell had followed him home. Alone and vulnerable, he massaged either side of his head. He squeezed his eyes shut, trying to think. What did he have to do to make it stop? Beau had told him he needed to mend his broken relationship with his parents and get right with God. All he had done so far was call them. Maybe he shouldn't wait until the morning. Maybe he needed to go home now.

Stiff with fear, he went into the bathroom and flicked on the light. Shards of glass riddled the floor and sink. His hands trembled as he retrieved the stone. Warily, he went into his room and packed a change of clothes. On his way out, he eyed the engagement ring he had set on the counter. He considered putting it away but was too eager to leave. It should be safe where it was.

Moments later, he was driving down a dark road, where dark things lingered in dark places. Menacing eyes of otherworldly beings watched from windows, doorways, and trees, stalking him. He pretended they weren't there and focused on staying between the lines. Maybe once he hugged his parents and apologized for his mistakes, the nightmare would end.

Chapter Five

Nobody's Home

Charles and the blonde stayed in the apartment while the living ones left for a nightclub. The lesson on how to drink and eat in the spirit world was quickly becoming the most frustrating thing Charles had ever experienced. He sat on a stiff sofa, eying one of many red Solo cups crowding a wooden coffee table. Ice slowly melted and shifted within a few of them. The clock on the wall read 12:30 am. He retrieved his pocket watch and felt the gears spinning within.

The blonde's heels tapped as she paced the length of the living room. "Just pick it up."

"Just pick it up she says," Charles muttered.

He glared at the red cup nearest him. It was wet with condensation and smelled sweet. A sliced lime was suspended in the ice. He tried to take it, and for the umpteenth time, his hand passed through the cup.

Charles propped his head on his fist. "I'm sick of this."

"Stop trying to snatch it." She took a breath and extended her hand. "All you need to do is pick it up."

Charles tightened his necktie. "I'll admit it's been a while since I've been in the land of the living, but I think I know the process of lifting a cup off a table, and the first step is to grab it."

"You've gotten it into your head that you can't do it. You have to believe you can."

"You haven't demonstrated that it can be done." Charles narrowed his eyes and folded his arms. "Perhaps you're toying with me."

"Am not." She smiled. "Not yet, at least."

"Then show me how it's done." Charles scooted on the couch to make room. "Help me believe."

"Watch and learn." She walked to the table and picked up the cup. The physical cup remained, but a faint representation of it was in her hand. She drank from the ghostly cup and placed it back on the table. An invisible force sucked it back to the true cup. "See? Nothing to it."

Charles glared back at the cup and visualized himself picking it up. He closed his eyes and went for it. Something *was* in his hand. It felt circular, flimsy, and plastic. He brought it to his mouth and a sweet taste splashed onto his tongue and burned when he swallowed. Ice fell onto his face. He brought the cup back to the table and shuddered.

"You did it," she said.

Charles wiped the wetness from his mouth. "What was that?"

"A watered-down margarita." The blonde sat next to Charles. "Wanna try again?"

"I finished it."

"Actually, you didn't. Look." She pointed at the cup.

"What?" Charles leaned closer. The contents of the cup hadn't changed. The lime was still sitting in the same spot. "That's strange."

"You're not drinking the actual drink," she explained. "What you're getting is its essence."

Charles adjusted his hat and took a quick sip. This time, it came more naturally. "It works the same way with food?"

"Yeah. Finger foods are easier. Silverware takes some getting used to." She walked over to the bar and took a ghostly potato chip from a green mixing bowl. "Come and have some."

He walked to her and tried one. It crunched in his mouth. Salty. He nodded his approval. "As much as I've enjoyed this, I must get going."

"I understand," she ate another chip, "but there are still some things you should know before you leave. Stay a little while longer. OK?"

"I can't." Charles glared at the clock and righted his jacket. He had spent more time with this woman than he had intended. Granted, some good had come out of it. "I should go."

"What if I give you my name?" She looked at his necktie and loosened it. "Stay a little while longer, and I'll give it to you. You could call on me whenever you want and no matter how much I resisted, eventually, I'd have to show."

"You're right next door to Daniel." Charles forced a handful of chips into his mouth. "We can meet up whenever."

"No," she said, squinting. "I'm more of a free spirit. I doubt I'll ever go back to that apartment again unless you call on me."

Charles sighed. He did like the looks of this lady, and her energy was contagious. Another lesson couldn't hurt. "Fine. I'll stay, but not much longer."

The woman hugged him rather hard. She spoke softly into his ear. "Thank you, Charles."

"Why thank me? I haven't done anything for you."

"I like you, I guess."

Charles reached for a small cup that sat by the bowl of chips.

"Don't drink that," she said, laughing. "That's dip."

"Dip?" Charles looked at the contents of the small cup, then back at the woman.

"Yeah." She took a chip, dipped it in the thick white substance, and ate it. "It's called that for obvious reasons."

Charles ran his fingers down his lapels and gripped them. "So, what's your name?"

"Emma." She leaned against the counter. Something glinted in her eyes. She seemed so pleased about this.

Charles tried the dip. "Are you sure your name is—Emma?"

She laughed. "You think I'd lie?"

"It's something we all do. Isn't it?"

"Some may, but not me." She dusted off her fingers. "So, before you head back to the apartment, I want to take you to a tavern. The same one where everybody else went earlier."

Charles rubbed the back of his neck. "I don't recall where they said they were going."

Emma took hold of Charles's lapel and gave it a tug. "It doesn't matter. All we have to do is want to be in the backseat of their car again and poof." Emma opened her hands to the sky. "We'll be there. Like magic."

Charles saw his reflection in the mirror. Even with his mother's eyes, he looked sick, like a dead man. He tightened his necktie. Beside him, Emma looked different—different meaning glorious. Maybe she was more powerful than he previously thought. He could use a powerful ally. "How do we get there? Do we both think about it? Hold hands or—"

Emma took his hands. "Look into my eyes."

In her light-blue eyes, his hideous smile reflected back at him. She was so lovely—too lovely. She came closer. He closed his mouth and swallowed. "What are you doing?"

Her lips moved slowly as she spoke. "Now close your eyes and have a seat."

It occurred to him that he did everything she asked. While it had paid off so far, it made him feel vulnerable. He already had three powerful demons who were skeptical of him. This job might be the cushiest thing he'd experienced since entering Hell, but it would require that he showed loyalty to either his friend or Satan. Who would he betray? And how was it even a question after spending nearly a century in Hell?

Despite his conflicting emotions, he obeyed like a good dog for its master. A slight wind rolled around him. The lower he sank, the more confident he felt he'd end up on the floor looking up at Emma, but when he was about to lose his balance and fall, he landed in the back seat of the same car as before.

"We're here," Emma said.

The car was parked near the trash bin that Charles had stuck his head through earlier that evening. He peered out the back window. Across the road stood the empty building where the Nothingness King had met with the overseers.

"Small world," he muttered to himself. Out in the darkness, in the shadows, under cars and trees, from blackened windows, Charles sensed the eyes of sinister things. Certainly, Satan had spies everywhere. If he were caught here with this woman... What if she wasn't a demon but an angel? Charles had a hard time believing an angel would help him, but if she were and demons caught him, it wouldn't be good. "I don't think I should be here."

"Why not?"

Charles turned to Emma. Her eyes seemed to glow in the darkness. She knew too much already. He didn't think it would be wise to tell her anything else. "I'm not supposed to be here. The last thing I need to do is draw the wrong kind of attention toward myself."

"I see." Emma looked about the parking lot. "You're worried about the overseers and their spies."

He was more worried about the Nothingness King and Satan but chose not to say so. "I should be where I'm expected to be, is all."

Emma turned to Charles. Her dazzling eyes were quite lethal this time. "Do you realize the opportunity I'm giving you?"

"You've helped me tremendously, but—"

"I've taught you more in a few hours than most figure out in a decade." She came closer and took his hands. "Most spirits like you fail because they have no idea what they're doing up here."

"What do you mean—spirits like me?" Charles glared at her.

She looked in the direction of the nightclub. "It's obvious that you're not a demon." She glanced at him and smiled. "It's rare that one such as you gets an opportunity like this, Charles. Don't waste it."

That stung Charles's ego. "I did more in a day than any real demons can dream of. I—" He nearly told her everything. How he guided Daniel and Beau from the base of the Purging Mountains to Satan in the bottommost pit. "I make the impossible possible. I get things done."

She touched the back of his neck. "You're not in that world anymore. What you did there doesn't matter—especially to the overseers. Pride is the downfall of many. The spirits that thrive in the land of the living understand there has to be some give and take in all this. Otherwise, your enemies will find ways to compromise you and send you reeling back into the flaming abyss."

Charles reached into his vest pocket and held onto his pocket watch. It was still. "I'm sure that's true."

"I'm not asking for hours." Emma took his hand. "The place closes soon."

He looked out the window into the darkness. "I believe I'm being watched. If I'm seen doing something other than my given purpose, my tenure here will be short."

"I can get us inside to a place where we won't be seen."

"There are demons inside there, too."

Emma rubbed his cheek. "They'll be too preoccupied to notice us. They won't see you, but you will see them. Trust me."

Charles tightened his necktie. Considering the hour and the arduous journey he shared with Daniel and Beau earlier, he imagined Daniel would be resting. Maybe he could spare a few more minutes with Emma to give him a better advantage in this world. "I'll go for a few minutes, but how do we remain unseen from the demons?"

Emma took his hand and said, "I hope you like to dance."

The world spun around them in shades of darkness and bright neon streaks. Charles became dizzy. The world sped around them. They seemed locked together in time. Noisy music engulfed them. The sound of a violin swayed through the air. Emma held on to his hands, guiding him around the far side of a crowded room. The living dancers were unaware of them. Emma twirled under his arm and came closer to him.

He looked over her shoulder. Demons were congregated around the bar. Some clung to men's and women's backs. Others sat on their shoulders, whispering into their ears. Those who weren't attached to anybody loitered about scheming among themselves and eavesdropping on conversations.

"Over here." Emma pulled Charles to a table in the far corner of the club. They sat on two tall stools. "You don't know much about dancing, do you?" It would've stung coming from someone less charming than Emma.

"Well, if you had warned me before we started…" Smaller demons gathered on a table near the bar and piled on top of each other. At first glance, it looked like a brawl, but it became apparent that they were coming together to become a single, larger demon.

Emma followed his eyes. "I brought you here so you could see that. You need to understand how they work."

Charles moved his hat farther back on his head and leaned into his chair. He remembered how a dozen of them came from one of the overseers' bellies. "Why don't they join together sooner?"

"They're all stubborn." Emma glared at them. "They make alliances and become legions as a last resort, and even then, if a leader hasn't been chosen, they'll quarrel."

"What's the point of them coming together if they can't cooperate?"

"It makes them stronger and smarter. If they don't join a legion, they die out within days. Even if they do, they rarely last a week, unless they find a human host."

Everything about Emma told Charles that she was no friend of demons. She had to be an angel. It wasn't only her looks that gave her away. The way she glared at them with outright disgust... She held pure disdain for these creatures. "If they're stronger and smarter, why do they hardly last a week without a human?"

The recently united legion of demons stood on the table as a single entity. It was stocky and broad, but only the size of a child in grade school. It lifted its pug-like head and stared down its flat nose at the tinier, Chihuahua-looking demons. Some bowed to it and begged to join. Others shrank away to darker parts of the bar.

Emma's eyes rose to the ceiling. "They're not as smart as they think."

A larger, bulkier demon, the size of a boulder, dropped from the rafters onto the smaller one on the table. There was a loud struggle between them. Tinier demons leaped into the giant as it wrestled Mr. Flatnose to the ground and beat it into smoke.

"There's always a bigger and better demon, I guess," Charles said.

Emma leaned closer and whispered, "They're not the only show in town. If they cross the wrong entity, they get put down."

"If they're smart, they'll join forces and become more powerful. Right?"

"If they get too big," Emma nodded to the black ceiling, "the saints come marching in."

Charles got out of his chair and eyed the ceiling. Nothing was there. He looked back at the largest demon in the club. It was standing with a group of men near a pool table. Charles looked back at the ceiling.

"Don't worry about the saints," Emma said. "Demons will deceive the living. They'll deceive each other, including you, if they get a chance. But remember this..." She took hold of Charles's jaw and forced him to look away from the ceiling and at her. "You have as much influence over them and others as anyone else. So don't let your guard down and don't be afraid to take charge of any situation. If you let them walk all over you, you'll get tossed for sure."

"They don't concern me." Charles fixed his jacket and peeked at them. He was more concerned about the saints. "They have nothing to do with why I'm here."

"They are a part of everything, Charles."

Charles looked into Emma's lovely eyes. Although he appreciated them, it was time for him to depart. "I'll call on you some time."

He closed his eyes and thought, *Mountain Brook Apartments. Building 3. Apartment 8.* The air rolled about him. The smell of yeast gave way to the scent of trees and earth. Warm, stagnant air changed to a cool, carefree breeze. When it stopped, he opened his eyes.

He was outside of Daniel's apartment door, standing, rather than lying on his face this time. He heaved a sigh and walked through the white wooden door. It was dark inside, although the kitchen light was on. Walking through the living room, he spotted the engagement ring sitting on the counter. Quietly, he turned into a short hallway. The bathroom sat at the end of it. The room to the left proved to be Daniel's bedroom.

He was gone. Charles scratched his head. *Maybe he went out with Kristine.* On his way back into the living room, he glanced into the bathroom. The mirror above the sink was smashed. Shards of glass were everywhere. The hairs on Charles's neck stood up. He headed back toward the kitchen, examining the carpet. Thin fumes rose from the floor. He went to his hands and knees and sniffed. *Sulfur.* Something from Hell must've visited Daniel, and Charles wasn't here when it happened. Did it take Daniel? Did he escape? Where was he?

Maybe he could jump to Daniel. After all, he was with him in Hell for the longest time. He closed his eyes and focused. Nothing happened. Charles groaned at the ceiling.

Satan's punishment for Daniel was in full effect, and it wasn't about to let up anytime soon. Charles stepped into the living room. Why was his chest pounding? He had no heart. He reached under his coat and took out his watch, which was shaking violently. What could he do? He had an idea but didn't like it. "What choice do I have?" He pocketed his timepiece. "Emma!"

Chapter Six

On the Road

Beyond the lights of Daniel's car, in the darkness, something bounded around him, never allowing a moment's peace. Sometimes, he sensed it soaring overhead and heard it speaking. *We are with you, always.* These words were not his thoughts. They were spoken as if whatever loomed out there in the blackness was whispering in his ear.

He tried the radio, but every station broadcasted muffled static, and in it, a garbled voice hissed curses and threatened him with death. The silence was less dreadful; the droning of the road was a small comfort. Within an hour, he was on I-77 South. The voice in his head diminished with each passing mile. It seemed to linger behind, watching him from afar. When he stopped for gas somewhere off I-20, he realized the voice was gone, but the bright fluorescent lights, their steady tremor, troubled him. He closed his eyes until the gas pump nozzle clicked off.

Another hour down the road, a new day began to dawn. Purple and red light bloomed over the trees that shielded the eastern horizon. It put him at ease, and hours later, he entered Dodge County, Georgia. It was almost 8 am when he stopped at Quincy's Quikstop to top off the tank and grab a snack. He was two miles from his parents' home, and this was his last chance to procrastinate. The store hadn't changed at all. Same layout, same products, and the same old man behind the counter.

"Hello, Mr. Quincy." The door rattled closed behind him. The stench of bleach and mold burned his nostrils and eyes. He went for a peanut butter Clif Bar and a 99-cent bottle of water.

On the way to the counter, Mr. Quincy scrutinized him from his stool behind the cash register; his bulky, gray-haired arms folded over his greasy red smock. Short, bald, and thick, he rarely smiled, and when he did, it was never in kindness—not for Daniel, at least.

He stared like a police interrogator. "Aren't you Paul's boy?"

"Yes, sir." Daniel set his items on the counter. He regretted coming in here. Mr. Quincy was no friend of his father's, and already he felt prickles of bad energy stabbing at his skin.

Mr. Quincy tapped on his old cash register. "How's the old town drunk doin'?"

Daniel sucked in a breath and closed his eyes. This was how he usually dealt with Mr. Quincy and anybody else who went out of their way to insult his father, but this proved to be ineffective. It had caused him to resent his father and feel ashamed, but he knew better now. He wouldn't remain silent anymore. "You know my dad stopped drinking the day I was born."

Mr. Quincy didn't seem to hear him. "It'll be $4.59."

Daniel's hand shook as he inserted his debit card into the card reader. Maybe if he didn't say anything else, Mr. Quincy wouldn't, either.

"You're shakin' like your no-good daddy used to." He smiled as if recalling a pleasant memory. "He'd stumble in here drunk lookin' for more liquor, and I'd toss him right on out. I sure did. Like it was nothin'."

Daniel's be-nice-o-meter malfunctioned. He had endured this sort of talk since he was a small child. Growing up, he figured it was just the way it was. You made any mistakes, even one, it defined you. He thought people like Mr. Quincy were justified in recalling the same old stories about his father. But now, after years away, he understood that the real problem lay with them—not his father.

Daniel took his items. "Aren't you tired, Mr. Quincy?"

The old man looked out into the parking lot. No one else was coming into his store. Daniel, however, did see something. It was faint, but it was there. In the reflection in the window, ghastly faces stared back at Mr. Quincy. They seemed to be caught within the glass somehow. They spoke in hushed whispers that Daniel couldn't quite make out.

"I reckon that I'm only getting started, boy. Why?" Mr. Quincy leaned onto the counter. His pupils were high in his socket. His jaw protruded with an underbite. "You got something you wanna say?" he hissed.

The faces in the window snarled with pleasure. Daniel glared into Mr. Quincy's empty eyes. The wrapper to the Clif Bar popped in his hand. "We aren't perfect. Me or my dad. No one on this earth is, including you, Mr. Quincy. The sooner you recognize that, the better off you'll be."

Mr. Quincy looked at the faces in the window. "Get on out of here before I toss you out, like I did your father."

Daniel started toward the door and felt a freedom he hadn't felt in ages. He didn't feel the need to lash out. Gossips, like Mr. Quincy, lived in the past. Lived a lie. He reached the door and looked back at Mr. Quincy. The man appeared tired; a lifetime of standing behind that counter with those evil faces looking in at him. He needed help, but what could Daniel do or say?

"I love my dad, Mr. Quincy, and I'm sick of how people talk about him. When will you let go of things that happened over twenty years ago and see him as who he is now?"

Mr. Quincy sank onto his stool in front of the cash register. He looked down his nose at Daniel. "Well, try not to knock your daddy to the floor with all that *love* you got for 'im."

Daniel gave a curt nod. "Fair enough. Take care, Mr. Quincy." He entered a cool breeze that ushered him back to his car. It didn't shock him that the people in town knew that he had pushed his father over a coffee table and walked out years ago. He had told a few friends about it before leaving for the military. That was all it took for the word to get across town.

He reached into his pocket for his key and brushed his fingers over the silky-smooth stone. It was warm in his car. He closed his eyes, longing for sleep. Mr. Quincy would have a field day if he dozed now.

It took everything he had to drive the last couple of miles to his childhood home. This last leg was dangerous. He drifted into the oncoming lane a couple of times. People would fly on this road, and it was a blessing that no one was coming.

Relief washed over him when he pulled into his parents' long gravel driveway. Maybe the demons would be done now that he was here, righting his wrongs. As tired as he was, he forgot how nervous he was supposed to be. He even chuckled, imagining the looks his parents might give him when they found him standing on their stoop so early in the morning.

He walked up the stairs and knocked. Standing straight was difficult. His body swayed no matter how he stood. The sun's heat jumped several degrees and poked at his neck. The beige vinyl siding reflected light that startled his eyes.

His father opened the door with a Georgia Bulldogs coffee mug in his hand. His mouth hung open slightly. "Son?"

"Hi, Dad." Daniel blinked hard.

"We weren't expecting you until later this afternoon."

"Yeah, I got an early start."

"You think?" he said with concern. "Get in here." He ushered Daniel inside, where it was cool and dark. The layout of the living room was the same as it was the night he had left, but his parents had replaced the coffee table. "What did you do? Drive all night?"

Daniel shrugged. "I couldn't sleep." His body still swayed. So tired, he almost mentioned how a demon attacked him in his apartment and that something far worse seemed to follow him for a time. Thankfully, he managed to keep that to himself. "Good to see you, Dad."

"I'm happy to see you too," his father hugged him tight, "but you should've rested. You look exhausted."

"I am." Daniel yawned. "It didn't hit me until the last bit, though. Where's Mom?"

"She left for the grocery store. Has this big meal in mind." His father closed the door and chuckled. "She was worried if she waited until after church, you'd show up while she was shopping."

"I'll stay up until she gets back." Daniel stifled a yawn. "Maybe I can have a coffee."

"Go get some sleep, son." His father nodded to Daniel's old room. "We'll catch up after church."

"OK. Can I make a quick call? Lost my phone yesterday and haven't replaced it yet. It's long-distance though."

"Let me guess. Your girlfriend?"

"Yes, sir."

He called Kristine but had to leave a message. After a little more banter with his father, he headed down the hall to his bedroom, which was on the left. It wasn't exactly as he had left it. Nothing was lying on the floor, but he took care of that when he kicked his shoes off. He eased himself under the covers. His head sank onto a fresh pillow. Not long after that, he slept.

Chapter Seven

Seeking Daniel

Charles paced the length of Daniel's apartment, saying Emma's name with every step. All he had to do was ruin Daniel and report to the overseers each night. Sounded easy enough, but apparently not. Things were already a mess. He walked into the bathroom and looked at the broken pieces of mirror for the millionth time. What happened here? Did a demon manifest in the mirror or something? He headed back into the living room and resumed pacing.

"I shouldn't have gone with her." He rubbed his forehead. "Emma!"

"For goodness' sake, what is it?" Emma appeared through the front door. Her eyes were wide with annoyance.

"He's gone." Charles gestured to the bathroom. "Something crawled out of the mirror and attacked him. The floor smells like sulfur, and Daniel is gone."

Emma stalked into the hall. "Oh, this isn't good."

"What am I supposed to do?" Charles stopped mid-stride and slapped his thighs. "I'm supposed to report to the overseers tomorrow, and I have nothing to say about this. Even worse, I have no idea where he is."

"Settle down." Emma came back into the living room with her hands on her hips. She squinted at Charles. "There's got to be a reasonable explanation for all this."

"Reasonable?" Charles disagreed. "What in the world is reasonable about this? I don't know where he is, and I'm pretty sure he's not coming back anytime soon."

"Stop panicking, you worrywart." She started for the bathroom again. "Wait here for a minute. I'll be back."

"Where are you going?"

"Don't call for me," Emma said over her shoulder before disappearing through the bathroom wall.

So much for asking for her help. She peeked in for hardly a minute and skipped out faster than a devil at an exorcist convention. He was sick of pacing but couldn't stand still. He moseyed over to the fridge and stuck his head through the door. It was cold, dark, stuffy, and smelly. He turned and leaned on the counter. A diamond ring, the engagement ring Daniel carried through Hell with him, sat right under Charles's nose, gleaming in the dim light of the kitchen. Something so valuable should be tucked away for safekeeping. Surely, Daniel would come back sooner rather than later, with this ring sitting out like this.

"Who in their right mind gets out of Hell and goes for a night out?" he muttered. "I mean, hello, what do you think got you there in the first place?" Charles folded his arms and gazed at the broken mirror. "That's bad luck."

It occurred to him that the walls in Daniel's apartment were bare. No pictures. No art. Not even a clock. Though the microwave in the kitchen read 3:45 am. The sink had a bowl with a few drops of milk in it, along with a large spoon. Charles dabbed his finger in the milk and got a taste. Warm and slightly sour. Trying his best to be patient and not call for Emma, he went into the living room and sat on the couch. Across from him, a large flat screen television sat on a table. Seeing his dark reflection made him uneasy. Was someone watching him?

Emma ran into the room. "OK. I know what happened."

Charles jumped to his feet. Finally, some good news.

"A demon that had been attached to Daniel for years attacked him. They said it begged him to let it back in, but he wouldn't. He got rid of it." She tapped her chin. "It's weird that he could see it."

"What's weird about that?" Charles asked.

"Most people don't see us." Emma leaned against the counter. "The ones who can don't see much."

Charles loosened his tie. "Is he all right?"

"It may have been traumatic, but all things considered, I guess he's OK. He drove off in his car."

"How did he get rid of it?" Charles asked.

"With a rock," Emma said. "Sounds crazy, I know. Sticks and stones may not hurt people, but apparently, they give devils their due." Emma smiled. "Oh, come on. Cheer up. Daniel's fine."

Charles took out his pocket watch and peered at his reflection. He came out of Hell with his watch, so maybe Daniel came out with the keystone. Would Daniel use the stone against him? Maybe, if he found out why he was put here.

Emma made a noise with her throat and sauntered over to Charles, smiling.

Charles took it as a hint for some gratitude. "Thanks. How did you figure it out?"

"This apartment complex is full of young people," she said. "Young people are very impressionable, so there are all kinds of spirits here vying for their attention. Some good. Some bad. Regardless, they're very nosy, especially now, since most people have left town for spring break."

"Did they tell you where he went?" Charles asked.

Emma frowned and shook her head.

"Can we jump to his car?" He took her hands. "You can get me there, can't you?"

"Sorry. Neither of us have been in his car, so no."

"Maybe one of the other spirits in the building has." Charles headed down the hall. "Come on."

"Actually..." Emma waited for Charles to turn around. "They were too frightened of Daniel's old demon to go near him."

Charles scoffed. "Well, I imagine he won't be gone too long without that." He pointed to the engagement ring on the counter.

"Speaking of that." Emma came closer to Charles and took his hand. "I found out where his girlfriend lives. I hopped over to her place before coming back here. Maybe you'd like to stick close to her since she'd probably hear from Daniel before anyone else would."

"Emma!" Charles almost hugged her but gripped her arms instead. "You're amazing."

She blushed. "It was nothing. Come on. I'll take you to her dorm room, but I can't stay, though."

Chapter Eight

A Spirit Named Clayton

Light peeked through the curtain and touched Daniel's face. The clock on his dresser read 11:30 am. His parents would still be in church. Prying himself out of bed was not an easy task. He shuffled his feet across his bedroom floor and into the hall, where framed pictures of him and his family hung along the walls. The lights were off, and a pleasant breeze blew from the vents.

The hall led into the kitchen, where an old-fashioned phone was mounted on the wall near the kitchen table. He dialed Kristine's number.

She answered, "Hello?"

"Hey." Daniel's throat was dry. He cleared it. "Good morning."

"Daniel." She sounded worried. "Goodness. Did you leave for your parents in the middle of the night?"

He eased into a seat at the table and spotted his senior picture displayed on the kitchen counter. Even then, he was too cool to smile. He rubbed his face. "I couldn't sleep, so I figured why not?"

"Maybe because you needed your rest," Kristine suggested. "You had a crazy day yesterday."

"Believe me, I know. I couldn't stop thinking about it and figured driving would help. I meant to ask you to come, but—" he yawned.

"I would've loved to, but I told my manager that I'd work today." She sighed. "Kinda regret volunteering to work over spring break. Too late to back out now, though. Anyway, you're home! How's it going?"

Daniel looked around the kitchen. It was spotless, like always. "I just woke up. My parents are at church."

The sound of footsteps echoed down the hall and into the living room. There was a long grunt, as if someone were sitting down. Daniel went to see who it was until Kristine asked, "How long are you going to stay?"

"I'll leave in the morning." Daniel propped his elbow on the table and leaned his head against the phone. "I'll stop at Bragg for Captain Jones's funeral but will head home after that."

"Want to get together when I get off work tomorrow?"

"Absolutely," Daniel said.

The person in the living room groaned. "Just one drink would be nice. No, that's overused. Gotta think of somethin' better than that." It was a man's voice, but not his father's. "It's a special occasion. The boy is back. Have one with him. If anyone gives you grief over one lousy drink, they're the problem. Not you."

"Kristine, I've got to go," Daniel said. "I'll call you later."

He hung up and crept into the living room. "Hello?"

An old man in a button-up blue shirt with yellow flowers all over it and plaid pants was sitting in his father's recliner. Thin gray hair was sticking out all over his head. He had long eyebrows that stuck out over his eyes like eyelashes. He leaned on the arm of the chair, staring at nothing in particular. "Oh, bother. What's the point? The man's incorrigible. He won't *drink* a *drop*."

"Who are you, and what are you doing here?" Daniel asked.

The old man looked over his shoulder toward the doorway that led to the hall. "Who is that boy talkin' to?"

"I'm talking to you."

The old man turned back to Daniel with wide, gray eyes. "You can see me?"

"I can hear you too." Daniel stepped closer. Something was off about this man. The way he talked about not *drinking a drop*. Was this about his father? "I asked you a question."

"Simmer down there, young chap." The old man raised his hands and slowly came to his feet. "Don't get all worked up now. I'm Clayton Docks, an old friend of your father's."

Daniel didn't like where this was going. His father had a few friends at the church, but he was certain that Clayton wasn't one of them. "You should leave before I call the police."

The old man let his arms flop to his sides. "Don't do that, boy."

"Don't call me boy."

"Fine. I'll call you Daniel, but don't call the police 'cause I'm pretty sure they can't see me. If I had any money, I'd bet you're the only one who can."

Great. Daniel closed his eyes and craned his neck. He's home but still seeing spirits. This thing didn't look like the others he had seen; a hideous version of himself crawling across the floor or a man in a top hat staring back at him through a mirror. He went to the couch and sat. "I guess you're some kind of ghost?"

The old man fidgeted with the buttons on his shirt. "Yeah. I've been a part of your family for—I don't know—about fifty years or so. Mind if I sit?"

Daniel rubbed his forehead. Here he was having a conversation with something beyond the physical world. This couldn't be good for his mental health. "Go ahead, I guess."

Clayton eased down as if he were liable to topple over or break. "I've been with your father for the last forty years or so. I was with your granddaddy, but moved on to your father because he listened better."

Daniel leaned forward. "Are you talking about drinking?"

"Yep." The old man pretended to drink from a cup. "Good ol' alcohol. I need it, but I can't get it on my own." He sat back and sighed. "I figured I'd have decades of steady drinks with your dad, but we both know how that turned out." He snapped his fingers. "I've got an idea. How about you bring home a six-pack tonight?"

Daniel scoffed at the thought. "Are you kidding me?"

The old man clasped his hands and bit at his fingertips. He looked to be on the verge of tears. "You know I haven't had a drink since the day you were born? He stopped cold turkey on me." His cheeks puffed. "I looked more your age back then. Now look at me!"

"Why not leave?"

"Ain't it obvious?" The old man sniffed and wiped away tears. "I'm stuck. Any time I try to get away, I get sucked right back to Mr. Goody-Two-Shoes."

"You're not with him now, so you can't be too stuck."

"You don't know how this works." The old man looked at Daniel incredulously. "I can be where he is or where he lives. That's it. I'm not going to no church, either." He folded his arms and raised one bushy eyebrow. "But I guess I'll be more likely to find some booze there than here."

"There you go." Daniel gestured to the door. "Go to the church and find somebody else."

Clayton folded his arms. "I would, but churches hurt my feet."

"Why can't you go with him to a store or something? There's bound to be someone else you can latch on to."

Clayton propped a foot on his knee and massaged it through his shoes. "I tried that and more, but somethin' about your daddy's resolve keeps me tied to him. I must say—" he huffed "—I don't much like your daddy no more."

"I can't believe this." Daniel looked at the floor. Was he going to have to chat with spirits for the rest of his life? "This is nuts."

"Beer goes good with nuts," the spirit said.

Daniel looked at Clayton. "You're not the first spirit that I've seen."

"Why are you so glum about it?" the old man asked. "You could use it to your advantage if you're smart."

"My advantage is going to drive me insane." Daniel pushed off the couch and started pacing. "When my parents get home, I'll have to see you and hear you. I can't deal with that." He stopped and stared at Clayton. "And to be honest, I can't tell the difference between you and everybody else. Other than your shaggy hair and crazy pants."

"What's wrong with my pants?" The old man seemed affronted as he brushed his hands over his plaid pants. He patted his hair, which did nothing to improve it.

Daniel almost laughed. "Nothing. You're not dressed like a normal person, is all."

Clayton swiveled his head as if he were shaking and nodding at the same time. "Well, I'm sure you'll figure it out. All the spirits I see are a little odd, in my opinion. The real bad ones look like little gargoyles to me. All sorts of sizes, but no wings. There are other spirits like me, though. Disembodied spirits, ghosts, or whatever." Clayton held up a finger. "None of 'em will think you can see or hear 'em. That's your advantage, boy—I mean Daniel."

Daniel walked to the front door and looked out the window. "It's not worth the trouble."

Clayton got out of the recliner. "Spirits are always plotting against you. You'll be one step ahead of 'em. Can you imagine what you could do with that?"

Daniel turned. "All I want is a normal life."

"Ain't no such thing, but I get it." The old man tapped a foot and then clapped. "Got an idea for ya. Try wishing it away. Pray or something."

It wasn't a bad idea. Daniel wasn't sure why Clayton was so anxious to help him. Maybe the old spirit was sick and tired of brainstorming ways to get his father to drink. This must've been a nice change of pace. "It's worth a shot." He bowed his head and prayed silently. When he finished, he looked up and saw the old man standing between the recliner and the coffee table, watching him. "You're still here."

Clayton scratched his head. "Try saying it aloud."

"Dear Lord. God Almighty. Please remove this spirit who influenced my father to drink alcohol. Amen."

The old man gave him an incredulous look. "I've never heard a less inspiring prayer."

"You want to criticize my prayers, or do you want to help me out?" Daniel began pacing again.

"When I walked this earth in the flesh, I prayed much better than that. I'm sure my most drunken prayers—"

"Hold up a second." Daniel stopped walking and studied Clayton's face. "You used to be human?"

"Not that it matters." Clayton stared out a window into the front yard. "Died in 1846. Alcohol poisoning."

"Why aren't you in Gluttony, then?"

"I never fell into it." Clayton looked to the ceiling as if he were trying to find a memory up there. "I was recruited to be a whisperer. Said I could have all the drinks I wanted if I could get with the right people. Worked out well until—you know."

"Do you still want that?"

Clayton shrugged and turned to Daniel. "I don't want to be stuck with your daddy no more. If I could get away from him, I'd find me a young buck with a taste for whiskey sour. Anybody, even an occasional drinker, would do well enough for me."

Clayton didn't seem like much trouble to Daniel, but he knew that given the chance, Clayton might ruin someone's life in order to get another drink. He pulled out the keystone, remembering how he got rid of the last evil spirit he ran into. "If you want out of this situation, I can help."

"How?" the old man winced at the stone.

"It—," Daniel had to choose his words carefully, "got a demon unstuck from me." He tossed it up and caught it. "This could work for you."

Clayton scrunched up his face and scratched his nose. "What happened to the demon?"

Daniel shrugged. "Don't know. He just disappeared."

Clayton seemed skeptical. His jaw moved side to side as if he were chewing up a decision. "OK. How do we make it happen?"

The last thing Daniel wanted to do was throw a rock in his parents' house. "Let's go into the backyard."

"Sunlight stings me." Clayton moved back to the recliner and sat. "Can it wait 'til dark?

Clayton had lived with his father without causing too much harm for the last twenty-three years. A few more hours couldn't hurt. Daniel returned the stone to his pocket. "OK. But do you mind telling me how you influence people who can't tell you're there?"

"Just talk. They don't hear us with their ears." Clayton jabbed a finger at his head. "It's all in here. Our words kinda become their thoughts. The easy ones will act on what we say—might repeat us word for word. We become connected. Soulmates in a way."

"I drank," Daniel said. "Why didn't you get stuck with me?"

"I didn't know," Clayton said defensively. "Besides, you had other influences, and one in particular hated everything, especially me."

Daniel thought about the demon he had destroyed in his apartment and picked up a picture of him and his parents. His parents were smiling, but not him. He stared at the picture, seeking a glimpse of the thing that Clayton had mentioned.

"You won't find it in no picture," Clayton said.

"What was it exactly?"

"You had this—" Clayton grimaced at the floor. "—this hateful demon. It was tolerant of you and your momma, but if anyone else got too close, it got nasty. That demon jumped at me and your daddy all the time. It was hateful and made you hateful, too."

Daniel stared out the window and saw his car sitting alone in the driveway. "You said it was tolerant of Mom?"

Clayton nodded. "It was with her before it jumped to you."

Daniel looked at Clayton. "My mom wasn't an angry person."

"She was oftentimes angry with your daddy before you were born. He'd go out with me, and she'd scream. I used that to keep him drinking." Clayton intertwined his fingers behind his head and leaned back. "Worked like a charm. Her hateful demon got what it wanted, and

I got what I wanted. That all died when your dad stopped drinking. That demon blamed me for your dad's change. Your mom stayed angry for a while, but her love, for you especially, weakened it. It ended up hiding in the crawlspace under the house, but one day, you got in trouble and went crying into your room. When you came out, it was on your back, licking at your head and whispering in your ear."

Daniel cringed and touched the back of his head. Outside, he heard his parents pulling into the driveway. "Think you can keep quiet 'til later tonight?"

"Sure." Clayton came to his feet and started down the hallway. "I'll mope around in your parents' bedroom. When they come to bed, we'll go outside so you can get me unstuck with that rock of yours."

Chapter Nine

We Solemnly Swear

When Emma touched Charles's shoulder, they shot through a blurry tunnel and came into a hallway lined with glossy white linoleum floor tiles. Charles felt nauseous, and his legs behaved like upright worms.

Emma pressed him to the wall. "You should've closed your eyes."

"Why don't you ever warn me before jumping?" The world slowly settled. Over Emma's shoulder, there was a bulletin board with all sorts of fliers and pictures tacked to it. "Is this where Kristine lives?"

"It's the dorm she lives in." Emma let go of Charles and walked toward the farthest end of the hall. Charles followed, using the walls to keep his feet under him. "This is her room." She pointed to a door to her right but continued down the hall.

Charles stopped at the door. "Where are you going?"

"Just checking on something." Near the end of the hall, she walked to the left and disappeared.

Charles checked his pocket watch. It wasn't vibrating, so he felt fine about clicking it open. The hands continued to spin wildly, and still, he knew not what to make of it. He closed it and returned it to his pocket.

What's taking her so long? He went to see what she was up to. When he reached the end of the hall, he found a glass door that led to a room full of spirits. None of them looked very pleased. A few were larger, dog-faced demons; others looked human, in need of serious medical attention.

"...you have to say it," Emma said bitterly to the crowd. She glanced at Charles before she turned back to them.

In the most unenthusiastic tone, the group muttered and mumbled a cacophonous response. "We promise."

Emma's smile looked forced and unkind; different from what Charles had received. "Good. You can't break the promise, so you may as well leave, lest you'll suffer far more than you could ever imagine."

Charles backed away as she came through the door. "What was that about?" he asked.

"They have no business being here." There was still an edge to her voice, though she tried to mask it. "Come on. I'll show you to Kristine's room."

"They're demons," Charles said. This was an opportunity for him to understand where her allegiances lay. If she proved to be an angel, he could use that. "They can be wherever they want."

"Pfft." Emma apparently didn't think that was the case. "Not if I have any say about it."

She walked down the hall toward Kristine's room. Charles peeked into the roomful of spirits before jogging after her. She didn't seem to like demons too much. Charles was certain now that she was an angel, and he was ready to find out for sure. "You know I'm a demon too, yet you're treating me *far* differently."

"Do you think I'm being unfair?" Emma spun around. Her eyes were fierce; her brow bent with serious discernment. It was kind of scary.

Charles scratched the back of his neck and checked the state of his shoes. "Um, no? But it appears to me that you have some sort of authority over others. You forced them to make some sort of unbreakable promise and have treated me like a student. Tell me, what would happen if they broke their promise?"

"Promises made to me can't be broken." Emma stopped outside Kristine's room and rounded on him. "With that said, my studious pupil, be careful what you promise and who you make promises to."

"You seem to care more than necessary, though." Charles took a step back because Emma looked as if she could deck him. For whatever reason, the possibility of displeasing her hurt him far more than he expected. "And you look far better than any other spirit I've seen."

"Oh, that's so sweet." Emma took him by his lapel and gave him a peck on the cheek.

He forgot where he was going with his line of questioning and stood there blinking dumbly.

"Wait here," she said.

Emma disappeared through the door. Down the hall, two spirits peeked from the room where they had made promises. Charles tipped his hat and they slowly drifted back into the wall.

Emma returned. "Come in. She's sleeping."

She took Charles by the hand and pulled him through the closed door. There were two wardrobes with pictures and school paraphernalia on the left, and a small bathroom on the right. Emma walked to the far side of the room where two desks sat underneath lofted beds. All the furniture was wooden, and only one bed was occupied.

The desk beneath it had several books opened, and a couple of items he didn't recognize. Pictures were taped to the wall. A couple showed Kristine with two older people, likely her parents. The woman had darker red hair than Kristine and similar facial features. One photo included Daniel sitting next to her in a dark place. They each had a dark brown bottle in their hands. Kristine was laughing. Daniel was frowning at something beyond the frame of the picture. Not the best picture of him, Charles imagined.

"I'm certain that Daniel will call her, so if you stay close to her, you'll figure out where he is," Emma said.

"Can I jump to him when he does?"

"Better not." Emma looked at him. "It's tricky. I've heard stories of novice jumpers getting stuck inside phones. One guy went into a phone with the intention of coming out in New York City, but they hung up before he got there. He was stuck in a phone for four hours." Emma suppressed a laugh. "The next caller was a spammer from India. Oh man, that poor guy never traveled by phone again."

Charles knew what a phone was but hadn't a clue about the word "spammer". He wanted to ask, but the gears in his head were clogged. He forgot his original question and touched the cheek where Emma had kissed him. "What was that you said?"

"Wait for me. OK?" Emma said. "I may not be free when she calls, but I'll help you as soon as I can."

"Why can't you show up when I need you?"

She patted his shoulder. "Because the world doesn't revolve around you."

That didn't sit well with Charles. He sighed and pointed at the things on Kristine's desk. "Fine. What are those two black things?"

"The big one is a laptop and the little one is Kristine's phone."

Charles wanted to know what a laptop was and how that skinny rectangular box was a phone, but he decided he'd hide his ignorance in these new world technologies. "So much has changed since my days."

Emma wrapped an arm around him and lay her head on his shoulder. "They sure have." She stepped toward the door to the hall. "And listen. I have to leave. Don't get caught up in the schemes you hear from other demons. That will distract you from what you should be doing."

"I won't," Charles said. He gripped his lapels and watched her.

Emma smiled. "You remind me of my brother." Then she disappeared.

Charles didn't think he liked the comparison. He wished he reminded her of anyone else. Anyone besides her brother. He sighed and looked at the dark rectangular phone and said, "Come on, lover boy. Call the girl who got you out of Hell."

CHAPTER TEN
A LESSON ON PAIN

The small wooden cabin sat among several spruce trees. It had two small square windows on either side of a light brown door. The roof covered the front porch that ran along the length of the house. Two rocking chairs flanked a table to the right of the door. A large pile of firewood sat to the left.

Memories of chopping firewood with his father on the side of the house caused Beau's forehead to tingle. They'd do that while Momma prepared dinner. Beau smiled as he recollected several conversations and moments of laughter for the first time in ages. Tears welled in his eyes.

Ralph massaged his shoulder. "Be thankful. Not everyone has fond memories of their parents."

"I remember them," Beau wiped away tears, "but it's coming back faster than I expected."

"What would you be doing around this time of day?"

Beau squinted at the dimly lit windows of his childhood home. "It's dawn, so I'd be gathering eggs from the chicken coop in the back for Momma. Depending on when this is happening, my dog, Dozer, would be with me. I'd feed him and the pigs after that." Beau turned to Ralph. "Are you sure this isn't Heaven?"

"Not quite." Ralph stepped onto the porch and took a seat in one of the rocking chairs. "Take a look in the window."

Beau's heart pounded with each step he took to the window. An oil lantern glowed upon the kitchen table. His mother had her hair tied back. She kept it like that, but at night, she'd untie it and brush it for a time. Young Beau came in through the back door.

Seeing a younger version of himself filled Beau with wonder. He had dark brown hair like his momma and was dressed in a gray button-up shirt and dark pants.

"Where's your father?" she asked him.

"Tending to the horse," Beau said.

"Still?" She set forks and knives beside the three plates. "What happened?"

"We found a copperhead near the chicken coop and had to take care of that first." The younger Beau stood behind his chair, looking down at his plate.

"Goodness gracious." Beau's mother placed a hand over her heart. "Did we lose any chickens?"

"No. Daddy said I was lucky that I saw it before it saw me. He took it and put it away."

Beau's mother scoffed. "I don't know why your daddy don't kill them things. They're dangerous."

Little Beau grimaced. "He said folks in town like to eat 'em for some reason or another."

Momma wiped a smudge from his cheek. "You know, that's right. Some folks do like to cook 'em up. Now sit down and eat your eggs. You gotta head on soon, or you'll be late."

The child looked at his plate and licked his lips. "I'm not hungry, Momma. Maybe I should get on to school. I get to play the piano when I'm early."

"That's right," older Beau said to Ralph. "I used to play the piano."

"Now Beau, you better eat," Momma said. "When you get home, you're gonna have to help your daddy with that fence, and you'll wish you did if you don't now."

"Yes, ma'am." The young boy cast his eyes to his feet and pulled his chair out. "Do you want me to wait on Daddy?"

"Get on to it. I'll fetch your father." Momma left through the back door.

As soon as she was gone, Beau sucked down his breakfast and ran to his room, which was to the right of the fireplace. When he came out, he was wearing a jacket and carrying a couple of books. He zipped out the front door and leaped down the steps.

"Goodness," Beau said. "I don't ever remember being in such a hurry."

Little Beau whistled. "Dozer? Where are ya, boy?"

The beagle sprinted from around the back of the house and trotted alongside the boy.

Ralph trotted down the steps and followed him. "Come on, Beau. You gotta keep up."

Beau scampered after Ralph. Young Beau hummed and whistled songs as he and Dozer left the farm and came along the main road that led into town. Warm sunlight lit up the world, but the forest kept them in the shade. All in all, the day was beautiful, not a single cloud in the sky. The brisk air caressed his face, and all sorts of wildflowers brought color to the green valley on the right.

"I'd usually pick a fistful of flowers on my way home for Momma." Older Beau turned to Ralph and chuckled. This weather suited him. It put him in a good mood. Maybe this wouldn't be as hard as he thought. "They're not as nice as the ones Daddy brought her, but she loved 'em all the same."

Ralph frowned and came to a stop, looking at the ground.

"What is it?" Beau asked.

A young man's voice spoke from behind. "Looky here, fellas. The coward thought he could sneak by us again." Three older boys sauntered from the woods. Beau remembered how they had taunted him for a time.

"Oh, no." Beau hid his eyes. "I remember this day."

"I told you that I didn't want any trouble," Little Beau said. Dozer barked at the three boys. They were all leaner and taller than him and had angry faces.

"Little Beau Peep and his little sheep," one said. The others forced a laugh. It was an insult they went to so often that even they had grown tired of it, but kept using it nonetheless.

Beau muttered to Dozer to be quiet, but Dozer wasn't having it as the three boys slowly came onto the road.

"I'm surprised you ain't tryin' to run, you ugly toad," another said.

"He's too slow." The smaller of the three boys picked up a rock and slung it at Dozer and missed. "We'd catch him easy."

"I know that," another said. He sprinted to Beau and pushed him down. "You fall pretty easy for a chunky boy."

Dozer ran a few feet away and barked some more.

"Your dog's as big a coward as you are, Beau Peep," one said. All of them smiled mischievously. "Y'all fetch that little rat while I take care of this coward right here."

The other two started after Dozer, who sprinted back toward the house. Beau got up to run after Dozer, but he was pushed back down. A foot was pressed against his back. "Now don't you go runnin' off, too."

"I'll tell," Beau grunted.

"Ain't nobody gonna help you." The boy kicked young Beau in the side. Beau cried out, gripping his hip. "School starts early today. Lesson one: stop being a coward." The boy kicked him again.

Beau squeezed his eyes shut. Throughout his life, the memory of this day often crept into his thoughts. *Stop being a coward.* He wished he could forget it again. His hands trembled. "Why do I need to see this?"

Ralph placed a hand on Beau's shoulder. "You need to remember."

"I remember already, so make it stop," Beau demanded.

Ralph sighed and looked back at little Beau. "I'm afraid there's more to see."

The other two came back panting. "The dog's too fast."

Beau got up and sprinted to town, but the three young men quickly caught up. They pushed him down and started kicking. It seemed to go on for a lifetime until Mr. Hicks came down the road on his wagon. The three boys took off, and Mr. Hicks came down off his wagon to help young Beau to his feet.

"Don't worry about them boys, Beau." Mr. Hicks glared at the boys as they ran to town. "They'll get theirs. I'll see to that. You alright?"

The day didn't look so beautiful anymore. Little Beau's face and shirt were bloodied and covered in dirt. His books were strewn about the road, and his pants got torn up too. The world froze when Mr. Hicks started to help him up onto the wagon.

Ralph walked over to little Beau and placed a hand on his cheek. "This was when you truly learned hate."

"Can you blame me?" Beau refused to look at his younger self, keeping his eyes in the direction of his family's farm. "Those boys were horrible. I wasn't the only one they did this to, either."

"I'm not talking about them." Ralph stood up and faced him. "You hated yourself."

Beau scoffed. "That's not true."

"Then why won't you come over here and look at yourself?" Ralph asked.

Beau glared at Ralph, who raised his brow in worry. He marched to his younger self. "I'll do it, but I don't see the point." He bent down. When he looked into little Beau's face, it broke his heart. Tears leaked over his younger self's puffed cheeks. His watery blue eyes stared at the ground. They were filled with an emptiness that Beau had never seen yet knew all too well.

"It's why I didn't want breakfast." Beau stood and looked away. "Those boys had tried to catch me on my way to school all week that week. All because I had bumped into one of 'em during recess. Challenged me to a fight there on the spot, and I backed down. It's why everybody called me a coward."

Ralph came up beside him. "After all this, you forgave them. Even after their halfhearted apology, you went on to become friends with these boys."

Beau pinched his trimmed beard and tugged. "You say it like I did something wrong."

"No, there's nothing wrong with that," Ralph said. "But you never forgave yourself. You were ashamed of who you were. You resented yourself more than they ever did."

"I did no such thing." Beau backed away. "I never resented who I was."

Ralph walked toward him. "You never thought that you deserved kindness. You thought you were worthless despite all the lives you touched."

Beau turned and looked to the east, where the sun was breaching the treetops. Its light warmed his face. He inhaled the fresh morning air. Over his shoulder, the town sat nestled in a green valley. Dust rolled along the ground. Three boys sprinted along the road. Then he looked at his younger self. "Those boys didn't know any better. Like you said, we became friends after this."

"Do you know why you were so angry with yourself?"

Beau wiped his eyes. "Because they were right about me. I was a coward. I was chunky and fell down mighty quick when what I should've done was stand up for myself."

Ralph nodded solemnly and snapped his fingers. Beau expected the world to start moving again, but it didn't. A dim veil stretched across the sky, darkening the world. The air seemed thicker.

Beau recognized this immediately. "The shadow realm?"

"That's right," Ralph said, "but not only shadows. Spirits of light and dark operate here. It's often called the spirit world."

Under the dark green canopies of the trees, ghostly eyes loomed. They weren't frightening but were full of gloom. Beau knew these creatures well. "I see shadow people in the forest."

"As you know, they're harmless," Ralph turned toward town, "unlike others."

Six dark creatures trailed after the fleeing bullies. Demons—the primitive kind. Shaped like small, hideous dogs, who often beg for their human hosts to act out in unbecoming ways.

"I would think they would have had more by the way they acted," Beau said.

"Take a look at yourself."

When Beau turned, his hand went to his heart. Three tall, gangly demons clung to little Beau. One sat on his shoulders. It had a hideous smile and a long-curved nose. The other two clutched his arms, whispering into his ears. Their bodies were green, warty, and bare.

"Three of 'em?" Older Beau asked.

Ralph snapped his fingers again. The world began to move. Mr. Hicks went to help younger Beau into the carriage. The demon on Beau's shoulders said, "We don't need your help, you simpleton!"

"Don't help me," the young Beau said tearfully.

Mr. Hicks nodded. "OK. You can get on yourself, then."

"They should be hanged, but they'll probably get away with a slap on the wrist," the demon hissed. "Vow to never forgive them, boy. Say it!"

Beau dropped his bottom hard onto his seat. "I'll never forgive them."

Mr. Hicks got on and took up the reins. "I know how you feel, Beau."

"He knows nothing. Don't listen to him," the demon growled. "Listen to me."

The two demons that held onto his arms agreed. "Yes, listen to us."

Mr. Hicks and Beau rode into town with three passengers they couldn't see. The one that sat on Beau's shoulders looked back at Ralph and bared its teeth.

"Can it see us?" Beau asked.

"No," Ralph said. "It senses the love from your family's home. It hates love."

The sky, the trees, the land and everything on it twisted into a mix of colors. Dizzy, Beau closed his eyes. His body began to tip, and Ralph caught him by the arm and sat him down in a chair. They were back on the front porch.

There was a tinkling noise. Beau chanced a look. Ralph was standing over him with a glass. "More lemonade?"

"Thank you." Beau finished it in a few gulps. "Please tell me that's all. That we can get on to Heaven now."

Ralph sat in the other rocking chair. "There's more for you to remember, Beau, but we can rest as long as you like."

Beau set his glass down on the table beside him. "Three demons? Did I ever get rid of any of 'em?"

Ralph rocked slowly beside him. "Those demons never fared very well with you, but every battle has its scars. You laughed and had many moments of happiness, but at the core, you were never happy with yourself. You were never good enough for you. You hid that from everybody, but you can't hide that from us."

"Did those devils make me hate myself?" Beau asked.

Ralph whirled a finger over Beau's glass, and it was refilled with lemonade. "The truth is that they can't make you do anything. Not even a legion of demons or multitude of hardships can overrule how you choose to see yourself."

"It's not fair. I was the victim."

"Don't feel defeated." Ralph crossed his legs. "Be at peace."

"Where were my angels?"

"Some things you have to do on your own, Beau." Ralph leaned back in the chair and let it rock back and forth. "You may not think so, but you did well."

Beau didn't think so. He actually understood why a lot of people couldn't finish the trip. Seeing those kids beat up his younger self hurt. And seeing demons all over him without a single angel in sight was demoralizing.

Ralph patted him on the back. "We'll get on with it when you're ready."

CHAPTER ELEVEN

RISE AND SHINE

It didn't take long for Charles to grow tired of watching Kristine sleep. He wanted to know what all the fuss was about. Why did Daniel care so much about this girl? How could it be that this woman could give a man the will to stomach Hell and return home? If not for her, Daniel would've dived headlong into the subterranean river of blood in the first chamber of Violence. This seemingly amazing woman was bundled up in a blanket that rose and settled upon each of her breaths. Red hair splattered all over her pillow and covered much of her fair, freckled face.

Charles stuck his head through the blinds and the window. The darkness was receding. Twilight colored everything in shades of blue and gray. He was excited for the morning. Not only would he see Kristine and likely find Daniel, but he would also see the sun in the sky, and all kinds of life for the first time since he had died.

He peeked at her. A slight opened-mouth snore told him she wasn't waking anytime soon. Maybe he should practice jumping. He closed his eyes and focused on returning to Daniel's couch. A sense of weightlessness washed over him as he slowly sat down. This time, he was confident that his bottom would end up on Daniel's living room couch, and it did. This was the fifth time he'd come over on his own. The first time, he was worried he might not make it back to Kristine's dorm room, but it proved to be much easier than he thought. All he had to do was think about being in her dorm room. With Daniel still absent, there wasn't a reason to stay, so he jumped to the rooftop, where he'd report to the overseers later that evening.

He had discovered that jumping to a standing position was a bit of a balancing act. This time, he stumbled but didn't fall. A majestic sky, with purple, red, and golden slivers of light bloomed and shone upon the trees and the brick buildings that cut through the green canopies. Cool air whipped about and nearly sent his bowler hat off his head.

Daniel could call Kristine at any moment, and Charles needed to be there when he did. He closed his eyes and felt the world change again. The sensation felt more familiar this time. The air warmed when he returned to Kristine's room. They weren't alone, however. Something had leaped through the door of the closest wardrobe when Charles opened his eyes.

"I saw you," Charles said. "Come on out."

"Why did that pretty girl bring you here?" a deep, growly voice asked.

Charles planted one hand on his hip and pressed his bowler hat lower onto his head with the other. The pocket watch resting in his vest vibrated slightly. It seemed to do that whenever he felt threatened, even a little. He looked back at the wardrobe. Demons were tricky creatures and had different ways to trip people up, but Charles was no sucker. "Never mind her. This is between you and me. Who are you and why are you here?"

"I'm Iffy," the demon said from the wardrobe. "I belong to Karen."

This demon couldn't be too knowledgeable, considering that it kicked off this conversation with a false name. Charles couldn't blame it for lying since names were so important up here, but lying right out of the gate seemed amateurish. He folded his arms. "If that's the case, why are you hiding?"

"I do not hide. I live here." Iffy climbed through the wall of the wardrobe. This creature didn't look like any demon Charles had ever seen. It looked more like a walking, talking stuffed animal. When it turned, its face looked like an earless rabbit, but with protruding golf ball-sized eyes centered over a large bulbous nose. A long, wavering smile stretched underneath it, as if a toddler made it with a black marker.

The sight of this demon was so ridiculous, Charles forgot what they were arguing about. "I didn't see you with the rest of your demon friends back in the other room."

"I eat demons for breakfast." Iffy opened its cavernous mouth and pointed inside. "See?"

Charles saw a gaping hole but no demons. "You have no teeth."

Iffy closed his mouth. "I do not like teeth."

"But demons have—oh, never mind. Why aren't you trying to eat me, *Iffy*?" Charles gripped his lapels.

Iffy waved off the question. "You have no taste."

"What?" Charles looked down at his clothes and tightened his necktie. "I'm teeming with taste. No other demon that I know of dresses this good."

Iffy scratched its head. "You want me to eat you?"

"No." Charles thought the judge he worked with back in Limbo, Baxter the Brittle, was annoying, but this guy might be infinitely more so. "Listen. I have it on good authority that her name isn't Karen. Didn't you hear my girlfriend—I mean the girl say her name earlier?"

"Yes." Iffy stood tall. Its head swiveled haughtily. "She used her old name."

"What is her old name, then?"

"I won't say." Iffy folded his arms and looked away. "She changed to someone else."

"OK." Charles knew this demon was trying to trick him into giving up Kristine's name, but he wouldn't. He gestured to the door. "You may as well leave because I'm still willing to use her real name, which means I'm more connected to her than you are."

Iffy took hold of its chin and tapped his cheek. "OK. I'll play nice. You can be my minion."

"Tell you what." Charles removed his hat and stepped closer to Iffy. "If I'm your minion, let me stay with her while you go do more important things."

"Good idea, minion," Iffy said. "I stay with Karen, and you go do the things."

"Actually, you should check the building for any more loose demons." Charles walked away from Iffy and lingered by the window, as if the discussion was settled. "Go eat those—delicious demons with your big, toothless mouth."

"I do this already." Iffy rubbed its belly. "Eat them like jellybeans. They're all gone now. More come later."

"Have you checked the roof, though?" Charles nodded to the ceiling. "They tend to hang out up there."

Iffy looked skyward. "Oh, I have never checked way up there. That would be fun!"

"Great." Charles clapped his hands together and pointed at Iffy. "You go have your fun, and I'll handle our little lady."

Iffy raised a thick, furry finger. "Very good idea, minion! I will have my lunch. Let me know when Karen wakey wakes." It walked through the door into the hall. Charles hoped it would stay up there for a while.

Soon after, Kristine stirred and climbed from her bunk. She wore red and black flannel pajamas. Rubbing her eyes, she tapped on her phone a few times and brought it to her ear. Charles neared her and heard

Daniel's voice. He knew it was a recording, though, so he didn't call for Emma. From what he heard, Daniel was in Georgia reconciling with his parents. Charles hoped Kristine would call him back immediately, but she set the phone down.

She walked through him and into the bathroom. It wasn't as bad as the car passing through him, but Charles felt as if his privacy was violated. He needed a moment away, so he stepped into the hall, which was empty. He figured there would be more demons loitering out here. *Maybe Iffy really did eat them for breakfast.* He took out his watch, which had calmed now that Iffy wasn't around. The hands had come loose from the center and were flipping around, counterclockwise.

The door opened behind him. Kristine came out wearing a long sleeve shirt and form-fitting sweatpants with her hair tied back. Her fingers tapped on her phone. She moved as if she were late for an appointment.

Charles followed after her, wondering what she was up to. She plugged earbuds in as she threw open a door to the stairwell and practically galloped downstairs. Why was she in such a hurry? Charles picked up his pace. Kristine reached the ground floor and pushed her way through the door to the first floor.

Charles lunged down two flights of stairs and sprinted out the door in time to see her jogging to the left. He ran out the glass double doors and trotted after her, but she kept getting farther and farther away. It was infuriating. What if Daniel called? Then he got an idea. He jumped to her.

He was right beside her within a second. Satisfied, he brushed off his palms, feeling like a real problem solver, but there was a new problem. She kept running. Charles rolled his eyes. "Well, I do need the practice."

Kristine jogged far longer than any normal person should. Charles jumped more times than he cared to count before she slowed to a walk. The entire experience of jumping every few seconds was exhausting. He might have preferred jogging. She went to her room, gathered a few things, and took a shower. Charles checked the wardrobe to see if Iffy or some other demon was in there. He found clothes and a tattered, stuffed animal that looked like a smaller version of Iffy seated up high on a shelf. There were plenty of demons outside, and everywhere else, but not here. Maybe Emma had them promise to leave. He doubted that Iffy could eat a single demon, much less dozens.

Kristine came out of the bathroom wearing a bathrobe. Her hair was wrapped in a towel. She went straight to her computer. When she got it started, her fingers went faster than her legs, tapping at all the letter buttons. He came up behind her and watched the screen. It was the strangest thing he had ever seen. She was writing, then reading, and then writing some more. So boring.

It didn't take long for Charles's patience to leap to its death. He paced the room, having a one-way conversation about the importance of staying in communication with your significant other. Of course, Kristine couldn't hear a word he said, but he continued nonetheless until that small rectangular phone rang on her desk.

The voice on the other end was female and apparently excited about something. Kristine smiled. Then her jaw dropped.

"What?" Kristine typed quickly on her computer. "We were there yesterday." An article came up on her laptop. The headline read: *Mysterious Cloud Spiraling Over Grandfather Mountain.*

"They say it's a lenticular cloud that's lasting longer than normal," Kristine said. She rested her elbow on the table and scrolled down the page, listening to the chatter on the other end of the line. "It does look like it's smoking, but there's no fire, according to the article. Weird."

Kristine clicked on an image of the mountain, making it larger. Thin plumes of smoke rose to a circular gray cloud over the peak. It reminded Charles of the Purging Mountains. If Daniel was there yesterday and the smoke was coming from an unknown source, the world could be in for a very hot summer. *What does this mean, though?* he thought. *Is Hell breaking loose?*

"No." Kristine pulled a strand of red hair behind her ear. "I have to work a double today. I'll go after work tomorrow if it's still a thing."

He couldn't make out what the girl on the other end of the line said and wondered what he would have to do to jump to her if he wanted to. Would he have to leap into the phone or something? Breathe into it?

"No." Kristine sat back in her seat and sighed. "We hiked there yesterday. It was crazy. A sinkhole or something opened up and Daniel fell inside it. I thought he was dead, but you know Daniel. He came out with some scratches and that was it." She paused. "No. He's out of town visiting his parents."

Charles gave up trying to hear the conversation and peered out the window. Overhead, the sky looked gray. It was clear and sunny a few minutes ago. Was the smoke affecting the weather? Would the clouds grow darker and loom over this town like it did Grayton?

"I promise I'll call you when I get off work." Kristine removed the towel from her head and dark wet hair spilled to her shoulders and back. "If I'm not too tired, I'll stop by. OK. Bye."

She hung up and sank back in her seat, reading the article.

Charles read over her shoulder. "See if there's another article about this."

"There's like four articles about it already," Kristine said as she typed. Charles grinned. *Interesting. Am I influencing her?*

She brought up a website for the local Boone news station. The article said the same thing about lenticular clouds and had a video of the smoke that seemed to have no source. A park ranger said that the smoke was most likely very thin nimbostratus clouds. Charles was certain that wasn't the case.

Her phone rang again. "Daniel" was displayed on the screen. She answered it.

"Hey!"

Charles loosened his necktie. "Emma." He waited and nothing happened. "Emma?" He came onto his toes and bounced lightly. "Come on. Emma."

She didn't respond. *Great.* "This is more important than your stupid appointment, Emma."

He said her name over and over, but she didn't appear. Charles gripped the brim of his bowler hat with both hands and grimaced. "Before you go, I have to tell you—Oh, OK. Talk to you later." She set the phone down.

"Go figure." Charles walked back to the window. He was brooding over the fact that Emma hadn't shown, and the two lovebirds had had the shortest conversation possible. Maybe he didn't need her. Maybe he could figure it out on his own. He already figured out that he could influence Kristine. He looked at her and whispered, "Let's go for a walk?" His voice seemed to echo in the small room.

"You know, I could use a coffee," Kristine muttered to herself. She picked up the phone and dialed a number. "Hey Mandy. I'm going for a walk. Wanna meet at Brewsters? OK. See you in a bit." She pocketed her phone and went to the bathroom to finish drying her hair. After that, she put on a light jacket and went out the door.

Charles wasn't sure if he'd influenced her or not, but just in case, he whispered, "Let's walk. OK? Taking it easy."

CHAPTER TWELVE
THE WIND AND THE RIVER

Azazel and all the other ancient demons who thrived in Hell, although intelligent and powerful, were flawed in one critical way. They underestimated the resilience of the human spirit and believed that given enough Hell, a person would acclimate to the terrors and embrace the horrors. Their ignorance worked in Chance's favor.

They believed that he'd drift through the winds of Lust forever, even though they knew he had been here before. The only difference this time was that he didn't have his hat. They didn't know that his trusty ol' hat hadn't helped him much in all the wind when he had extracted his brother years ago.

The ropes on Chance's wrists and legs slid off. Slowly, the winds carried him downward until he was walking along the desert floor.

Counterclockwise, bodies whirled overhead in this never-ending storm full of flies. There were two ways out of this realm of Hell. He could head to the eye of the storm, where a pit would take him down into Gluttony. That would be counterproductive, since that wasn't the way he needed to go to get back to Grayton to find his brother, Harrison. He was the only person Chance could trust, now that his teammates had betrayed him.

The winds of Lust pushed against Chance's back, ushering him toward the River Styx, where Charon served as the ferryman. The demon wouldn't willingly give him a lift back to Limbo, but Chance was certain that he could best him. After all, the angry boatman wanted one thing more than anything else, and that was to be on time. The smallest delay vexed him, so all Chance had to do was weather his wrath for a short while.

Several bodies rocketed from right to left. One struck Chance and he tumbled several yards before he regained his feet. If he'd had his hat, he would've reacted faster. In fact, he'd already be at the River Styx and back in Grayton. He was thankful that he didn't have it, though. The winds could have carried it away, and it would've taken an act of God for him to retrieve it. Come to think of it, it was probably an act of God that kept his hat in Limbo rather than here in the first place.

After four more miles of dodging bodies and mustering swarms of flies, Chance leaped through the outer walls of the storm and came to the still shores of the River Styx. When Chance touched the greenish-brown waters with his fingers, he felt the slightest tug to the right. That meant Charon was delivering souls to deeper hells. The demon would be en route to Limbo when Chance faced him, which meant it'd be more apt to give Chance the ride. He touched his fist to his chest and then pointed skyward.

"Thank you, Lord."

Chance walked in the direction of Grayton in the shallows of the river. It would likely take him a week to get there this way, but he didn't like the idea of standing around. The River Styx wasn't a fishing hole. If anything was in those waters, he didn't want it biting him. Period. The sloshing of his feet and the slow yet steady change of scenery helped him to think, anyway. So much had happened yesterday. Strange that today seemed equally hectic. What did it mean for tomorrow?

Best not worry about tomorrow. Today has its own worries.

Azazel, along with his army of minions, didn't march into Limbo every day. They preferred to stay in their realms, where they held dominion over others. Something was amiss, and he believed it had everything to do with Daniel Strong, who'd fallen into Hell alive and had returned home with God's favor upon him. This couldn't be about revenge, though. Azazel's actions were too tactical; too extreme of a response over one man escaping Hell. They were digging into the Purging Mountains, where souls fell into Hell. Was it possible they could reach the land of the living? He would need to be back in Limbo to find out.

The water changed. The current pressed against his heels. He turned. Charon wasn't in sight yet, but was heading in his direction in a hurry. Water sloshed as Chance trudged out into the middle of the river. The deepest point came to his waist. Charon would run aground if he tried to go around him. The current pressed harder. Chance took a step back and braced himself against it.

The water cut around him as if he were a boulder. It retreated toward the deeper hells. The river receded until there was no water around or behind Chance. A wall of it rushed toward him, and on the crest was Charon with his skiff.

Charon stood near the stern. His bulbous head stood out from his long, bony, gray body. He held a staff before him, parallel to the ground. When his black eyes fell upon Chance, he scowled, revealing a mouth full of quill-like teeth.

A message blared in Chance's head. *"Move!"*

Chance shook his head. "I'm coming aboard. Like it or not."

Right before the wall of water struck him, Chance leaped and took hold of the hull. The speed of the boat and the pressure from the water nearly sucked him under, but he held on. Charon, in a fit of rage, threw his pole down and marched to Chance. He must've assumed that Chance was, like all the others, damned to this wretched world. With the pole out of Charon's hand, the boat slowed to a drift, allowing Chance to pull himself aboard.

Charon took Chance by the arm and tried slinging him ashore, but found that wasn't happening. Even without his hat, Chance was slippery quick. He whirled his arm around Charon's hand and knocked the demon off balance long enough for him to sprint to the stern and grab the pole.

Charon hissed. The sound of his words didn't travel through the air. They hopped straight into Chance's head again. *What are you?*

"Just a poor wayfaring stranger." Chance winked. "Promise me you'll take me to Limbo, and I'll give your pole back."

Charon lunged, and Chance swatted the pole at his head. The demon shrieked at the sky of stone. *Give it! Now!*

"You can't control me like you do others." He held the pole defensively. "If you want your pole back, you have to do as I say."

Charon thrusted an open hand toward Chance. Chance felt the pole tugging toward the demon, but he held it tight. His feet slid a few inches closer to the boatman.

Give it back!

"Make the promise!" Chance strained against the invisible power drawing the pole closer to Charon's hand.

They glared at each other. Hundreds of veins bulged over Charon's face. His hand shook with fatigue. The force that pulled on the pole diminished. Charon dropped his hand. *I promise to take you to Limbo!*

Chance sighed in relief. "Thank you." He tossed the pole to Charon and stepped to the bow of the boat to be as far from the demon as possible. This wasn't out of fear, but a simple courtesy for a demon with a reputation of vehement anger.

CHAPTER THIRTEEN

THE JOYOUS ONES

Tiny little lights zipped around Daniel's parents as they exited the car. He thought it was his imagination at first, or perhaps he was seeing stars flaring up in his vision, until he heard them squeaking excitedly. They flew about and would float momentarily to beckon and speak to one another. As his parents approached the house, Daniel could see the little things were wearing tiny red hats and sparkling yellow tights. Their faces were bright and stretched into blissful smiles. When they caught sight of Daniel, they waved and somehow became even more excited than they already were.

Daniel's parents were far more composed than these tiny creatures, but the joy in their glowing expressions caused him to chuckle. He opened the door, and the little sprites jetted over and hugged him, snuggling their faces into his cheeks and around his neck.

We love you!

So happy to see you!

Welcome home!

They were very distracting, but Daniel kept his eyes on his parents and did his best to look sane. One little flying person hovered in front of his face. It looked male and had orange hair that stuck out from his red hat. Freckles dotted his flushed cheeks. It squeaked a few times and blinked as if confused. It seemed to ask Daniel why he wasn't hugging back.

Daniel muttered, "Not right now."

The sprite seemed relieved and squeaked at his flying companions, all of which darted past him and into the house.

"My son is home." Daniel's mother hugged him deeply. She was dressed in a navy-blue dress and smelled like her favorite perfume. His father wore a black sweater, tan khakis, and a tie.

A chubby little person with transparent butterfly wings sat on his mother's shoulder, beaming with delight. "Hello," she said. "Don't be alarmed. We're happy fairies. My name is Orna Joyous, the elder of our clan."

Daniel felt a little on the spot. He couldn't strike up a conversation with a little fairy lady named Orna in front of his parents. "Hello."

Orna waved like a happy child. His mother took him by the hands.

Daniel looked into her bleary eyes. "It's so nice to see you."

"Come here." His father was next. There were no little fairy things loitering on his shoulder, but he gave Daniel a hearty hug and several pats on the back before letting him go.

"We're doing all this on the porch." Daniel's mother touched his shoulder. "Let's go inside and have some lunch."

The house seemed a little more magical when Daniel walked back inside. The fairies squeaked and flitted about aimlessly. Some seemed to dance in the air. The female fairy on his mother's shoulder said, "Oh no. We're distracting you." She came to her feet and struck a metal triangle with a tiny stick. "Little ones. Oh, little ones. I need your attention."

"Are you OK?" Daniel's mother touched his forehead. "You look like you've seen a ghost. Have a seat. I'll make you a glass of sweet tea."

"That sounds great. Thanks, Mom." Daniel walked to the couch and sat.

"Let me help, honey," his father said, heading into the kitchen.

Daniel heard Orna speaking. "While we all have good reason to be excited, we must settle down. Daniel can see us and hear us, and it's causing him distress."

The fairies let out a long "Awww." Five of them peeked around the corner and waved.

Daniel waved back awkwardly. It wasn't as bad as seeing demons, but these little guys had enormous energy.

"Let's allow him some quality time with his parents," Orna said.

"Get enough rest?" Daniel's dad came into the living room and handed him a glass of iced tea, then took a seat in the recliner.

"Oh, yeah." Daniel still had his ear on the kitchen. The fairies were silent. "I needed it. How was church?"

"Well," Daniel's father chuckled. "You won't believe this but—"

Clayton, his father's old demon, came out of his parent's bedroom flailing his arms. The fairies were buzzing around his head, kicking and slapping him. Orna flew over and broke it up. "Leave him alone," she said smartly. The fairies reluctantly stopped. Orna turned to Clayton, who was hunched with his arms shielding his face. "Return to your place. We'll leave you be." She neared Clayton's face as he slowly lowered his arms. "For now, that is."

The other fairies each gave a curt nod. They stood rigid in midair, glaring at Clayton. He gazed at them warily as he stepped back through the master bedroom door.

"You're still a little tired, aren't you?" Daniel's father looked concerned. "You can get some more rest if you need to, son."

"I'm good." Daniel turned to his dad and focused the best he could on him, rather than the squeaking argument transpiring in the hallway. "Just some lingering cobwebs. What were you saying?"

"That old demon can't ruin this occasion," the lady fairy said. "Now go on into the kitchen and whirl around the lady of the house, but keep it down." They gladly obliged.

"The preacher called for prayer requests and praises, and your mother leaped up and shouted, 'Our son is home!'" His father smiled so big his teeth showed. That was a sight he'd rarely seen growing up. "The whole church gave her a standing ovation."

Daniel's mother peered around the corner. Orna was back on her shoulder. "There's a potluck tonight, and everybody wants to see you. But I told them it's up to you."

"Please say yes," Orna said, her hands folded before her as if praying. Daniel chuckled. "I'd love to."

His mother beamed and disappeared back into the kitchen, where the other fairies squealed with a cheer.

Daniel turned back to his father. Never had he seen him so content, but with all the anticipation and emotion lingering in the room, they didn't know what to say. His mother came in from the kitchen and set a plate of crackers, cheese, and salami on the coffee table. "I got so excited that I started making dinner." She sat in her favorite chair and fidgeted with her hands.

His parents didn't seem to know what to talk about, so Daniel brought up Kristine. From there, the conversation drifted naturally. They told funny stories of things that happened with friends and family since Daniel left. A couple of extended family members had passed away in his four-year absence, which made him regret ever leaving home in the first place.

"Mom. Dad." Daniel looked at his folded hands. "I'm sorry."

"It's OK, son," Daniel's father said.

"I know I was wrong for what I did." Daniel didn't know what else to say. "I wish I could take it all back, but I can't."

His mother took his hand and squeezed. "We're glad you're home."

"We love you, son."

Chapter Fourteen

Terror in the Cabin

Beau ignored an intuitive tug to go inside the cabin and instead walked about the grounds. Behind the chicken coop, he found a tree he used to climb. He had carved his initials on it. To the left of it, a wooden fence surrounded an acre where they had grown sweet potatoes.

The horizon was shielded by countless spruce trees. He gazed above them at the clear sky, remembering all the colors and shades of the many sunsets he'd experienced during his life. He wished Ralph brought him here for that rather than the darkness that loomed inside his childhood home.

Ralph waited on the porch. He had given Beau more space since the encounter on the road, where Beau had witnessed demons clinging onto his younger self. Did he truly hate himself? Without a doubt, he cared about others. He could look into anyone's eyes and find the good within them. However, gazing at his own reflection made him sour, and he wasn't sure why. The path to finding out led to the cabin.

He took a seat on a stump where he and his father would cut firewood. Footsteps came from behind him.

"Want me to get going, huh?" Beau asked.

"When you're ready." Ralph took up the axe that was stuck in the chopping block a few feet from Beau. He placed a log on it and sliced it in half with a single downward stroke. "Are you worried about what's ahead?"

Beau scratched at his beard. He stared at the chopping block, unable to meet the angel's gaze. "No. I'm fine. Just taking everything in."

Ralph set the ax on its head and rested his hands on the handle. "You know, it's OK to be scared."

"I'm not." Beau snatched up a shard of wood and rolled it in his fingers. If he had a knife, he'd whittle it down to something. "I'm home for the first time in ages. It feels good."

"Oh. My mistake." Ralph looked about the yard, smiling. "It is nice out here, but inside the cabin—maybe not so much?"

Beau cringed. He dug his finger into the wood grain and peeled a skinny fiber off the shard. "I always liked it out here better."

"Why is that you think?" Ralph set another log on the block and sliced it.

Beau looked the angel in the eyes this time. Sure, Ralph bore the semblance of a good-hearted person who meant no harm, but he wanted Beau to experience whatever nightmare waited inside. "You know as well as I do that if I go inside that house, something bad's going to happen." Beau slung the small piece of wood to the ground. He stormed to his feet, pacing. "No wonder no one makes this trip. For you, it's nothing. I'm the one who has to feel all this."

Ralph nodded. "It hurts."

"You're doggone right, it does." Beau wiped his eyes. "And I don't know why. I don't want to know."

Ralph walked to Beau and hugged him tight. "I can't take your pain away." Beau let his tears roll onto the angel's shoulders. "But you are not alone. You never were."

"That's not true." Beau pushed Ralph away. "I've been nothing but alone for ages."

"As a shadow, yes," Ralph said, "but you chose that."

Beau narrowed his eyes. That couldn't be right. Could it? "I chose to be a shadow?"

Ralph nodded sadly.

Beau looked over at the exterior of his cabin home. The frames around the windows were white, but beyond the glass was darkness. "That demon that clung to me. Did it have anything to do with my decision?"

Ralph took Beau by the shoulders. "It was yours and yours alone."

"I turned down Heaven to be a shadow?" Beau couldn't believe it. "Why?"

Ralph shrugged. "We're here to find out."

"Very well then." Beau headed to the porch. His heartbeat thumped louder with each step he made. He paused at the steps, resting his hand on a handrail that he and his father mended many times over.

Ralph walked by him and stood at the door. "Whenever you're ready."

Beau looked at his sandaled feet. Despite the quiet, he was reeling inside, squirming like a worm whose flesh had been pricked by a hook. After a deep breath, he went in.

It was warm. The fireplace was going. Save for an oil lamp and a few candles, all was dark. The daylight was gone. Darkness blotted the windows. Something about his parents' bedroom door drew his attention. He walked to it, ignoring the tolling of his heart.

He passed through the door. In the darkness, Beau saw his father lying there; eyes wide with fear. Upon his chest sat a creature with red eyes that looked like a short, shadowy version of a man. All around the room, shadowy beings lurked about. Beau got the feeling they were tethered to the thing on his father's chest somehow.

His father's lips shook, but the rest of him lay still. He seemed to mutter a plea to the creature. It lowered its head to Beau's father, snarling, taunting, tapping a four-inch-long talon to his chest.

Beau reached for his father, but his hand passed through him, like it did the door. "Dad?" he whispered. "Can you hear me at all?"

"He can't." Ralph was beside him, arms folded. His eyes glowed as blue as the sky.

"I think this is the night he died," Beau whimpered. Although he knew it would be in vain, he tried to shoo away the creature sitting on his father. It didn't react. "I can't watch this."

Beau started to leave. Behind him, his father groaned. He struggled for air and said, "Honey..."

Beau's mother stirred. "Jerry?"

The creature vanished along with the others, but Beau's father clutched his chest, grimacing. "I love you both." Those were his father's last words.

Jerry stilled. Beau's mother sobbed and shook him. A shadow came up from under the bed and placed a glimmering black stone in Jerry's hand. A blue light, the same shade as twilight, shot skyward.

Beau knew this process well. "He went to Heaven." He wiped his eyes. "Good. He was a good man."

"Still is," Ralph said.

Beau kneeled by the bed and stared at his father's unblinking eyes. "Why am I supposed to see this?"

"Come with me." Ralph walked through the wall that separated little Beau's bedroom from his parents'.

Beau was reluctant. He took a second glance at his parents before heading through the wall. On the other side, his younger self lay on the bed, wide awake, staring into the corner of the room. There, a tall figure, shrouded in black, wore a top hat. Its smile stretched like a skeleton's mouth. Dark eyes glared at young Beau.

"Go away, Devil Man," young Beau blurted. "I said my prayers. You can't hurt me."

The devil man inched closer to his younger self, raising his cane, taunting, daring angels to intervene. The boy curled up under the blanket. His eyes were likely squeezed shut.

His mother shouted for him. "Beau!"

The devil man dissipated, and young Beau ran for his mother. Beau stood there with Ralph, gazing at the empty bed. "I saw that thing many times." He wiped his face and held onto his beard. "Where were you guys? If I was never alone, why didn't you protect me?"

Ralph's chin sank to his chest. He looked pensive rather than upset. "He never touched you."

"Is that what it would take for you to act?" Beau asked. "He can hover over my bed and stare at me all night? And what about that thing that killed my father?"

Ralph walked over to Beau's bed and sat down. "Something was protecting you. It's why he never touched you."

"I saw that monster almost every night." He heard his mother and young Beau crying through the wall and bit his fist.

Ralph sighed. "You let him in, Beau. You let him in, and your fear gave him dominion over you. All you needed to do was remember that God was with you. That would've given you the confidence to command it to go."

"I told it to go."

"Not with authority." Ralph started toward the wall. "Come with me. There's something you need to see."

"I'm not going back in there," Beau said.

Ralph passed through the wall, and Beau stood alone in his darkened room. He felt great relief in the solitude. No demons or angels prodding him to do this or that. He was at peace. At least on the outside. Inside, a storm ensued. Clouds in his head. Lightning in his arms. Thunder in his heart. Rain from his eyes.

Through the wall, he heard his mother sobbing. Young Beau's feet ran outside, going for help. A fruitless endeavor, but what else could he do? Beau looked back at the wall and rubbed his beard. Surely, time would stand still until he reentered his parents' bedroom. He pushed off the bed and stomped across the room and through the wall.

His mother buried her face in her husband's chest. Her hands clutched his. She was surrounded by a haze of colorful lights that stretched from the floor to the ceiling, filling the entire room.

Ralph was beside him, staring skyward. "Get closer to your mother."

When Beau did, the hazy colors that surrounded them took shape. They looked more like people wearing different clothing from different generations and cultures.

His mother cried harder. "Please. Please. Not now. Never."

Beau kneeled and closed his eyes. He reached for his mother's shoulder and felt it.

She gasped and gazed at the ceiling. When Beau looked up, there was no ceiling. They were at the center of a golden tower with columns that sparkled with lights. Thousands looked down from banisters, their hands raised, heads bowed. Higher overhead, angels drifted downward and surrounded Beau's mother. Among these angels, Beau found his father.

"Dad?"

Beau's father nodded. He reached for Beau. "Son."

When Beau took his hand, the room became empty. His mother and father were gone. Only he and Ralph remained.

"Were we there?" Beau looked at Ralph. "In Heaven?"

"Almost."

"I don't understand." Beau sat on the empty bed. "I didn't do anything. Didn't learn anything. Why would we be closer now?"

Ralph sat next to him. "All your life you found peace in solitude. You thought it was peace, but now you realize the truth."

"I was hiding." Beau looked at Ralph. "Avoided everyone I could for as long as I could. I kept quiet, thinking it would preserve my life, but the things I was trying to avoid were still there. Watching and waiting."

"When you're alone in your fears, you become easy prey."

Beau walked out of the room into the main living area and sat in his father's chair. Why was he putting himself through this? Wouldn't it be easier to go back?

Chapter Fifteen

A Stroll and a Coffee

A cool breeze mingled in the warm sunlight that illuminated everything it touched and darkened everything that it didn't. Kristine plodded from one sidewalk to another. She moved eagerly and confidently, but Charles wondered if she were lost in this strange maze of concrete paths that cut through lawns and ran alongside roads. Not many people were out and about. Perhaps they were stuck at a dead-end staring at a wall.

Those who were ambling about smiled and nodded at Kristine as they passed. Charles didn't understand it. Why were they so happy to see each other? Look at us! We're walking about aimlessly along paths that seemingly lead to nowhere. Oh, look a person! What a pleasant sight. Rather than ask for directions, I'll nod and smile like a buffoon.

He looked out for other demons. Although there were dozens in any direction, the foul things didn't seem to enjoy the sunshine. They lingered in and under trees and shrubbery. Others peeked out from the windows of cars and buildings. Some demons, though fewer in number, did enter the light; those types clung to people's heads, necks, and backs like a baby mammal would its mother. They didn't seem concerned with him or Kristine, which was a relief. The less drama he had to deal with, the better off he'd be. After about a half mile, Kristine came to a busy road lined with many small shops. She crossed it and walked alongside the strip until she entered a door with the words Brewster's Café written in curvy letters.

The shop's tinted windows kept it nice and dark. The sweet scent of coffee caught him off guard. He loved the scent of smoke, but this—this was so pleasant. Without a doubt, he would remember this place so he could slink back here to take in as many euphoric inhalations as he desired. There were tables and chairs everywhere. In a corner, there was a couch that looked much cozier than the one in Daniel's apartment. And there was art all over the wall. Although he didn't understand why anyone would bother painting steaming coffee cups or dark brown beans, it did put some life into this place. On the opposite side of the counter, fluorescent lights lit up a menu listed in colorful chalk. Beneath this toddler-drawn menu, sat several metallic machines that produced noises which Charles figured were engineered to make patrons thirsty.

"Finally, my favorite customer." The man behind the counter had his hat on the wrong way. He wore a black shirt and looked too smug for Charles's taste. His dark brown eyes gleamed as if he might break down and cry at the sight of Kristine. "Whatever you want is on the house."

"How about your head on a plate," Charles folded his arms, "but with the hat on the right way?"

A small voice from an unseen person squeaked, "How dare you speak of the mighty Adam that way?!"

Charles figured it came from the other side of the counter, but soon the small demon revealed itself. It climbed up Adam's neck to the top of his head. It had the face of a hairless cat and the body of a gray, tailless lizard. "Oh, great."

The little demon grimaced. "He's handsome and everybody likes him."

"Hey, Adam." Kristine walked to the counter, staring at the menu. "I appreciate it, but I prefer to pay."

"Seriously, it's on me." Adam blinked like a puppy in a pet store window. "Your usual? Caramel macchiato?" His overt attempt to speak sweetly sounded more like knives slicing and scraping along ceramic plates. Charles wished his bowler hat was a little bigger, so he might pull it down over his ears.

"Not today." Kristine smiled. "I'll have the Loca Mocha, please."

"Wanna make it a large?" Adam asked.

"Medium's fine." She dropped a couple of dollars in the tip jar.

A bell rang and the door swung open. A young brunette came in wearing black slacks and a buttoned-up sports coat. Her heels clacked on the floor as she came over to Kristine and hugged her. "Hey, girlie."

"Mandy!" Although he tried, Adam couldn't quite mask the displeasure in his voice. He forced a smile. "Good to see you."

The demon on Adam's hat leaned over. "You know, you could have both of them."

"Yeah, right." Charles gripped his lapels.

"Stay out of our business," the demon hissed. Its little lizard chest bowed.

If Charles were the size of a hamster, he might've been intimidated. "What are you going to do if I don't, shorty?"

Along the counter, thirty or so miniature demons emerged. Charles lost his composure and bent over with laughter. It was a good laugh. He hadn't laughed like this since his thieving days. "Oh, I'm so scared now."

The little demons melded together. The one on Adam's head leaped in last. They became one muscular demon with a potbelly, but it was hunched terribly with a horn protruding from its forehead. Its skin was purple and scaly. The face still looked like a hairless cat.

Charles laughed so hard it pained his side. He stumbled to the counter and braced himself until the hulking demon backhanded him well enough that he fell through a table and onto the floor. This was the last thing Charles expected at an establishment as aromatic as Brewsters Café, but when he peered up, he was reminded that he was in the spirit world, for the table and chairs were still in place. Beyond them, on the counter, the weird-looking cat demon with the steroid-induced dad bod seemed to have a taunting look on his face. "Funny now?" Its voice was deeper and somehow managed to sound dumber.

"What's going on out there?" Another demon, extremely small, stuck its head out of Mandy's purse. Its hair was long and wavy, like Mandy's. "Get back on the job. We don't get chances like this every day, you numbskulls."

The muscular demon seemed to fall apart. The hairless one jumped back to Adam's shoulder as he prepared a cup for Kristine.

"What are you having, Mandy?" Adam asked, pushing and pulling at the noisy thirst-machines.

"Make it on the house for her too," the demon in Mandy's hair suggested, as Adam went over to the register.

"I'll have an iced latte." She came to the counter and opened her pocketbook.

Adam waved his hand. "Don't worry about paying. I got you."

"You're going to go broke if you keep that up," Kristine suggested.

Adam shrugged. "You two are worth it."

"Aww." Mandy took out a ten-dollar bill and dropped it in a tip jar. "You are too sweet."

"Why did you let her say that?" the hairless one hissed at Mandy's demon. "You know it hurts his confidence."

"I know what I'm doing." The demon climbed out of the purse and up Mandy's arm. She perched herself on the edge of Mandy's shoulder and held up a mirror, puckering its tiny, swollen lips. "Stick with the plan."

Another demon was sniffing Kristine's shoe. Charles got to his feet and punted it across the room.

The hairless one growled at that, as did the others.

"Here you go, beautiful." Adam set a cup on the counter. Ugh, he winked.

"Thanks," Kristine said. She blushed as she took her free drink to one of three tables by the large, tinted window.

Mandy joined her. "He likes you." The demon on her shoulder whispered frantically into her ear.

Kristine sipped her mocha. Her eyes flared, almost taking offense at Mandy's comment. "I'm with Daniel, remember?"

"Mr. Mean Streak?" Mandy rolled her eyes. "Girl, you deserve much better than him. He's trouble."

Charles came up behind Kristine. "Tell little miss Mandy that you don't need relationship advice."

Kristine sat back in her chair and stared at her cup, twirling it. "Daniel's changed a lot, you know."

"No. I don't," Mandy said. "He got into a fight two nights ago."

"He told me about it." She took her drink with both hands and sipped.

"Did he?" Mandy's eyes went wide. "That is—wow!" The demon on her shoulder caressed her neck. "I didn't think he'd fess up about choking somebody."

"What?" Kristine brought her cup down hard.

"Oh, he left that little detail out, did he?" Mandy flipped her hair over her shoulder and shifted in her seat. She seemed to lock eyes with the little demon, who nodded reassuringly.

"Don't listen to her," Charles said. "She's lying."

"It's OK," the demon on Mandy's shoulder whispered. "She's listening. Besides, it's now or never. It's either you or him at this point."

"Daniel punched a guy and then jumped on him," Mandy said, cringing. "He choked him until someone pulled him off. It was terrible."

Kristine's face paled. She closed her eyes, shaking her head. "Unbelievable."

"She's lying." Charles came closer to Kristine and spoke intently. "She can't even tell you this while looking you in the face."

"Look at her and nod," the demon on Mandy's shoulder coached quickly. "Keep nodding. Look sad."

Adam came over and set Mandy's coffee on the table. With both girls sullen, Mr. Lovey Dovey had to ask, "What's wrong?"

"Don't worry about it," Kristine said dryly.

Charles tightened his fist in triumph. The shriveled smile on Adam's face sent the hairless-cat-faced demon into a growling tantrum that wasn't much different from the noises of the thirst-machines.

"She's upset because her boyfriend keeps getting into fights." Mandy smiled and sipped her drink. "Mmm, this is so good, Adam."

"Goodness, Kristine." Adam put his fist to the tabletop and flexed to show his chiseled arm. "What do you see in that guy?"

"It's a lie!" Charles shouted at Kristine. Ratlike demons climbed up Kristine's legs and chair. Charles swatted them off. He'd had enough of these little demons. "You know what? We should leave, Kristine."

"I think I should go." Kristine pushed her chair back. Adam winced and quietly made his way back behind the counter.

Mandy took her hand. "Don't be upset. It's not your fault. Here, I have to show you this." She took out her phone. "Did you hear about the lights shining around Grandfather Mountain last night?"

"I heard about the cloud," Kristine said as she stood.

"Check it out." Mandy tapped on her phone several times and handed it over. Charles peered over Kristine's shoulder. A video with night vision showed lights blinking and moving around the base of Grandfather Mountain.

"I thought this only happened at Brown Mountain." Kristine handed the phone back.

"Until last night." Mandy took it. "No one knows what's causing all this. Wanna go up there tonight to see it? It'll be fun."

"Not tonight. I'm working a double. I should get going."

"Kristine," Mandy got out of her chair and hugged her, "I'm sorry, but I had to tell you."

Charles stared down at the demon on Mandy's shoulder. "She'll find out the truth, and you'll feel pretty dumb when she does."

The demon on Mandy's shoulder balled its fists. "Who do you think you are? This isn't your business. I'm reporting you to the overseers."

Great. Just what he needed. A little tattle-telling demon. "It'll be the last mistake you ever make if you do, little one."

"I'll call you later." Kristine let go of Mandy. "Take care, Adam."

"Catch you later." He winked from behind the counter.

Charles followed Kristine through the door. She waited to cross the road and didn't look back into the café. Charles did. Mandy's little demon was standing on the table yelling at her. In Mandy's downward gaze, he saw regret. She peered up from the table in time to see Kristine cross the road.

Chapter Sixteen
A Heavenly Library

The clan of joyous fairies tapered off throughout the afternoon. Around 5:45 pm, Daniel sat in the back seat of his parents' Honda Accord and watched his hometown slip by on their way to church. A magical feeling swept through him as his eyes darted from one building to the next. They brought back memories of the days his parents drove him to school. Back then, he was so ready to grow up and get away, but now, he longed for those old days.

The church parking lot was almost empty when they arrived. Inside the community center of the church, a couple of men were setting up tables and chairs. Daniel knew they were his father's friends, but he couldn't remember their names. They stopped to greet Daniel, and although they would've heard about how he had behaved the night he had left, neither of them gave him the evil eye and seemed genuinely happy to see him.

The Reverend and his wife arrived soon after. More people trickled in and greeted Daniel, asking him questions, and thanking him for his service. It quickly became exhausting, so he slipped into the sanctuary for a moment of peace.

Stained glass windows brightened the red carpet and the wooden pews. The walls stretched up and came together at the center of the ceiling. Eight light fixtures hung from chains. So many times, he looked up at them, wanting nothing more than for the preacher to end his sermon so he could go home and watch football.

"Reminiscing?" someone asked from behind him.

When Daniel turned, an alarm went off in his head. It was the old man he had encountered on Grandfather Mountain moments before he had fallen into Hell. Daniel took several steps back and almost sat in the front pew. The old man stood there with a fedora in his hand.

"You," Daniel managed to say.

"Yes. Me." The old man ambled over to Daniel. A new fear entered Daniel's mind. What if he was never meant to escape Hell, and the old man was here to send him back? Would the ground beneath his feet fall away and send him tumbling into the valley of death? But the old man seemed to be in a much better humor than he was when they had first met. He held Daniel at arms-length. "And *you*. So good to see you, Daniel."

Daniel chuckled in relief. "Oh man. I thought something bad was about to happen."

"Why?" the old man asked, squinting.

"The last time I saw you, things didn't go so well for me." Daniel sent a hand through his hair. "Am I the only one who can see you?"

The reverend came in from the community center. "He's in here with Gabriel." He patted the old man on the back and started back to the community center. "Come on, you two. We're all ready to eat."

"Gabriel?" Daniel gazed at the old man in wonder. His gray eyes had flecks of gold in them. "I assume they don't know you're *the* Gabriel."

Gabriel gave a warm smile. "Go visit with your friends and family. We'll chat soon."

All the questions running through his mind made it very difficult for Daniel to walk away from the angel. A sense of dread also kneaded his heart. How long must he witness the unseen? Fairies and demons. Even angels now. Was he on the verge of death? Was he losing his mind? Will it ever stop? He entered the community center to a round of applause.

Shame and embarrassment nipped at him like biting flies. He smiled and nodded at the gleaming faces of people he used to know. Most of them were his parents' peers. Over their heads, fairies zipped about like bottle rockets. Everyone wanted to hug him or shake his hand. He didn't deserve their praise or this homecoming feast, but seeing true joy in so many faces touched him, and he embraced it as best he could.

When he reached his seat, the reverend said a prayer. Shortly afterward, people lined up for food. Daniel wasn't hungry. He had his eye on Gabriel, who spoke with several other older men who leaned in to hear whatever he was saying. A fairy soared over the angel's head so fast that it looked like a light blue halo. He locked eyes with Daniel and gave a slight nod.

Across the table, his father and mother beamed as they spoke with another couple. Never had he seen them so happy. It pained him to know that in the morning he'd leave for Fort Bragg, but at least this time it would be on good terms.

Someone took him by the arm and spoke in her usual twangy voice, "You remember me, don't you, Danny?"

It was his former babysitter. He remembered her and many others. Most of his old friends had either left town or they no longer attended.

"I heard you had a few words for Quincy this morning," one of his father's friends said, taking a bite off his fork. His face was red from laughing.

Daniel forgot how quickly rumors spread in this small town. "I stopped in for a snack and some gas. He wanted to talk about things that happened over two decades ago, and I didn't want to hear it."

Daniel's dad chuckled. "Two decades ago is a lot like yesterday for Mr. Quincy."

"Well, you should tell 'im to get over it." Daniel's mom stabbed her fork into a chunk of chicken. "That man can be so rude. I have it in mind to march into that rathole of his and slap him upside his empty head."

Daniel's mother didn't like it when anyone spoke ill of her husband. Clayton had said she used to be hard on him after he quit drinking, but those days predated Daniel's earliest memories. He looked down at a plate someone had graciously made and brought to him and moved his potatoes a little farther from his macaroni and cheese.

"Don't worry, Daniel," his father said. "Your mom's just blowing off steam."

"Somebody should." His mother stabbed another piece of chicken. "You're a good man, and all they talk about is the past."

"Hittin' Quincy upside the head ain't gonna change him," another said. "No amount of head slappin's gonna help him or his miserable friends. They're stuck in their ways."

Daniel thought about the demons he saw in the glass at Quincy's store. They were saying things that only Quincy could hear. "Maybe you should invite Quincy over for dinner sometime."

The table went quiet. Everyone stared at Daniel as if a crowd of fairies were dancing on his head. Someone attempted to lighten the mood. "You could poison the beans. I hear he loves beans."

"I'd rather eat the beans myself." Daniel's mother set her fork down. Shame shone in her eyes. "I know you mean well, Daniel, but Mr. Quincy is not welcome at our house."

A thin, nearly flat green head peeked over his mother's shoulder; curiosity, fear, and incredulity in its yellow eyes. It whispered in his mother's ear. "He comes home for one day and wants to tell you what to do."

Daniel couldn't bear the sight. He turned away, wiping his mouth. What could he do? Walk over there and have a debate with this thin, leafy-looking lizard? No one else could see it but him. He needed to help his mother but didn't know how.

"I don't think Mr. Quincy would accept an invitation to our home, Daniel." His father looked concerned. "Even if we did, I don't think much good would come of it."

An uncomfortable silence followed that. The fairies stayed away from their table. Daniel saw Gabriel standing by the door. He put on his fedora and stepped outside.

"Excuse me." Daniel got up from the table. "I'll be back in a minute."

He hurried to the parking lot and pushed through the door before anyone could stop him.

Gabriel sat on a bench to the left. "You have questions." He gazed over the parking lot at the tall evergreens stretching to a clear sky. "Have a seat."

It occurred to Daniel that the trees weren't supposed to be there. Light passing through the branches broke off into thousands of colors. The parking lot looked to be paved in white gold. The church behind him shone like a diamond. Only the door was the same.

"What's this?" Daniel touched the walls of the church. It was smooth and cool to the touch, like glass. "Heaven?"

"It's home." Gabriel had changed. He looked younger and wore a white gown with a yellow sash. His eyes were bright orange, and his hair was dark.

Daniel hid his face. He wasn't worthy of this.

"No need to bow or feel ashamed." Gabriel's voice was deep and warm. "If it's too much for you, we can return to the church."

"I think I'd like to stay awhile, if that's OK." Daniel looked about. Through a golden haze, many floors stretched into the sky farther than he could see. What he thought was the sun was an enormous chandelier dangling high above, twirling slowly. "How high does this go?"

Gabriel walked over and stood next to Daniel. He seemed uncertain of the answer. "It doesn't end."

"And what about the chandelier?" Daniel asked. "It looks larger than the moon."

Gabriel gazed at the sparkling, spinning structure overhead and nodded. "This is but one of many libraries. I chose this place because it is quiet, but if you'd like to explore, we can."

Daniel's eyes adjusted and he looked about. This area looked like a lobby. Unvarnished chromatic tiles covered the floor. The walls were a pastel purple with faint green holographic flower patterns scattered out symmetrically. A thick black post stood at the center. White signs with elegant letters written in gold hung from it and pointed in the direction where they could find escalators, elevators, and even stairs if they preferred. Of course, there were other rooms, and several exits they could use should they choose.

"I imagine I could be here for years and never see enough," Daniel said.

"A year in this place is shorter than half a second in your world," Gabriel said. "We could scale every floor of every library, venture into every nook and cranny of a billion castles, and still have you home well before anyone noticed you were gone." He headed back to the bench that sat along the wall of this magnificent lobby. "While all that sounds wonderful, we both know that your heart is already yearning to return."

He sat down and crossed his legs. "When you're rich with purpose, time spent in leisure troubles the soul."

Daniel joined Gabriel on the bench, looking about in different directions. "That's an understatement, Gabriel. I'm going insane. I'm seeing things I shouldn't." There was so much to say, but he struggled to articulate the heavy blackness clouding his heart. He closed his eyes. "I can't unsee Hell."

"It is overwhelming for you." Gabriel offered Daniel a small something that was wrapped in crinkly burgundy paper. "Seeing things as they truly are can be difficult, but you need to. It's the truth that'll set you free."

Daniel untwisted the wrapper and found a yellow piece of hard candy. He popped it into his mouth and lemon-flavored goodness melted onto his tongue. He closed his eyes and savored the taste. Given that this was candy from Heaven, he wondered if it would cause something miraculous to happen.

Gabriel seemed to know his thought when he said, "It's only a simple piece of candy, but simple things can put us at ease. Praise God for the simple things."

"Nothing is simple anymore." Daniel bit into the candy. "Waking in the night to demons prowling my floor, appearing in my mirror—looming in the blackness. Sprites twirling about my parents' home in broad daylight like a bunch of maniacs." Daniel leaned over, resting his forearms on his thighs. "I never saw this stuff until I got out of Hell. It's like it came out with me."

Gabriel's face bent with discernment. "You see the world around you differently, but yet you see yourself the same."

A knot tightened at the back of Daniel's throat. He gripped the armrest on the bench and took a deep, inward breath. "Yeah, I'm still me so. . .What?"

"You've changed, Daniel Strong," Gabriel said. "The only thing about you that hasn't changed is the Holy Spirit which is in you."

"The Holy Spirit wasn't attacking me in my apartment." Daniel came out of his seat. "It wasn't flying around in my parents' house attacking my father's old demons. It wasn't sitting on my shoulder when I watched a demon whisper hateful things to my mom."

Gabriel lowered his head. He seemed to be praying. "You suggested to your mother that she invite Quincy over for dinner. You did this hoping to get Quincy away from those demons at his store. You planted a seed. It may take root. Should it grow, so shall she in the ways of the Lord."

"That's nothing." Daniel rubbed the back of his neck and reached into his pocket. He pulled out the keystone. It behaved differently in this heavenly library; geometric shapes rolled about the surface while a dim blue light pulsated within. "I used this to get rid of a demon yesterday."

Gabriel peeked at it from the corner of his eye. "It's not as effective as you think."

"But planting seeds?" Daniel brought his hands up and let them fall. "It may or may not beat a demon, but this kills it."

Gabriel leaned closer. "That demon that was whispering to your mother is gone. It went too far. Lost its grip. That happened without you casting a stone."

"But I won't know what to say to people," Daniel said, "and don't get me wrong, I'd love to help, but I don't want to see everything, either. I need to be able to turn that off from time to time."

"Pray on that." Gabriel came to his feet. He seemed like he was ready to leave. "Before I go, you should know what has come of Beau and Charles."

Daniel never thought he'd hear their names again. Although it had hardly been a day, it seemed as if years had passed since he entered the bottommost pit of Hell with them by his side. "Are they—all right?" *What a silly question.* They were in Hell. How could they possibly be all right?

Gabriel's thin lips curled into a smile. "Beau caught the bus. He's on his way to Heaven. It's not an easy journey, so pray for him."

Daniel brought his hands to his head and laughed. He reached toward the chandelier and said, "That's great! If Beau can go through Hell to save me, I'm sure he can make it here. I know his memories were coming back—he remembered his daughter."

"It's easier to fall than to fly, Daniel." Gabriel raised a hand, and his feet came off the ground. Upon lowering it, he jetted skyward. A powerful gust of wind sent Daniel scrambling to keep his feet. Gabriel returned within a second. "What is natural to me is not so for others. For you, it'll come more naturally than Beau. He hid in the darkness for too long. So long that the light of Heaven may be hard on his eyes."

"I'll pray for him." Daniel crossed his arms. "What about Charles?"

Gabriel's expression was plain, but his voice seemed solemn. "Charles is in your world, looking for you."

"What? Why? How?"

"He's been tasked with following you. To ruin you."

"He agreed to that?" Daniel ran his hand through his hair. He thought Charles cared about him. While Charles was power hungry and had deceived him, there was good in him. That couldn't have changed overnight. Could it?

"Charles is a deceiver," Gabriel said. "Plain and simple. He deceived you and many others. He's even deceived himself. The devils don't trust him, but they do trust their schemes to a fault." He nodded. "Yes. They believe Charles will ruin you to avoid being cast back into the Seventh Ditch of the Malebolge without his eyes or watch."

Of course, Satan would send someone Daniel had befriended in Hell to come here and fill his head with lies. Maybe the first week, or even the first year, things would go swimmingly, but it would only take a second for Charles to walk Daniel right off a cliff. Even if Charles failed, Daniel would be pained by the horrible fate of his friend. He looked at the stone in his hand.

"What should I do?"

"You already know."

Daniel chuckled. "Would it kill you to give me a direct answer for a change?"

Gabriel walked to the door. "You want a direct answer? Fine." He pointed at the stone in Daniel's hand. "Don't put all your trust in that."

Daniel flipped the rock over. It wasn't about trust for him. It was about getting things done. "Where would it send him?"

"It'll send any demon it touches straight back to Hell."

Daniel pinched the bridge of his nose. It was hard to see himself do it—send Charles back to Hell, but he would without a second thought. "How do I get back?"

Gabriel opened the door, and brilliant light spilled to the floor. A breeze that smelled fresh with honey warmed Daniel's nose. Gabriel stepped through the door and said, "Pray."

"Wait." Daniel bolted up.

"Yes?" Gabriel peeked back.

"Tomorrow, I'm going to a funeral. My friend killed his brother and himself in front of his oldest son." Daniel felt nervous but had to ask. "Can you come? Help those boys?"

Gabriel dropped his gaze. "I am only a messenger, Daniel. If you want to help, you must pray for them. Take time with them. Show them love."

Daniel's eyes teared up. He blinked them out. "Yeah, but I can't be there all the time. That family needs more than what I could possibly offer. They need God, and you're a lot closer to Him than I ever will be."

The angel looked solemnly at Daniel and turned away, as if ashamed of what was said. "God is with you always, Daniel. Have faith." He closed the door, leaving Daniel to himself in this heavenly library.

He closed his eyes and prayed for home and for his friends—even Charles. These small, unspoken words seemed powerless, like wishful thinking. When he opened his eyes, he was back on the bench beside the door to the community center.

The crowd in the dining hall had slowly thinned. He sat at the table with his parents and peered down the dark hallways, wondering if Charles was watching. Why did he feel as if a maniacal killer was stalking after him? Charles was no killer, but would do anything to avoid going back to the Malebolge.

CHAPTER SEVENTEEN
THE RUINS OF GRAYTON

Charon kept his pole raised horizontally before him. This simple act somehow propelled the skiff upriver, against the current, at an unnatural speed. Through a pink haze, distant mountains burned with fire. Black smoke billowed above them, dissipating under the fiery stone sky. Flaming rocks fell from its cracks and smashed into the vast red plains of Limbo and into the River Styx.

The great cloud that loomed over Grayton peeked over the horizon. The south side of the sad town inched into view. Buildings lay in ruins. Their foundations jutted from the ground like broken teeth. Slivers of walls pierced the everlasting thundercloud. Chance placed a boot onto the gunwales of the boat. Though it was unnecessary, he gave the boatman a nod before leaping into the river.

When he came ashore, he entered the ruined city. Steaming rain poured onto concrete slabs and bent steel railings. Although it was humid and hard to breathe, all souls were better off in here because the cloud protected them. It sheltered them from the heat and reduced falling boulders to dust.

The sound of gritty rain comforted Chance. He knew his way around the rubble well. Those who were damned to Limbo didn't take refuge in the ruins, they preferred the northern side of town where the buildings were intact. The south side was quiet, and there was no trouble at all. That wouldn't be the case anymore. Not for Chance or Harrison.

His team, the traitors, were well acquainted with the ruins and likely came here to search for his brother. There were plenty of places to hide, but Chance had hidden Harrison in the most obvious place, the tallest remaining structure in the ruins, and likely the first place the traitors would look.

Chance walked the perimeter of the tower, using his eyes and ears for any sign of intrusion. When he was satisfied, he entered. Much of the building's structural material had fallen and decayed, but he and his brother had reinforced a stairwell and several floors with steel. He climbed to the fourth floor and entered the first room on the right.

Light shone through a thick sheet of glass they had placed over a large hole in the room's ceiling. Dark shadowy beads darted about the walls between snake-like streams. Water dripped and slowly oozed to lower floors. A desk, a filing cabinet, and a wardrobe sat huddled at the other end of the room. Behind them was an old mattress, three blankets, and a tub full of water. It was everything his brother needed to remain comfortable until he decided to catch the bus.

Everything was here, but his brother wasn't. He sat at the desk and rested his head in his hands. "Where are you, Harrison?"

"We figured you'd show up here," a familiar voice said from the doorway.

Chance turned. It was Miguel. He looked about the room. "Where's Marlin and Jethro?"

"They're on the north side of town." Miguel stepped into the room, eying the glass that covered the hole in the ceiling. "Nice touch."

"What did you do to my brother?" Chance stood and squared up with Miguel.

Miguel peered at the floor. "We chose not to seek him out—not for Satan. We were wrong, Chance, and have been praying for forgiveness."

Chance watched Miguel carefully. He appeared ashamed, but it could be an act. "Why'd you do it?"

"No good reason." Miguel wiped his brow and leaned against the door frame. Slowly, he sank to the floor, crying silently. "We wanted out. Out of Hell. Out of the war. Out of it all."

Chance stepped closer. "You should've known better."

Miguel nodded and gazed at Chance; his eyes intense and watering. "We aren't like you. We don't deserve the Lord's grace. We don't deserve forgiveness."

"Spare me the pity party." Chance was out of patience. "I've had it with all that whining. My goodness." Chance craned his neck and took a deep breath. "Why are you here, Miguel? To send my brother back to the Second Hell?"

"No." Miguel stood. "We knew you'd escape and come looking for him. I'm here to find you." Miguel stared back at Chance. "I promise it's the truth."

"What do you want with me?" Chance said harshly. "You threw me to the wolves once already."

"We want to make it right." Miguel's body shook. He blinked out tears. "We want to take it back, somehow."

"Take it back, huh?" Chance laughed. "You can't change what you've done, but you can change. Start by getting to work. No more sulking and start fixing what needs fixing." Chance considered a solution for Miguel and the team to focus on. "Maybe you ought to make sure that bus stop stays open."

"We can't." Miguel shook his head. "The demons destroyed it already."

"Then build a new one," Chance grumbled. "Those demons won't be around forever."

"They're not leaving."

"How do you know?"

Miguel shrugged. "Why would they? Grayton is a lot nicer than where they came from."

"But it's not home for them." Chance walked over to Miguel and helped him to his feet. "The souls in Limbo are too benign. The environment isn't harsh enough. It's too cold for their taste. They hate this. That's why, Miguel."

"Then why have they come?" Miguel asked. "Why are they trying to get back on Earth?"

"Because they always want more." Chance needed to find his brother. "Are you going to do it? Get the bus stop back in order?"

Miguel nodded. "It's the least we could do, but do you need us for anything?"

Chance shook his head. Although he wasn't sour with Miguel, he probably looked it. "Make sure you get on the next bus out of here. I don't think you boys can handle another day in this mess."

"Will God take us back?"

Chance patted Miguel on the arm and squeezed. "I forgive you, so I know He will."

Miguel nodded and then hugged Chance. "Thank you, brother."

Chance wasn't much of a hugger, but he slowly wrapped his arms around the heaving man. He patted him on the shoulder and started off. "I'll see you later—in Paradise."

He headed toward the north side of Grayton. There was a particular rooftop he told his brother to go to should the hideout ever be compromised. From there, he was to get on the bus. Unfortunately, the bus stop had been dismantled by demons. While that wouldn't deter the bus driver, it might deter Harrison and any other soul willing to leave.

A few low-level demons stayed in town, but Chance suspected they would likely be on the mountain partaking in the excavation. When he knew that his brother was safe, he'd head there himself to see what he could do about getting his hat back.

He hopped over one of many concrete barriers that divided the north side from the south. There was some rubble along the road. It was still quiet, but the sounds of rioting roared in the distance. The protest occurred late every day. Hundreds of participants walked about the streets expressing their grief and sorrows. It was a sad, open prayer that often turned sour. The lamenters would beg for mercy and when the sky didn't open up to reveal God, they took their anger out on the streets. They sought an extravagant sign rather than the simple one that stood next to the bus stop.

The hospital came into view, and beyond it, protestors turned onto the street that led to City Hall. Chance took the road that ran parallel with the march. Three blocks down, he climbed a fire escape. At the top, he climbed a railing and leaped to the roof. His brother wasn't there. Where was he? Remaining hunched, Chance walked to the other side of the building. From there, he saw that demons had ripped the bus stop sign out of the concrete. They did a poor job by leaving the bench there. The sign was simply laying on the ground.

Chance sat back against the ledge. Where was his brother? Waiting somewhere in the ruins for nightfall? He figured he should wait for an hour or so before heading on to the mountain.

Chapter Eighteen
Any Last Words?

It was dark when Daniel's father pulled into the driveway, but he and his mother were still taking trips down memory lane. Daniel loved hearing stories about how his parents had met and all the happy moments that happened along the way, but as he got out of the car, a sadness swept over him and his parents. They knew in the morning, Daniel would leave.

He ambled up the driveway toward his parents' front door. Clayton waved through the blinds. Daniel kind of liked the old spirit, but he wanted to free his father from the burden.

He reached into his pocket and squeezed the stone. Clayton wasn't his only worry, unfortunately. Daniel was on the lookout for Charles as well. Not to mention that dark thing in the top hat he'd seen the night before.

Daniel's father broke the silence. "I'm sure glad you came home, son."

"Me too." A slight cool breeze pushed against his face. Images of Heaven seemed to peek out from the distant streetlights. "I'll come back during summer break and stay longer than a day next time."

They filed through the front door into the living room. Clayton Docks moved to a far corner. He had slicked his hair back and wore a black buttoned-up shirt with pineapples all over it and pale blue jeans. He gave Daniel two thumbs up and said, "Ready when you are, buddy."

Daniel would look foolish if he responded, but he nodded and placed his index finger to his lips. They put away the dishes they brought home from church. Leftovers went into the fridge. They then sat at the kitchen table and played Scrabble. It was often their Sunday night family ritual. His mother went to bed first.

Clayton entered the kitchen from the living room. "Would be nice to have a couple of beers with the boy, don't you think?" He leaned against the countertop. "You could make a quick run to the Quikstop. Get a six-pack. It's not a crime, you know."

Daniel gripped the stone in his pocket.

His dad folded the Scrabble board and returned it to the box. "Will you have breakfast before you head out?"

"Sure." Daniel would have time. He'd need to leave by nine in the morning to make it to Bragg before the funeral.

"Come on," Clayton said. "Have a drink with the boy before he goes. It couldn't hurt. You deserve one after all these years."

"Well then." Daniel's dad patted him on the shoulder and headed to bed. "See you in the morning. Good night."

Daniel locked eyes with Clayton. "Good night, Dad." When he heard his father's bedroom door close, he asked, "You bug my dad like that all the time?"

"Nah." Daniel pulled out a chair so Clayton could sit. "Thank you kindly. I figured I'd try once more before closing up shop. I must say, though, I'm not keen on getting struck by some magic rock."

"About that." He set the keystone on the table. "A good source told me that it'll send you to Hell." He regarded Clayton. The old spirit stared at the stone. A mixture of fright and intrigue in his eyes.

"Hmm." Clayton rubbed his chin nervously. "Figures. I guess I'll have to wait until your daddy dies."

"Maybe there's another way to get you out of this."

Clayton stared out the window into pitch darkness. "I'm not concerned. Your grandfather passed at seventy-six, which means your daddy has maybe thirty years left on him." He sighed deeply. "Yeah, think I'll wait it out."

Daniel didn't like this idea. If Clayton stuck around, maybe he'd eventually get the better of his father. If not, it would only be a matter of time before Clayton found another person to influence. Another person to ruin with alcohol. But Hell seemed too harsh a punishment to Daniel. He knew what would come of Clayton and didn't like it. He looked to the ceiling, hoping a better answer was up there somewhere.

"You can go outside," Daniel looked at Clayton, "but how far can you go?"

Clayton winced in thought. "I can make it to the car before I get pulled back here. It's sort of like jumping. What goes up must come down. The car is as high as I can jump."

Daniel scratched his head. "What if I walk with you? I'm my father's son. Maybe I can get you past that, and maybe—maybe that'll break the chain that has you tethered to him."

Clayton nodded more emphatically as Daniel spoke. "Yeah. Yeah. Maybe. It's worth a shot. Let's try it."

Clayton walked to the door more willingly than Daniel liked. He hated how well his lie worked. Daniel took the stone and trailed after the good-natured, yet ruinous, spirit. He reminded himself that Clayton tormented his father for years and would do the same to the next person.

Daniel followed him outside. The thick night air cooled his skin. The fresh scent of spring invigorated him. He could do this. He could do what must be done. Rid the earth of this heathen—this demon. Out in the forest, which stood darker than the night sky, entities with deep red eyes watched them descend the steps and walk into the yard.

"Any last words, Clayton?"

Clayton stopped and lowered his gaze. "I should've known you'd do this."

"I can't let you go. You'll ruin somebody else. Another family." Daniel didn't need to explain this to Clayton but needed to convince himself that this needed to be done.

Clayton peered up to the sky and tearfully asked, "Will you give me a moment?"

Daniel gripped the stone in his hand. "Sure."

A few seconds into this given moment, Clayton sprinted toward the end of the yard. If he reached the car, he'd return to the house, where Daniel couldn't throw the stone. He still wasn't sure he wanted to throw it, but he did—as hard and as true as he could.

Clayton was slow. The world was even slower, especially compared to the blue stone that crashed through Clayton like a raindrop through smoke. The spirit stopped a few feet from the car. He turned. His wide eyes found Daniel staring back at him. He dropped to his knees, whimpering.

"It was me," he said.

"What do you mean?" Daniel ambled toward Clayton. The old spirit pressed a hand to his wound, where smoke seeped and sank into the ground.

"I told your father to tell you to go. And he did. It was the first time he heard me in years. The last time."

"You wanted him to take another drink."

Clayton nodded and coughed. He went to all fours. Smoke oozed from his chest. His body had thinned and aged horribly. "Tell me. What's it like? What's going to happen to me down there?"

Daniel went to a knee. "You'll fall into a valley at the foot of a burning mountain and be judged on which hell they should send you to." Daniel felt responsible for what was to come of this poor man. Who was he to put someone there? "Listen, Clayton. When you wake up, run. There's a city not far from the mountain. Get to the bus stop in that town. It'll take you to Heaven. Just pray that the bus finds you before anyone else does."

Clayton's arms sank into the ground. Seconds later, the spirit was gone. Daniel wiped his eyes. The keystone lay glowing several yards away. He retrieved it. The red-eyed entities no longer watched from afar. Hopefully, they had decided to stay away, but that was wishful thinking.

He went back inside and sat at the table. It was best to send Clayton to Hell. One less evil influencer in the world. But still, he felt terrible about it. The melancholy that weighed over him needed to be lifted. There would be no sleeping otherwise, but he knew what to do. He'd been thinking about it since earlier that morning. He picked up the phone and called Kristine.

Her sweet voice answered, "Hello." There was a lot of noise behind her. She was at work, so she wouldn't have much time to talk. He was lucky she answered at all.

"Hey," he said. "I know you're working, but do you have a minute?"

"I'm taking a break." She sounded flustered. Her tone was on edge, as if she was having an epically bad shift. "I need to talk to you."

"Yeah?" Daniel sat up straight. Something was off. "What's up?"

The noise on the other end of the phone quieted. Kristine breathed heavily as a door closed behind her. "I heard more about that fight you got into."

A black snake slithered out from under the kitchen sink. Daniel stomped on it, and it turned to smoke. What did she hear? If it was more than what he had told her, it was a lie, but he'd have a hard time convincing her over a phone call. "What did you hear?"

"I heard it was more than a punch." She exhaled. "Mandy said you choked the guy, too."

Daniel came out of his chair. More shadowy snakes reached out from corners, curtains, and cracks. "That's not true." Daniel walked into the living room, where there were more of these snake-like demons. Their hisses sounded like screeching shrills. "I punched the guy once and that was it. Mandy's either mistaken or flat-out lying." Daniel sighed. He didn't like accusing Kristine's best friend of lying, but what else could it be? "Ask Jimmy. He was bartending that night."

"Yeah, she didn't seem herself when she told me." Kristine sounded relieved. "She's never been a big fan of yours, but it's not like her to lie, either."

She believed him. Daniel gave a silent thanks to God. He went back to the kitchen and sat back down. The shadowy snakes thinned out. Those that remained looked like long worms.

"Well, I have given her more than enough reasons to not like me." A new thought occurred to him. What if demons were trying to get at him from another angle? What if they're trying to destroy his relationship with a lie? He needed to get back there. Stop it somehow, but he was so far away with promises to keep. It would have to wait until tomorrow night.

"I have to get back to work." Kristine sounded tired. This unnecessary drama had put a horrible weight on her. "But before I do, you need to know that... Do you remember what you said about falling into Hell?"

"Yeah." Daniel's heart began to beat harder. "Why?"

"Since then, there's been this cloud spiraling around Grandfather Mountain. It's lasted all day, which has everybody talking." Daniel came out of his chair and started pacing. "And I also heard there are mysterious lights around it too, like Brown Mountain."

Daniel massaged his head. Did Gabriel mention something about this? He couldn't remember. Whatever it was, he didn't want Kristine to worry about it. "I'm sure it'll blow over in a day or so."

"Yeah, but it would be kind of neat if it didn't. Well, I have to go. Call me when you can tomorrow."

"I will," Daniel said. "Love you."

"I love you too." Before he hung up, electricity zapped his lips and ear. He dropped the phone. It dangled by the cord, swinging like a pendulum. Static electricity tickled his skin. A new scent entered the house. It smelled familiar. Footsteps came from the living room. He recognized the cadence of the gait and the clicking of a pocket watch.

The footsteps stopped. Daniel gazed up from his chair at the slender silhouette in a bowler hat. "Well, if it isn't Heartless Charles." He put as much venom as he could muster into his words.

Chapter Nineteen

So You Didn't Miss Me

Hours before making the jump to Daniel, Charles discovered that Kristine had the worst job in the world. Earlier, she was reading books on human anatomy and typing on her computer, but now she took orders from this person and that person. She brought whatever they asked for and spoke kindly with everyone, even the snooty people with perpetual looks of displeasure etched on their not-very-smart-looking faces.

He grew tired of chasing after her from the kitchen to the dining area. Back and forth she went. On the bright side, he did manage to get his hands on a ribeye steak. Shamelessly, he grabbed the ghost steak with his hands and ripped it in half with his teeth. The mashed potatoes were delicious too but quite messy. Luckily, nothing stuck for more than a few seconds. Eating lost its fun, though, because it did nothing for his thirst or his hunger. *Go figure.*

He meandered about the restaurant, pitching thoughts at employees and customers to see if he could get a rise out of anyone. No one seemed to hear him, unfortunately. They were busy with their food and conversations. Some stared at televisions while others played with their cellphones. He watched a child play a game where a spaceship shot gigantic bugs. If the world were to rely on him for saving it, humanity would be lost for sure.

"There you are." Emma twisted around on a barstool. She wore a purple dress that hugged her body. Her hair curled down her shoulders and back. "Tell me you got some steak," she said excitedly.

Charles didn't fall for her charms. No. He would not get on her wavelength right now. He needed her to know he was upset that she hadn't shown up earlier. "Daniel called."

"I came back as early as I could." She patted the seat next to her. "Come here. I can't stay long, but I have enough time to teach you how to travel through electronics, so you'll be ready the next time he calls."

Sure, she couldn't stay long, Charles thought, sliding into the seat beside her. "You said it was too difficult for a novice like me."

"It is without any training." She swiveled to face the television.

Charles propped his elbows on the countertop and steepled his fingers. After a few seconds of silence, he blurted, "Well, I'm all ears."

Emma smiled but squinted ever so slightly. The look in her eyes told Charles that she hadn't quite figured out how to handle him now that he wasn't so keen to fall for her sweet charms.

"Good." She looked back at the television. "You've learned that by thinking of a person or a place that you're familiar with allows you to jump to them. The same works with what you can sense." Emma nodded to the television, where grown men bounced a ball around an arena filled with people. "If you focus on this game, you can follow the path the signal took to make it here and find yourself there. Go ahead and try."

Charles watched the television and ignored his surroundings. The volume was turned down, and the view bounced from one angle to another. He found this very distracting. "I can't hear anything, and it won't stay still."

"That doesn't matter," Emma said. "It's all in one place. Focus. Imagine that you're there."

"What if it starts showing all those advertisements?" Charles broke his gaze and gestured to another television that was displaying depressing images of sad puppies. If he ended up there, he'd never forgive her.

"Aww, those poor babies." She turned back to him. "Don't focus on the advertisements. Focus on the game."

Charles squinted back at the screen. The floor of the basketball court had shapes painted on it. There was a circle at the very center of the court. It wasn't showing now, but he knew it was there. He closed his eyes and imagined what it was like inside that circle.

Loud. Smelly. Cool.

He opened his eyes. Thousands of people were on their feet shouting. Large, awkwardly tall men ran past him, bouncing a ball to the other side of the court.

"What a strange game."

Lights shone from higher, and oddly enough, there was a lot of darkness beyond those lights. A chill hung in the air. He smelled popcorn, soda, and beer. The men came zipping by him again. They smelled like sweat. Did he stink this bad when he was alive? He wondered how he might smell to them.

"You!" a man in shining armor shouted over the noise. He leaped over a barricade. What a showboat.

"Great, an angel," Charles muttered.

This guy couldn't bear the thought of hiding his allegiance. His long, dark hair was shiny and straight, which was laughable. Charles might have laughed, but the angel pulled a long sword from a scabbard that dangled by his side. This psycho would slice him to pieces, considering the intensity in his eyes.

"You don't belong here." He held the hilt with both hands and marched onto the floor.

Charles took several steps back, raising his hands. "I'm leaving."

The angel continued toward him. Basketball players zipped by them. Charles wanted to leave, but the angel was all he could focus on. He couldn't think of a name or place to go to. The angel whipped the sword back to strike. Charles fell back and yelped. Not his proudest moment, by any means.

The space between them seemed to bend as if an invisible tube was sucking away reality. Emma appeared, as if stepping from behind an invisible veil. "Stand down, soldier."

The angel stopped mid-stride. He looked from Emma to Charles and returned the sword. "Get him out of here," he said.

Emma bowed. "Thank you, friend."

The angel walked away. Emma turned to Charles. She looked marvelous in that huge arena. While it would be unlikely that she could've competed with the giant men playing the primitive game, she could've won the hearts of everyone else in attendance with that smile of hers. She touched his knee, and they were back on the bar stools. There was a commercial on for conquering headaches. Charles was sure it wouldn't have helped much if that angel struck him with the sword.

Although her cover was blown, Emma didn't seem fazed. She quietly regarded Charles, as if playing a game of silence. The first to speak would lose. Charles was very good at this sort of thing, but he was in no mood. "I had my suspicions."

"Never mind me and what I am. You did well. Ready to try a phone now?"

"Don't change the subject. You're an angel."

"Yeah." Emma twisted her seat toward him and crossed her legs. "Is that a problem?"

Charles wasn't sure. Despite getting him off track, she had done a lot for him. "Why are you helping me?"

She flipped her hair back over her shoulder. "Have you heard about the cloud over the mountain? The lights they're seeing around it at night?"

Her concern for this confirmed what Charles was thinking. "It has something to do with Daniel, doesn't it?"

Emma leaned closer. "They're trying to breach that pit. We've been handling the scouts, but soon there's going to be a full-scale invasion." She left it at that and studied his face.

"Don't ask me. I don't know anything." Charles pretended to care about the ridiculous game where he almost lost a limb—or a head. He was sour with Emma. All of her pandering was about getting information he didn't have. Oh well, at least he'd be able to focus more on his mission now.

"I wasn't going to ask about it," Emma said. "We know what we need to know. But you need to be aware of this—that Hell is trying to break loose."

"What good would it do me to know about it? It's not my problem. I've got enough to worry about." He expected her to lash out, but she didn't.

"See that family over there?" Emma pointed.

A mother and a father were coloring with their children, two young boys. They seemed content, waiting for their food. Emma wanted to pull on his heartstrings, but he wouldn't let her win this time. "Wow," he said with false wonder. "What a credit to humanity. The next Rembrandt may come from that very table."

Emma frowned at that. "Everyone in this world will be in for something horrific if we don't do something about it."

Charles looked away. His eyes kept finding those kids. Why did they have to be so happy? It didn't help him at all. He spotted Kristine hustling by with another food platter. He cared more than he should, but he wouldn't let Emma know that. "And I guess you want me to wave a magic wand or something?"

"You can help us," Emma said, leaning closer.

"Maybe I don't want to," Charles said. "Maybe all I want is to tell the overseers the name of a particular angel. Show them that not only can I hand deliver souls to Satan, but I can get whatever I want out of an angel as well." He regretted every word he said. He swallowed to hide his anguish.

"I see." Emma's jaw tightened. Her eyes glistened. She got up from her seat.

Charles broke his composure. "Look, I'm sorry."

"Do whatever you think you must," Emma said plainly. Her sweetness was gone. She sounded businesslike, and her expression was stoic.

"I won't give them your name." Charles knew this much, but he might dangle it as bait should the overseers threaten him with expulsion for failing to find Daniel. "I don't know why I said that, but you have my word."

"The words of a man who once thought he was a demon." She took Charles's necktie and loosened it. She spoke kindly, almost motherly. "What good is that? I could make you promise. Promises made to me cannot be broken."

"Then I—"

"No." Emma held a finger to his lips. "I won't hear any promises from you today, Charles Thorne. I see what you need, and I'm giving it to you. You have my name. Do with it as you will. Your choice."

Charles gazed at his shoes. "I already told you I won't tell them." When he looked up, she was gone. He looked back at the family of four. They were eating now. The youngest one held two chicken nuggets up to his eyes, swaying side to side with a gaping smile. Charles turned away.

The clock read 8:13. The light outside had diminished. The overseers might be on the roof waiting on him right now, and he had little to share other than an angel's name. Even if he did tell the overseers, he wasn't sure if that would be enough to assuage them.

He followed Kristine everywhere, becoming more anxious for her phone to ring. Rarely did she pull it from her pocket. It seemed unlikely that she'd answer even if he did call. Around 9 pm, she received a text from her friend Mandy asking if she'd ride out to Grandfather Mountain to see the lights. Apparently, they were more active tonight than the previous one. Little did they know it was a battle between angels and earthly demons.

Kristine declined Mandy's invitation, which relieved Charles. Another moment with that annoying little demon of hers and he'd be apt to spend the evening with Iffy, the monster who claimed to eat demons for breakfast.

It was dark outside, and Charles still refrained from reporting to the overseers. Surely Daniel would call Kristine soon; however, no matter what, he would report at 10 o'clock.

Finally, Kristine pulled the phone from her back pocket and answered it. It was Daniel. "I'm taking a break. I need to talk to you." She hurried to the back of the kitchen and walked through the back door into the parking lot, where much of the staff took cigarette breaks. He had to run to catch up with her.

"I heard more about that fight you got into. I heard it was more than a punch." Charles tried to get close so he could hear Daniel on the other end, but Kristine was pacing around. "Mandy said you choked the guy, too."

"Will you please stand still?" Charles said.

Kristine did stand still. He could almost make out what Daniel was saying on the other end. He closed his eyes and focused on the voice.

"Yeah, she didn't seem herself when she told me." Kristine sighed and tucked her hair behind her ear. "She's never been a big fan of yours, but it's not like her to lie, either."

Charles put his ear as close to the phone as he could. He heard Daniel say, "Well, I have given her more than enough reasons to not like me."

Kristine started for the back door. "I have to get back to work. But before I do, you need to know that... Do you remember what you said about falling into Hell?"

"Yeah." Charles clearly heard Daniel this time. "Why?"

Kristine stopped at the door and peered over the wooden fence that bordered the rear of the parking lot. "Since then, there's been this cloud spiraling around Grandfather Mountain. It's lasted all day, which has everybody talking. And I also heard there are mysterious lights around it too, like Brown Mountain."

The line was quiet. Charles figured Daniel hadn't heard about this yet. "I'm sure it'll blow over in a day or so."

Charles focused on Daniel's voice; his body prickling with static as if someone had dropped him into a cup of fizzing soda. All around him was darkness. Where was he? Somewhere inside the phone? He wished he'd let Emma teach him how to do this rather than wing it.

"Yeah, but it would be kind of neat if it didn't." Kristine sounded distant. Her voice came from under his feet. "Well, I have to go. Call me when you can tomorrow."

"I will," Daniel said. His voice was very clear. "Love you." The conversation was nearly over, but Charles wasn't there yet. He squeezed his eyes shut and focused.

"I love you too."

Charles opened his eyes. He was in a room with sofas and chairs. Relieved, he took out his pocket watch, which was acting calmly for a change. He clicked it open and snapped it shut, looking for any sign of Daniel. A dull light shone in the kitchen, so Charles walked in there, and finally, he found Daniel sitting at a table, nursing his lip.

"Well, if it isn't Heartless Charles." Daniel couldn't sound more unenthused. He took the phone, which dangled beside him, and hung it up.

Charles had hoped for a pleasant reunion, but Daniel's tone and appearance seemed defensive, maybe even hostile. "I've been looking for you," Charles said softly, stepping closer.

"I've heard," Daniel said. "Stay where you are." His eyes were fierce. He must've heard about Charles's mission.

"Who have you been talking to?" Charles asked. "Emma?"

"I don't know anyone named Emma." Daniel's eyes told Charles he wasn't lying. "Why?"

Charles loosened his tie. "You look like you could kill me."

Daniel's expression didn't change. "Why are you here?"

Charles looked about at nothing in particular, hoping to seem less threatening. "They tasked me to follow you around. I have to report to them soon."

"You forgot the part where you're supposed to drag me down? Ruin me?" Daniel reached into his pocket.

"I have no intention of doing what they tell me," Charles said, "but I do need to report soon because I'm late."

Daniel brought something out of his pockets. It glowed blue in his fist. He leaned forward and whispered, "Go on then, but don't come back here."

"Daniel—"

"I can't trust you." Daniel's eyes were darker than the shadows of the room. The thing in his hand shone pale between his fingers.

Charles's balance wavered. He was a little surprised to find that he was hurt by this. "But I can help you."

Daniel raised his chin. "I don't want your help." He held up the shining thing in his hand. "Remember this?"

It shone like the stone Beau brought into Hell, but the color was different. Charles nodded.

Daniel cradled it in his fist. "I can send evil spirits to Hell with it. I've done it twice already. If you come back here, you'll be the third."

Charles didn't know what to say. He wanted Daniel's trust, so he blurted out the first thing he thought Daniel should know. "They're trying to plant lies in Kristine's head. I've been helping you. Where do you think I've been all this time?"

"What part of *I can't trust you,* don't you get?"

Charles wiped his face. What did he have to do to get Daniel to believe him? "The name I mentioned. Emma. She's an angel. I don't think she would want you to banish me."

Daniel shook his head. "I'd be a fool to believe anything you say."

Charles nodded. "Have you forgotten? Demons speak truth when it suits their purpose." He walked to Daniel. "I won't betray you."

Daniel stared at Charles's chest. He seemed to consider that. "Report to whoever you need to report to. Tell them whatever you want. As for me and Kristine—stay away from us."

A lump ballooned in Charles's throat. It surprised him that he nearly cried. He masked his disappointment the best he could and managed to swallow. Tears wanted to roll, but he refused to let them. "We worked well together. Remember?"

"You lied. Remember that?"

"Yeah." Charles did what was best for him, and in the end, got what he thought he wanted. "I'll be back, Daniel. If you choose to send me to Hell with your magic rock, that's your prerogative."

"I meant what I said."

"Either I stick with you or with Kristine." Charles looked around the room. "It's all I can do to help you."

Daniel moved toward him with glaring eyes. "Stay away from her," he growled.

"See you soon, old friend." Charles touched the end of his hat and thought of the overseers' rooftop. It was colder and windier there. The sounds of cars passing on the nearby road intermingled with muffled music from the tavern across the street. Only one of the three overseers was there—the man in overalls.

"Where have you been?" he growled.

"Sorry." Charles walked to him. "It's been a busy first day."

He grabbed Charles by the neck and slammed him onto the roof. "I'll have you tossed back to the depths, fool."

Charles hated to use his leverage so soon, but this raging lunatic seemed ready to go through with his threat. "Wouldn't you rather know the angel's name? She seems to have a lot of pull around here."

The demon's grip loosened. "You know nothing."

"She's blonde," Charles grunted. "So beautiful it's intoxicating."

The overseer released Charles and stood. "She gave you her name?"

Charles coughed and nodded. "So you know about her."

"Give me her name if you know it."

"Oh, that's the thing." Charles came to his feet, brushing off his pants and coat. He checked that his hat was still on his head. "If I tell you, I'd gain nothing. So I'm not saying it. Not yet."

The overseer cocked a fist back. "You slimy little—"

"I'll tell you," Charles said, backing away, "but not today. Not until you can assure me that I'll remain here for a long time."

The hateful overseer seemed to consider this. With a growl, he dropped his fist. "Not all things are decided by me, but if you give me her name, you'll be in my favor for a time."

Good. Seemed like Charles would avoid an early exit from the spirit world after all. But he needed to change the subject. "I have more to report. As I said, Daniel is watched over by an angel, whose name I shall share after we reach an agreement. Another thing is that there are lesser demons who are working to upend the relationship between Kristine and Daniel. I disapprove of this."

The overseer pointed at him. "Don't you interfere with that. Of the many things that have gone awry, that has gone as expected."

"It's not working. It's creating a rift between Kristine and Mandy, and you need Mandy if you want to break them apart."

The demon neared Charles. His breath reeked of death. "Maybe if you weren't so privy to assert yourself in the coffeeshop, there'd be no rift."

"It's too easy to disprove." Charles stepped back and attempted to wave the stink away from his nose. "Kristine's no fool. Let me work on ruining the relationship. Leave those no-brained little rats out of it."

The angry overseer spat and folded his hairy arms. "You said you've been busy, yet this is all you have?"

"I'm not finished." Charles pulled his pocket watch out. It vibrated more violently than usual. He wondered what would happen if he opened it right now. He let it drop back to the bottom of his pocket. "Daniel has a stone that can banish demons. He's done it twice already."

The anger that dominated the demon's face sank into an expression of fear. He swallowed and looked at his boots. "How do you know this?"

Charles delighted in how this information troubled this overseer when it seemed of little consequence to him. "He threatened to send me back."

His eyes widened. "He can see you?"

"He can." Charles didn't want to tell the overseer anything else. "I'll leave you with that. See you tomorrow evening."

"I'm not through with you."

"I have nothing else to report, and from what I can gather, I gave you plenty."

The overseer pointed at the roof. "Stay put until I say."

Charles looked down at the spot where the overseer pointed. "If you ever wish to learn the angel's name, you must trust me. I have nothing else to report. Now, good night."

Charles thought of Daniel's apartment. He dropped onto the couch and stared at his reflection on the television. "Oh, what a day."

Chapter Twenty

WHEN BEAU MET EVELYN

Beau sat in his father's chair, staring at an empty fireplace. The younger version of himself and his mother weren't there. Ralph was outside, giving him time and space to think. Beau needed it. Memories flooded in like an endless intake of breath, and he needed to exhale.

He lay his head back and stared at the ceiling. Remembering was so much harder than forgetting. Knowing there was more ahead seemed daunting, so he thought about his father.

Those who knew his father considered him a merry man, but they didn't know him like Beau did. His father smiled and spoke kindly to everyone, but a cloud of melancholy lingered about him. At night, he'd spend hours watching the fire, reading and contemplating with tears in his eyes. Beau's mother would console him, but it seemed to do little good. Beau didn't understand why his father was so sad in those days and couldn't bring himself to ask.

His father had tried to mask his sadness for the sake of others. He hadn't wanted anyone to worry about him. It was why he had waited until night to weep. How was he supposed to know that his son had heard him through the closed door? Then again, maybe he had known.

Maybe that was why his father was so tender compared to the other men in town. Most of them would take their boys hunting. Beau's friends often bragged about whatever game they happened to kill on their excursions, but Beau's father didn't take him hunting. Instead, he'd take him on long walks through the forests.

They'd walk every trail, and on these little adventures, which Beau cherished, his father taught him about flowers and foraging. He remembered how his father would gently pluck vegetation from the earth and talk about its nature and how it was useful to mankind. Although he could have gone into great detail about each of them, he usually shared stories, personal ones, about how the plant had helped to shape his life.

His father would have him pull up the dandelions they'd come across on these walks, and they'd pile them into a basket, which would be filled to the brim by the time they returned home. That evening, they'd used some of them for a salad and garnish. The rest were stored in jars and shelved for later use or to trade with neighbors. For some reason, others in the town didn't care much for foraging plants, but for Beau and his family, it was a tradition.

Four empty baskets sat beside the front door. After his father died, Beau didn't go foraging for weeks. The thought of doing so felt wrong. Everything felt wrong, even sitting in his chair, but his mother had urged him to go as their stock began to dwindle.

Beau thudded his way over to the wicker baskets and took one. It felt right in his hand, almost like an extension of his arm. He pushed the door open and stepped onto the front porch.

The sunlight outside was hard on his eyes, and it warmed him more than he liked. Fortunately, he remembered a trail that wasn't too far from home. It provided plenty of shade and vegetation.

"Mind if I go for a walk?" Beau looked down at Ralph, who rocked in the chair by the door.

Ralph looked up with a glint in his eyes. "Sure. We'll catch up soon enough."

Beau stepped off the porch and headed toward the main road. He turned left, which was away from town. After about a quarter-mile, he climbed a small hill that had a beaten path leading into the woods. The shady green canopies allowed light to shine upon the foliage like diamonds. The soil was dark and wet. A patch of blackberry bushes was perfect for picking and sat nestled within the tree line. Not far from there, he found several patches of clover to add to his basket, as well.

He heard footsteps and turned, expecting to see Ralph, but it was his younger self walking along the trail with two baskets of his own. He was about fifteen. A shadowy creature was latched to his back, likely the same one that latched onto him the day he was beaten up by the bullies. Three smaller demons trailed behind him, sniffing at mud and growling at each other.

At this point in his life, young Beau walked the trails only to forage, not to gander. If the house was short on a particular item, he'd head into the forest as if it were the local grocer. He'd gather whatever was needed and return home.

Ralph followed Beau's younger self. "Well, you gonna sit there all day or what?"

Beau joined him, wary of what horrible thing he'd have to remember this time. "What is this all about?"

Ralph shrugged. "I don't know, but it must be important."

They crested a hill and started down the other side. There was a spring a few yards to the right. It couldn't be seen from here, but the cattail weeds marked it. Young Beau went straight to it and began pulling them up. Ralph remained on the trail and leaned against a tall gumball tree.

Beau came up beside him, wracking his brain, trying to remember what could have happened on one of his foraging trips that would warrant a revisit.

"Hey! What are you doing?" a feminine voice shouted from behind him.

Young Beau turned. His face screwed up in confusion. Beau looked over his shoulder and saw her. His heart jolted. He gasped. Again, a flood of memories rocked his head. His legs buckled, and he would've sunk to his knees if Ralph hadn't caught his arm and kept him upright.

"It's OK," the angel whispered.

Beau hardly heard him. He gazed into the young woman's face. She seemed curious about what young Beau was doing. "Are you landscaping the forest?" she asked with a hint of laughter.

Young Beau didn't respond right away. His younger self was infatuated and completely caught off guard. This was Evelyn. She had moved into town a few weeks ago. Her father was a dentist and her mother assisted him. Evelyn had quickly won the hearts of everyone in town, including Beau's, but never did he dream he'd speak to her. She had dark black hair and brown eyes. On this particular day, she wore a long yellow dress. It wasn't the thing someone wore on a foraging expedition.

"Are you OK?" Evelyn asked, taking a few steps forward.

"Yeah," young Beau said. "I'm gathering cattails for dinner."

"Cattails?" Evelyn laughed. "Is that what those things are called? They look like impaled sausage links to me."

Beau laughed, as did his younger self. "Oh, she had the most wonderful sense of humor, Ralph." He wiped his eyes. "How did I ever forget her?"

"You didn't." Ralph patted Beau's shoulder and gave it a rub. "You remembered her until the end of your life."

"Well, they're not as tasty as sausage links." Beau came up from the creek carrying two fistfuls of long cattail weeds. "But they are good. I can show you how I get 'em ready if you want."

Evelyn looked down at her dress. "I promised Mother that I wouldn't dirty up my dress."

"Don't worry." Young Beau came onto the trail. "I'll do all the dirty work." He kneeled and started processing them. "To be honest, I'm surprised you'd come out here alone."

Evelyn cocked her head to the side. "Why? Is it dangerous?"

"I don't think so," young Beau said, "but—oh never mind."

Evelyn folded her arms. "Would you have been surprised to see me alone if I were a boy?"

"Probably not." Beau spoke as if he had been reprimanded. His movements slowed. "It's just that you're so pretty, and while it's peaceful around here, I can think of several men who I wouldn't trust around my mother if they were alone."

Evelyn lifted her dress and kneeled down. "I heard about your father. Everyone in town misses him. I bet you miss him even more."

"Believe me, I do." Beau sighed. "He taught me all about foraging." He cut a cattail stalk into smaller pieces and placed them in the basket. "Hard to do any of this without thinking of him."

"You should think of him." Evelyn touched his hand. A wave of color flashed through the world. All things seemed a little brighter. The demon attached to Beau and its minions shrieked and scampered away. "There's nothing wrong with that."

From that point on, young Beau seemed more at ease around Evelyn. Once he finished processing the cattails, he went back and grabbed several more. Evelyn carried a basket, and the two of them headed back to Beau's cabin, where Evelyn met his mother. That day was the last day Evelyn walked any trail alone. Beau always strolled with her, teaching her what his father had taught him. Her parents took a liking to him. They were impressed with how well he maintained his teeth and how he found food on simple strolls.

Beau turned to Ralph as they watched young Beau and Evelyn walk carefree out from the forest into the dazzling sunshine. "We were inseparable."

Ralph nodded toward a cluster of trees. Three shadowy demons peeked out from behind the trunks. Their yellow eyes glared at Evelyn. "You two had a special connection, and these types can't stand it."

A bitterness blossomed within Beau. It welled in the back of his throat. Did they do something to her? Beau couldn't remember. So often he and Evelyn had walked trails, foraging along the way. They talked about everything and spent much of their free time at each other's homes. Oftentimes, Beau found himself sitting at the piano at Evelyn's house, playing merry tunes, surrounded by friends and family singing along. "The days we spent together. . ." Beau rubbed his eyes. "Every day was so much the same, but something changed. Something had to go bad. Right?"

"Do you remember the wedding?" Ralph asked.

Beau lifted his gaze. He was standing in the backyard of Evelyn's parents' home. Everyone from town, including a few from the next town over, was in attendance. They sat in chairs, and behind them were tables of food that awaited the banquet that followed. The reverend read scripture. Evelyn and Beau made their vows, and the celebration began. Evelyn wore her favorite dress. It was light blue, and she'd worn it to church only a few times before. She looked like a fairytale princess in it.

Beau wore his father's old suit, which was dark brown. Despite its age, it looked nice.

It was a festive event. After the meal, there was dancing that lasted well into the night. Evelyn and Beau didn't go home, to Beau's cabin, until the following day. All this time, Beau had expected something horrible to happen, but it didn't. "I don't understand. I thought you were going to show me the dark times of my life. Not my happiest moments."

Ralph took a seat in a nearby chair. "We're on a journey of remembering, therefore it is one of healing. Your life isn't one of pure darkness, but there is still much for you to remember." He looked over at young Beau dancing with Evelyn. "Yes, this is a happy time for you. Be thankful for those times because they are truly special."

Chapter Twenty-One

Meanwhile at Smokey's

Something about the stillness of Daniel's apartment didn't sit well with Charles. He walked about, glancing into the darkness beyond the doorways, the emptiness that covered the bare walls, and the broken pieces of mirror in the bathroom. What stood out to him was the engagement ring on the counter. If it hadn't been for Charles, Daniel would've exchanged it for a lousy flask. Where was Daniel's gratitude for that?

He walked into the narrow kitchen and stared at the ring. The Nothingness King had told him to ruin Daniel. That was the job. That was his purpose, so why was he upset over Daniel's reaction? Was it because he was failing in that purpose, or was it more sentimental? Did he care enough for Daniel to not do as he was told?

He picked up the ghost version of the ring. "You don't trust me." The ring blurred and trailed back toward the actual ring. "I must do what I must do."

There were other things that concerned Charles, like the strange happenings on the mountain where Daniel had entered Hell. The children who colored with their nitwit parents. *Poor kids.*

Charles scratched his chin. Why weren't the twin overseers at the meeting with their hateful counterpart? Were they in the thick of whatever was happening on the mountain? Possibly. Then again, maybe it was common to only have one or two of the three in attendance.

Something about their ugly little offspring got under his skin. He shuddered.

The demons back in the coffeeshop were similar. They had likely come from the twins. Were they scheming up something special for Kristine? *Where would she be now?*

Charles checked the time on the microwave. It was 10:30 pm. She should be off work. The world folded in on itself. The periphery of his vision blurred, and he passed through a transparent tunnel until he slammed face down in the backseat of a car. He retrieved his hat from the floorboard and sat up. Kristine was driving. Quiet music mingled with the sound of the road. Where was she going? It didn't feel like she was heading home. Her eyes seemed to be searching for something other than a pillow.

He climbed over the console and sat in the front passenger seat. "Where are you going?"

His words didn't affect Kristine. She was too focused on the questions that spun in her head. She pulled into the parking lot of Smokey's Ale House and Bar-B-Q.

She parked and headed for the entrance. Charles followed close behind, still wondering what she was up to.

It looked larger on the inside than it did on the outside. The floors were hardwood, and the walls were black and bare, save for a few tacky-looking mirrors with gold-painted frames. Dim light fixtures hung from a dark ceiling, making this place look more like a dungeon than a place of leisure. Loud, thumping music blasted from speakers, yet no one was dancing. They were gathered around the bar, where televisions displayed more games featuring tall people bouncing a ball.

Kristine and Charles walked by four unoccupied pool tables and a wall of dartboards. Other than Charles, no one was aware of the shadowy demons scurrying about the floor like rats, stalking one person or another like ravenous dogs. A few people had child-sized demons sitting on their shoulders, whispering into their ears. Dark vines reached out from under the bar and wrapped around the legs and waists of those near it.

Kristine found an opening at the bar and took it. A vine stretched from under the countertop toward her ankles, and Charles stomped on it. A small band of demons spotted him and darted to the far right of the bar. Charles watched them warily until they were out of sight.

The bartender came over to Kristine. "Haven't seen you in a little while. You doin' good?"

"I'm OK. How about you?"

The bartender looked about the crowd, filling a glass of beer. "It got crazy on me."

"I can see that." Kristine leaned onto the counter. "Were you working last Friday?"

"No. Why?"

"I heard Daniel got into it with somebody."

"Is that so?" The bartender didn't sound surprised and shook his head as if disappointed. "Nobody told me anything about it. You want something to drink?"

Kristine sighed. "No, thanks."

"Hey girlie!" Mandy came up from the right and hugged Kristine. She wore dark mascara and lipstick. Looping earrings hung from her ears and golden jewelry shined on her chest. "Why didn't you tell me you were coming?"

Kristine pointed to the door. "I was about to leave. I thought you were going to see the lights."

Mandy's eyes widened. "I didn't want to go without you. We can still get out there now if you want."

"Not tonight." Kristine shifted her feet toward the door.

The same little demon from earlier crawled onto Mandy's shoulder and whispered in her ear. Charles folded his arms. He was hesitant to interfere, having already drawn too much attention to himself from his actions at the coffeeshop earlier.

Mandy gripped Kristine's arm and said, "I followed up on what you said. You were right. Daniel didn't choke anybody. I'm so sorry about that."

"Oh." Kristine's face lightened. She seemed less tense. "It's OK."

"No, it's not," Mandy said. "I need to make sure I have my facts straight before I say stuff like that. I'm so sorry."

The demon on Mandy's shoulder grinned. Charles found it hard to believe it would back off so easily. Then again, he was very convincing at the meeting. He gripped his lapels, feeling quite good about himself.

"It's OK." Kristine pulled a strand of hair behind her ear. "I'm glad it's cleared up."

Several demons were sniffing at Kristine's feet. Charles shooed them away.

Mandy took Kristine's hand. "There's someone I want you to meet."

"You don't want to go with her right now," Charles said. The sooner they got out of here, the better. This place reeked of trouble. "She's trying to get in the way of you and Daniel."

"You better not be trying to set me up with somebody," Kristine said.

"No, this one is for me." Mandy led her to a back door that led outside to a patio, where three iron hearths sat between two rows of tables. Only one table was occupied. Two men clinked beer mugs together, laughing. Another girl sat next to them, playing with her phone. A crowd of little demons scurried past them to the twin overseers who had missed the meeting. *So this is what they were doing.* They looked much younger now. Their long black hair blended with their matching black dresses. The tiny demons emitted smoke from their hands while the women inhaled it.

When there was no more smoke for them to breathe, one of them snapped at the little demons. "This isn't enough. Bring us more."

The demons sprinted through the wall, back inside Smokey's. Mandy led Kristine to the table.

The girl set her phone down and hugged Kristine. "Hey girl. You doin' all right?"

"It's been fun," one of the two guys said. He downed his beer and sighed as he set it down. "Catch y'all later."

The girl who hugged Kristine said goodnight and left with him. Mandy sat near the man who stayed behind and introduced him to Kristine as John.

"Come here, Charles." The overseer closest to him held her hand out like an overturned, writhing spider.

The other sneered. "You interfered at the coffeeshop."

Charles inched his way to them. He had already told the male overseer a decent enough lie why he did. All he had to do was stick to that. Besides, it was true. It wouldn't have worked. The lie was too easy to disprove. "I had to, because your little people are poor liars." He glared down at the little demons, who hissed at him. "Why do you think she's here?"

"She is here because we wanted her here, you imbecile." The twin to Charles's left snatched Charles's coat and slung him to the far corner of the patio. The pride Charles felt about the meeting was utterly dashed. "But you are supposed to be with Daniel, not our girl. Be gone. Back to Hell with you!"

They called Kristine *their girl*. Were they planning to take control of her? Charles needed to find out. "About that…" He pushed himself off the deck. No time to feel sorry for himself. "If you had come to the meeting, you'd know that I have vital information." He brushed dirt off his sleeve. "The other overseer—the angry one. He still wants me around and for a good reason."

"This is true," one said to the other. "Rogknot relayed this much to me."

Charles hid his delight at hearing the name of one of the three overseers.

"You gave his name to this simpleton," the other overseer responded.

Charles was no simpleton but knew better than to challenge the notion.

"It's not like he can do anything with it if we're sending him back to Hell."

"All three of us need to be present to do so," the other said.

"Oh, if that's the case, maybe I should call on him so we can take it to a vote," Charles said slyly. He couldn't hide his smile and wouldn't want to if he could. The fury in the air was palpable. *Who is the simpleton now?* Charles thought.

The twins glared at him like scorned lovers ready to stab him countless times out of a fit of passionate anger. His watch bounced around in his jacket like a pinball caught inside a crowd of bumpers. He maintained his poise. "I can keep a secret if you can. Tell me what you need from me so that I'm back in your favor."

"What did you tell our counterpart at the meeting?" one asked.

This was interesting. Either Rogknot didn't relay the report, or they were testing him. It felt like the latter to Charles, but there seemed to be some tension between the twins and the angry one. "I have come across the name of an angel. Also, Daniel can see into the spirit world and carries a stone that sends demons to Hell."

"Give us the name."

"Give it now."

"Not yet." Charles raised his finger and wiggled it. "Not until I know for sure that I'll be here for a long, long time."

"Consider it done."

"The name. Now."

"Your word isn't enough for me, I'm afraid." Charles looked at Kristine sitting at the table. So much for getting out of here quickly. "I need to hear it from the Nothingness King."

The twins didn't like that. Their faces contorted in a mix of anger and anguish.

"You do not get to make demands of us."

"His Majesty would destroy us all for such a petty thing."

"I won't give the name otherwise." Charles gripped his lapels and relaxed his arms. He knew they wouldn't ask. It would be considered a sign of weakness if they did, but making such a demand allowed him to keep the name hidden.

"You have until tomorrow to give it to us."

"Fail to do so and you're gone."

Charles pretended to consider this as if it were optional. "Fine. We'll circle back on the topic of the angel's name then."

"Leave."

"Now."

The twins walked to the table where Kristine sat with Mandy and the man named John. Charles gazed at Kristine. She seemed fine. The demons kept their distance from her, but with the twins stalking after her, how long would she be safe? He started to place Daniel's house in his mind but looked to Smokey's rooftop instead. A second later, he was standing on the ledge of the roof, looking down at the patio.

"You didn't give them my name," a voice whispered behind him.

He turned. Emma was beaming in a black suit that covered every inch of her but her face and glorious golden locks. She held a mask in her hand.

"Oh great, you're a ninja too?" he said.

She wrapped her arms around him and squeezed. Her body pressed against his. "I'm so proud of you." She pulled away and donned the mask. Her blue eyes were so vivid. "Stay a few feet back. You stick out like a sore thumb up here." She crouched at the edge of the building and peered down at the patio.

"Don't be too impressed with me," Charles said. "I dangled your name like bait."

She raised her index finger. "Shhhh."

Charles took a furtive step forward and peeked over her head. The patio had become a cesspool of dark, shadowy beings. Darkness slithered about the deck. Like vines, they rooted Kristine to her seat. "Are you going to do something about this?" he whispered.

"No." Emma's attitude seemed too passive, considering the infestation of demons beneath them.

"Why not?" Charles asked. "Who knows what sort of lies they're filling her head with?"

Emma turned and regarded him. Somehow, he knew she was smiling beneath that mask. "Was Daniel alone when you found him in Hell?"

Realization washed over Charles. Daniel hadn't been alone. A powerful spirit had been with him. "So you're saying that Kristine, Mandy, and John are protected by the same thing as Daniel?"

"Only those who choose Him." She turned back to the patio. "Which isn't everybody, I'm afraid."

Mandy eased into a seat beside John at the table. She caressed his back as if she were playing a harp. A demon walked along her arm and climbed onto his shoulder, whispering into his ear. The twins leaned closer to Kristine and muttered something to her as well. She took a deep breath and exhaled. "I better get going. It was nice meeting you, John." She started for the door. "I'll be around tomorrow if you want to catch up. Maybe head up to Grandfather Mountain."

"OK," Mandy said. "Just call me."

Kristine was gone, and the two overseers trailed after her.

"Are you sure Kristine is all right?" Charles looked at Emma, who didn't seem very happy at all. She was as still as a mouse in a snake's cage. "What's wrong?"

"Mandy's in trouble," she said.

"What?" Charles said. "What about Kristine?"

"She'll be fine. She has a lot to live for. But Mandy—" she looked up at Charles, "she'll need help."

"Look at her." Charles pointed, as if Emma was mistaking Mandy for some imaginary person. "She's happy and having the time of her life."

Emma looked back at Mandy, almost as if she wished it were true. She seemed to observe Mandy giggling and fidgeting with the man for a time and then said, "No. She's not happy at all."

Charles watched Mandy. Her eyes were fixed on the side of John's face. He never looked at her. Instead, he typed on his phone. She spoke lovingly to him, but he seemed too preoccupied to care. "She wants him, but he doesn't want her."

"He's married," Emma said. "She knows it, but she doesn't want to be alone anymore. The man will go home with her, but he won't stay."

"It's not like they're children." Charles reached for his pocket watch. It had settled down considerably, vibrating slightly. "They can do as they please."

Emma took Charles's hands. Her eyes stood out in the night. "Will you look out for her tonight? Please?"

Charles pushed his hat down on his head. "Why can't you?"

Emma peered at him and seemed to consider telling him something important, but said, "I can't tell you why."

Charles gestured to Mandy. "If she is so important to you—"

"Please, Charles." Tears welled up in Emma's eyes. Charles looked at Mandy, John, and the little demons.

How did she get him wrapped so tightly around her little finger? "Fine."

Chapter Twenty-Two

Harrison's Promise

The rain always poured in Grayton. During the hottest hours, it quickly evaporated and returned to the cloud overhead. Rocks that fell from the sky exploded within it, feeding its rage. Grainy beads of sand sprinkled over Chance as he waited, hoping his brother would show up on this rooftop.

Where was he?

The rioting subsided as more placated city-dwellers ventured from their hiding holes to clean up the streets. Little progress was ever made, however, because they tended to gather around and gossip, and there was much to talk about today.

"Chance." The voice was faint, but he knew it was his brother's. He turned and saw him roll onto the roof, coughing.

"Harrison." Chance hurried over and knelt beside his brother. His face and clothes were burned. He must have left the protection of the cloud. "You were supposed to come here."

Harrison nodded. "I know, I know. But something strange is happenin' up on the mountain. You know about it?"

"It's my job to know. Did you go up there?" Chance didn't like his brother taking unnecessary risks. If demons had found him, who knows what they might've done? "You have no business up 'ere. You leave things like that to me."

"They're digging their way to Earth." Harrison gripped Chance's jacket and pulled himself up. "I heard a few talkin'. They think they'll breach the surface anytime."

"How would they know?" Chance asked. Relieved that his brother was safe, he sat back along the ledge of the roof. "The only way out of here is through the bus, which you're taking tonight."

Harrison scratched one of his reddened arms. Thin, jagged cuts ran along his sensitive flesh. "The bus is no longer an option from what I've heard."

"We're already handling it," Chance said. "Those demons hardly did anything to the bus stop. All we need to do is set the sign back in place." They sat in silence. It didn't suit Chance. He had too much to say and even more to do. "My team betrayed me. They went looking for you but never found you."

"I know. One of your angel buddies, Azrael, told me to leave." Harrison stretched out his bleeding arm. "Can you do anything about this?"

"I already told you I can't heal anything unless God wills it." Chance said. "You'll have to wait until the cold comes. Maybe if you hadn't left the city—"

"Goodness, Chance." Harrison pushed to his feet and stepped away from his brother. "Our sister asked me to go check on the mountain. OK?"

"What?" Chance didn't understand why Emma would do this. "She called for you, not me?"

"She tried, but you didn't answer, so I had to step up."

"Seriously?" Chance caressed his forehead. They must really think these demons could dig their way out of Hell. "Doesn't matter. You goin' up 'ere wouldn't change anything. You should've stayed here. If you get caught, we'd be in even worse shape." He stood up and ran his fingers through his hair, feeling a little more exposed without his hat.

Harrison chuckled. "I'm sorry, Daddy."

Chance hated it when his little brother did this. Harrison may be a grown man, but he needed direction. He had a habit of getting into trouble and making poor decisions, such as sleeping with every single woman that struck his fancy.

Chance pointed at him. "Don't you do that. Not today."

"Stop treating me like a child and I won't." Harrison gazed along the rooftops. The world had darkened to a deeper red. "Look. I'm sorry. Word was that they got you and your hat, and I didn't know what to do."

"Why'd you come back then?" Chance asked.

"Are you kidding?" Harrison scoffed. "You're all I got, and you told me way back when that there's always hope and that my prayers are heard. I didn't have anyone else to turn to, so I came back in case you found a way. And, by golly, you did."

Since they were kids, Harrison had the uncanny ability to do outrageously dangerous things and rationalize his actions enough to avoid a verbal lashing. It was part of who he was. And probably why no jealous husbands shot him dead on account of his dirty deeds.

Chance rubbed the back of his neck. "Did Azrael tell you anything worth tellin' me?"

"Nope." Harrison pointed in the direction of the mountain. "But I heard about a demon who works incredibly fast up on the mountain. They say he's wearing a hat. Sound familiar?"

Charles set his hands on his hip and stared through waves of steaming rain. It didn't make sense. "That hat won't rest on just anybody's head."

His brother shrugged. "Well, maybe they found a way. Tied it down or somethin'."

Chance looked toward the Purging Mountains. He didn't like the idea of a demon wearing his hat. "Well, I guess I should see to it. Stay here until I get back."

"I'm coming with you," Harrison said.

"No." Chance walked to the back of the building and leaped to the top landing. "You'll slow me down. If you don't want to wait here, go back to the hideout. Once I get my hat, I'll catch up with you."

"Are you kidding?" Harrison gestured to the city surrounding them. "I don't want to stay around here by myself with everything like it is. I'm goin' with you."

"Tell ya what." Chance rubbed his chin. He had asked Harrison to promise to go to the bus stop in the past, only to be shot down, but those were for lesser things. Maybe today was the day. "Promise me you'll catch the bus the next time it runs, and you can come along."

Harrison's eyes were mad. His lips were pressed into a thin line. "OK. Fine. I promise. Doggone it."

Chance smiled. Maybe his time in Hell would end after this day. "You have to say the full promise."

"Doesn't matter. I'm getting out of here if I can."

"Come on and say it now, Harrison," Chance pleaded. "You're holdin' me up."

"I promise I'll catch the bus the next time it runs. That good enough for you, or should I sing it along the way to make you happy?"

Chance was stunned. For ages, he'd tried to get Harrison to catch the bus. He must truly be worried, to make a promise he couldn't break. "You think your singin' can make me happy?"

They went down the fire escape and wove their way through back alleys toward the burning mountains. With all the trouble he'd dealt with the last few days, Chance hadn't thought to listen out for his sister. He'd need to keep an ear out for her from now on.

"What's she gotten herself into this time?" he muttered.

Chapter Twenty-Three
Joy and Tragedy

Beau and Evelyn's first year of marriage couldn't have gone any better. Evelyn became pregnant and continued to help her parents at the dentistry, which was quite successful. Customers came from surrounding towns because there weren't any other dentists within seventy miles of their practice. They were skeptical at first but warmed up to it when word-of-mouth reported alleviated toothaches and better-looking smiles.

When she wasn't helping her parents, Evelyn spent her time knitting and cooking. In the evenings, Beau would come in from working his mother's fields, and they'd forage nearby trails. Their walks were always filled with laughter. The land provided plenty if you were willing to explore it. They gathered more than they needed and offered the extra portions to the neediest families in town.

Some evenings, they'd take a trail where Beau had cleared out an area atop a cliff. There, they'd sit and watch a healthy, sunlit stream cut through the valley below. This was their favorite place to picnic until a strong summer storm compromised it.

When Angela came into the world, she proved to be the most content child the midwives had ever known. Rarely did she cry, and when she was old enough to follow directions, she did so with an eager smile.

Beau and Ralph watched years pass in a matter of minutes. There weren't any dark entities lingering about as far as Beau could tell. Most days were the same. They went about their lives working, raising their child, and loving each other—faithfully devoted.

After a brutal winter, many folks were relieved when spring arrived. They didn't expect it to become a season of death. Mr. Willsbury was the first to go. He had left town to attend his brother's funeral. The flu that had taken his brother came back with him. It soon found its way into the lungs of many of the townspeople. Beau's mother, along with Evelyn's father, died within the first month of the epidemic. They rose one morning seemingly healthy, but by midday grew so ill they could hardly move. Their skin filtered through deathly colors until turning blue. Shortly after that, they were gone—like hundreds of others.

In these days, fear ruled the town. Beau and Evelyn, like many others, chose to stay home, only venturing out to forage and work on the farm. They still provided extra portions to needy families, leaving baskets on doorsteps.

One morning, however, Evelyn was slow to get out of bed. Beau and Angela took care of the early chores: gathering eggs and feeding the chickens. But when they came back in, Evelyn lay still, staring past the ceiling. Her face was pale blue. Beau closed her eyes and took his daughter out into the yard.

He sat on the porch with a bottle of whiskey and a pipe full of tobacco. For hours, he cried silent tears. When Angela took his hand, it startled him. "Hey Daddy. When is Momma goin' to get up?"

He tried to mask his sadness, but his voice was broken. "I don't know, darlin'." He pointed to the yard. "Why don't you get back to playin' now? You worked hard this morning." His chin trembled. "A girl your age needs playin'." Beau broke down and sobbed. Angela brought his hand to her cheek. He pulled away. "Go play now."

"Momma's dead," she said plainly. "Isn't she, Daddy?"

Unable to speak, Beau sobbed and nodded.

"I don't want to play. I won't ever play again!" She tried to run inside, but Beau caught her by the wrist and pulled her close.

"You gotta stay out here," he whispered. "Understand?"

"I don't wanna play," Angela cried.

"You don't have to, love." Beau wiped the wetness from her cheeks. "You can sit here if you want."

They sat on the porch for hours. The sun set over the trees. Beau waited until she fell asleep before he dug a grave in the backyard close to the forest and the road. He worked well into the night until he laid her gently in the hole. He buried the love of his life and lay there in the dirt singing her favorite songs. The next morning, he woke with his daughter curled up in his soiled arms.

The sickness took many others that year, including Evelyn's mother, who never accepted that her daughter had died. She was delirious in her anguish, believing that Beau had locked Evelyn up in an effort to protect her from the sickness. By the end of summer, the dying subsided. Beau foraged the land with his daughter, but it wasn't filled with any more laughter. Quiet somberness had replaced it. Every outing had become a death march.

Angela forgot that they were supposed to be sad. She spoke cheerfully and skipped about the path, singing the songs she heard in church and at school. "Why don't you play the piano anymore, Daddy?"

Beau took a long swig from his bottle of whiskey. "I forgot 'em all, darlin'." He stumbled over a root but caught himself on a tree. "Ain't no point to music anyhow."

"But you're the best player in town, Daddy." Angela pulled up several dandelions. "I heard Pastor Joe ask you to play for the church. Why'd you say no?"

Beau kept his back pressed to the tree as he sank down to his bottom. "I done told ya, darlin'. Ain't no point to it."

Angela lay the dandelions in her basket and looked at her father. "Are you gonna take another nap, Daddy?"

"Just a little one this time." Beau sounded on the verge of tears. He closed his eyes. "How about we play hide and seek? Go hide and I'll come find you when I've finished napping."

Naps and hide and seek had become commonplace on their walks. It had worked well, too. Angela would run about, seeking a nice place to hide, avoiding any unpleasant people who might come along the trail. Several bands of bad people frequented the area these days, looking to take things left behind by those who had died. Most of it was long gone, leaving the looters angry, and they were happy to take their rage out on innocent bystanders.

"You didn't come looking for hours last time, Daddy."

"I'm sorry, darlin'," Beau's eyes closed. "Tell ya what. If I. . ."

Beau fell asleep. Angela took up her basket and looked along the trail. She bounded a couple of hundred feet into the forest and nestled down in a patch where sunlight broke through the trees. She took out her dolls and set up a tea party.

The real Beau stood over this patch of green next to Ralph. "I was a horrible father."

"You were grieving," Ralph said. "People you trusted said the whiskey would help. By this time, you knew it wouldn't, but you'd grown too accustomed to it."

Daylight waned, and Beau continued to sleep. Angela went to her father and shook him. "Time to wake up, Daddy." It didn't help. She grew frustrated and slapped her father hard across the face. He blinked. "Wake up, Daddy! Time to catch me."

Beau eased over to all-fours. "What happened? Where's your mother?"

"Can't catch me." Angela laughed as she sprinted back in the direction where she had left her dolls. "Come on, Daddy. You promised."

"Wait!" Beau came to his feet and fell. "Don't run that way, darlin'."

"Gotta catch me!"

"No!" Beau got to his feet and pressed his palms to either side of his aching head. Angela stopped and turned to him, smiling. "Come on back. We'll play catch at home, OK?"

"Nope!" Angela shook her head. "Catch me now, like you said."

"I'm not chasing you out here. It's not safe."

"Oh, yeah?" Angela laughed. "Then you better catch me fast!"

She took off. Beau chased after her, but she was quick and agile in the thick forest. Beau was clumsy. He tripped over rocks, stumps, and roots, bumped into trees, and swatted at branches that smacked his face and whipped his arms. "Stop!"

She looked over her shoulder and kept sprinting. "Can't catch me!"

Older Beau saw it happen again. His daughter sank from view as she ran off the cliff where he and Evelyn would watch sunsets. He had never brought his daughter here, afraid that she might fall. He ran to the ledge. Her screams gave way to thuds as she fell down the rocky cliff. When he peered over, Angela lay still and silent, staring up at her father as if shocked.

All around him, dark entities slithered to Beau, coiling up his legs and around his body. A larger one climbed onto his back and whispered, "Leave her. There's nothing you can do. The animals will take care of her for you."

Beau went to the ground and pounded his fist. He let out a scream that sent birds from the trees. "I have to bury her."

"Better get a move on then." The demon wrapped his arms around Beau's neck and pulled. "You'll need a couple bottles of whiskey after all this."

Beau climbed to his feet and stared down at his daughter's body. He considered jumping but was too afraid. On his way back to the trail, he passed the baskets and the dolls laying in a clearing. He took up his bottle of whiskey and went down the trail to a place where he could reach Angela.

The real Beau glared at his younger self. Ralph was right. He did hate himself. He walked over to where his daughter was playing, picked up a doll, and held it tight. "I'm sorry, darlin'."

"It's OK, Daddy." Angela's voice echoed from the sky.

Beau staggered back and looked about the forest, turning in every direction. "Angela?" Ralph was beside him. "Where is she?"

"We're getting close, Beau, but we're not there yet."

CHAPTER TWENTY-FOUR

DEALING WITH MANDY

Charles worried what the twins might do to Kristine, but trusted that Emma knew what she was doing. She seemed confident and intelligent regarding spiritual battles. He turned his attention to Mandy and the married man. They didn't stay long after Kristine left.

He didn't follow them from the back patio into Smokey's. The last thing he needed was a demon to spot him and go tattling to the overseers. He walked along the roof and waited above the entrance.

Mandy and John came out into the parking lot moments later. The same little demon sat on Mandy's shoulder. Charles closed his eyes and jumped to her. He ended up right behind her and swatted the demon off before hiding behind a nearby car. The little demon went scampering and leaped into what Charles believed was Mandy's car.

They came to the rear of that car, and John took her by the waist. They gazed at each other, but not into each other's eyes. Charles crept closer to them, keeping out of sight in case there were any demons watching.

"You can ride with me if you want." Mandy ran her fingertips along John's chest. "I don't live far."

"It's better if I follow you." The man gently pushed her away and made for his car. "I can't stay long, so we should get going."

Charles watched them get into their cars and plopped through the passenger-side door of John's sporty ride and sank into a smooth leather seat. "Ooh, this is nice."

John pushed a button and revved the engine. He gazed at Mandy through the passenger window. She smiled and winked before backing out.

Charles loosened his necktie. He wasn't sure if he could influence John, but considering his bad behavior, Charles believed it was possible. "Compensating for something? I mean, look at you. You're a married man, driving this beautiful car to places full of loose women. I'm sure no one suspects that you're an utter douchebag."

The man grew rigid and backed out of his parking spot. "Shut up." He pulled up behind Mandy, who was waiting to turn out onto the road.

Charles smiled. This was going to be delightful. "So you can hear me. Congratulations! Do you ever listen to your wife?"

"I do all the time." John sounded agitated. He looked into the rearview mirror and shook his head. "It's all I ever do."

"Sure." Charles lay his head back and relaxed. "Say, do you know if your wife will get your car as part of the divorce settlement once she wises up to your late-night shenanigans? Oh, man. I sure hope you don't have a kid."

"Don't talk about my little boy. You leave him out of this!" The man tightened his grip on the steering wheel. "This is a onetime thing. All right?"

"Oh, that's so virtuous of you." Charles turned in his seat. This was going so well. "Someone should put you in for family man of the year. Only cheated one time? Make sure you mention how honored you are during your victory speech. And don't worry about your poor little boy. He'll be proud that his daddy found more than one way to compensate for his midlife crisis."

"I'm not having a midlife crisis," the man growled. "I work hard. I should be able to cut loose every now and then. Besides, Mandy gets me."

"What does that mean? That she won you as some consolation prize for being the runner-up of the poor choice awards?" Charles wasn't sure. Maybe it was a figure of speech that came about some time after he had died. It likely meant that she understood him, but he doubted that was the case. John was making lame excuses that would not serve him well in Hell. "Never mind. It doesn't matter that she *gets* you. You don't get her. The only reason you're doing this is because you're selfish. You don't care about Mandy."

"I'm not selfish." John's bottom lip puffed out. "I care about her. I care about a lot of people."

"Does that include your family?" Charles asked. "Why aren't you with them, rather than chasing after young girls?"

John didn't answer and appeared sullen. Ahead of them, Mandy pulled into an apartment complex and parked. John, however, didn't. He pulled up behind Mandy's car and pushed a button to make his window go down. "Hey." He patted the steering wheel nervously. "I gotta go. My son is sick and asking for Daddy."

Mandy sucked in a breath and folded her arms over her stomach. The demon on her shoulder whispered in her ear. "I'm sure he's sick. You know who else is sick? Me. This was your idea. I had other plans, but I gave up on them to be with you."

John glanced at her and then at the steering wheel. Charles got out of the car but crouched to remain hidden from Mandy's demon. "I know, and I'm sorry. I've been leading you on—"

Mandy cursed at him quite creatively. Charles was impressed. She stomped away to the sidewalk and didn't turn back. The demon on her shoulder did. It hissed at John as he peeled out of the parking lot. The smell of burned rubber reminded Charles of the tar pits in the

Malebolge. Not wanting to draw the demon's attention, he watched Mandy enter her apartment before he approached.

He went to the window and listened. Her keys slapped onto a wooden table as she muttered hatefully to herself. She went to another room and slammed the door behind her.

"Why is she so upset?" Charles said. "Goodness. I've seen pigs that were more handsome than him. That poor kid of his…" He shook his head. "Let's hope his mother is better looking. Then again, if she were…"

Charles entered through the door. The apartment had decent furniture. Nice leather chairs and a bigger television than Daniel or his parents. The walls had a nice mix of art and pictures. Sobs burst from the bathroom. Charles rolled his eyes. He didn't understand. *Why is she in so much pain?*

He walked to the door and wondered if he should go through it, even though there was a little tattle-telling demon in there with her. He leaned closer, listening.

"You lied to your best friend." This wasn't Mandy's voice. It was her little demon. "Nobody likes you. Look in the mirror and say it, you hag."

"No one likes me," Mandy whispered.

"I'm worthless," the demon grumbled. "Say it!"

"I'm worthless," Mandy repeated.

"Indeed," the demon said. "You shouldn't live like this. You can end your troubles painlessly right now. Stop being a burden on your parents and your friends. You know which bottle to use. We've talked about this."

Charles needed to intervene, but he didn't want to risk exposing himself. The demons who were attached to Mandy would report him, and he'd be back in Hell for sure.

He removed his hat and scratched his head. On the hallway wall, there was a picture of Mandy holding a small dog. An older man had his arm around her. There was some likeness in their faces. It must be her father. Why did Charles feel so sad for this man in the picture? He and Mandy seemed so happy in that moment. Did he know what his daughter was going through?

What do I do?

In the periphery of his vision, in the darkness of the bedroom, he noticed something darker within. He turned and saw nothing there. Although he saw nothing, he felt something. There was a change in the air. *A shadow-man.* Beau was a shadow-man, and Beau had said he'd used a horn to frighten off demons when they'd torment the living.

Charles went into the bedroom. "What are you doing hiding in here? Aren't you going to help her?"

"There's nothing I can do," the shadow-man spoke slowly, as if he were on the verge of sleep. "There's too much light."

"You don't need to go in there." Charles could barely make out the shadow-man in the darkness. "Just blow the horn."

The shadow-man shifted. "Are you sure you want that?"

"I'm not a demon. Go for it." Charles gestured toward the bathroom. "Hurry. She needs you now."

The shadow didn't move. Nothing did. Time might have frozen, but Mandy's sobs didn't. "I hate myself."

"You should, because you're a coward," the demon said. "Stop stalling and take the pills."

Charles gazed at the dark silhouette. "It's now or never."

The shadow-man walked to the threshold of the bedroom and eyed ambient light from the living room and seemed to fumble with something. "There's too much light."

"Get over it," Charles said. "Come on. Save her."

The shadow-man inched into the hall and brought the horn to his lips. He stuck the large end through the door. The demon hissed and the horn sounded.

It was deafening. The world seemed as if it were on the brink of exploding. Charles fell to the floor, fatigued. He blinked and stumbled to a chair in the corner of the bedroom. When the horn stopped, Charles peered at the ceiling. The shadow-man hovered over to him. "It's too late. She's set on taking the pills."

"Stop her."

"I can't. All I can do now is wait for her to die."

Charles scoffed. "You're the lousiest shadow-man I've ever met." He marched over to the door and entered the bathroom. It was bathed in light. Mandy had a prescription bottle in her hand. She popped the lid off.

"Don't do it," Charles said.

Mandy stared into the mirror. The makeup around her eyes had been smudged. She looked beaten and was a tearful mess. She dumped the entire contents of the bottle into her hand.

"Don't," Charles said. "You have too much to live for. All those pictures on the wall. People love you. They need you."

Mandy poured the pills back into the bottle and sank to the floor, sobbing. "I hate my life."

She heard him. Charles loosened his necktie and sat down on the toilet seat. The horn had given him a horrible headache. He didn't know what to say, but felt as if he needed to say something. "Yeah, well, I hate my afterlife." He crossed his legs and used his thumb to wipe a smear from his shining shoes. "What I don't hate is myself. Do you honestly hate yourself, Mandy?"

Mandy lay her head against the wall and stared at the overhead light. She seemed to be contemplating the question. "I don't like who I've become."

Charles crouched beside her and whispered in her ear. "Because this is not who you are. You know the difference between right and wrong. Use that and you'll change for the better."

Tears rolled down Mandy's cheeks. She wiped them away. "I can change?" She took a quivering inward breath and exhaled. "My gosh, I don't know where to start."

"Start by getting some sleep." Charles stood and stretched.

Mandy pulled herself from the floor. She took a long look in the mirror and dropped the bottle of pills into the trash. The intensity had changed. The apartment was calm and quiet.

Charles went into the living room and sat in the darkness while Mandy took a shower. He tipped his hat to the shadow-man who watched him from the kitchen. "We did it. We saved her." He felt so good that he could barely stand himself.

Charles looked at the shadow-man. "If I hadn't become a thief, I might have been a mind changer." He interlocked his fingers behind his head. "Whatever that is."

"What are you?" the shadow asked.

"Call me Charles." He kicked his feet up onto the table and closed his eyes.

"You aren't supposed to help them." The shadow-man moved closer. It seemed to be curious. "That's not what your kind does."

Charles held up his finger. "Easy on the generalizations, shadow-man." Charles closed his eyes and wondered about Beau. What was he up to? "Have you ever met another shadow-man named Beau?"

"Beau? There was one called Beau. He worked in this area, but he's no longer a shadow since entering Hell."

"That's him." Charles sat up. "He helped me save someone from Hell."

"But," the shadow-man sounded pensive, "we're not saviors. Only senders."

"Are you sure about that?" Charles asked. "You helped me save Mandy when you blew that horn. There's more to you than you think. Beau used to think he was always a shadow, but when he entered Hell, he took on the form of a man and remembered that he once lived, even had a daughter."

"Strange." The shadow-man came closer to Charles. Whatever reservations it had about him earlier were gone. "I feel as if I've always been a shadow, but I can't remember when I began."

"Do you have a name?"

"Windsong."

"Weird name. What's the earliest thing you remember?"

"It's all fragmented." The shadow seemed to bend forward, as if burdened by an invisible weight. "When I think about it, when I try—it pains me. I find it more suitable to not remember."

"Well, you should try it from time to time," Charles suggested. "Tell me, what do you know of the overseers and the Nothingness King?"

"The Nothingness King reigns in outer darkness. He sometimes steals souls from us. He tricks them into pleading fealty to him," the shadow-man said.

"Why don't you stop him?"

"He's too powerful."

"Is he too powerful for Azrael?"

Windsong shook his head. "No, but the Nothingness King is slippery, and it takes time to save souls from outer darkness once they're imprisoned."

Charles rubbed his chin. Mandy hummed a tune from the bathroom. He listened and looked at the picture where she was with an older man. If that were her father or grandfather, did he have any idea how much she was struggling? How close he had come to losing someone he loved?

"What about the overseers?" Charles looked to where the shadow-man was, but it was gone. "So long, Windsong."

CHAPTER TWENTY-FIVE

LET IT SHINE

Mandy went to sleep in her bed, and Charles relaxed on the comfy sofa in her living room, enjoying the quiet darkness until the television in the neighboring apartment blasted to life. "Grandfather Mountain is temporarily closed. We'll go live on the scene right after the break. Suffering from chronic joint pain..."

This was quite fortunate. Charles stuck his head through the wall. He didn't see any spirits, but the hairy man sprawled on the couch in Star Wars-themed pajamas leveled a remote control at the television and changed the channel.

"Change it back," Charles suggested, stepping through the wall into the man's apartment. "You'll want to hear about Grandfather Mountain."

The man's face twisted with thought. "I'm sick of the news. I wanna watch some Star Trek." He set the remote on the table.

Charles's words seemed to go in one ear and out the other, but at least the man could hear him. All Charles needed to do was to persuade him somehow. "It'll only take a few minutes."

The man smiled as an odd-looking spaceship traveled through darkness speckled with tiny white lights. *This must be Star Trek.* It gave Charles an idea.

"You know, whatever's happening on Grandfather Mountain likely has something to do with aliens." He came closer to the man and tried to sound enthusiastic. "Don't you think it's strange how nobody can explain it? They try to put some spin on it, but nobody's buying it."

The man shifted slightly. He rubbed his nose—or was he picking it? Charles wasn't sure. Despite the man's empty-headedness, he pushed on. "It's gotta be aliens, but the government won't admit it."

"Yeah." The man flicked something.

Charles scoffed. *Definitely a pick.* How could he communicate with such a person?

"Doesn't matter," Mr. Pajamas said. "They'll cover it up like they always do."

"But they're going live," Charles said. "There's no hiding live footage, you know. You should record it. Imagine. People would pay you to see footage of a real alien."

"I've seen this episode too many times. Maybe I'll check on the news for a minute." The man changed the channel back to the original station. After a series of commercials, the television flashed a graphic with the words "Special Report". A well-dressed man, whose thoughtful facial expression seemed stern and somewhat idiotic, stared back at Charles through the television. "Hello, and welcome to this special report. We are live in Linville, North Carolina, tonight to give you the latest updates on an interesting phenomenon..."

The television turned off.

Charles gasped. "What about the aliens?" he asked desperately.

The man yawned and shuffled back to his bedroom, flicking the lights off on his way to his bedroom, leaving Charles in pitch-black silence once again.

"Great."

Charles needed to see what was happening on that mountain. If he could jump there, he would. He tried saying it, even hopped while doing so, but nothing happened.

He rested his chin on his palm and thought about what he should do next. Go to Daniel? Kristine? The rooftop? Sitting around here wasn't doing him any good.

Maybe he should peek in on Kristine. The twins had told him to stay away, but he knew the building and felt confident that he could check in undetected. Then again, if he hopped to Daniel, maybe his ungrateful friend would look up Grandfather Mountain on a computer. He doubted Daniel would send him to Hell, but then again, Daniel was quite upset when Charles left.

He closed his eyes and spoke his thoughts aloud. "What next?"

The air changed. He entered through another translucent tunnel without the slightest idea of where it would take him. It seemed to take longer than usual. Did he get himself stuck in this portal with his indecision? Emma had mentioned that it happened with phone jumps, but that seemed to occur when callers hung up before the jump completed.

Looking about, he realized this wasn't a tunnel, but a bubble. The surface was thin with chromatic swirls moving about like some global weather pattern. Beyond that, everything seemed silvery, almost mirror-like.

He jabbed a finger at the surface, but it didn't even quiver. He tried to jump to numerous places but couldn't. It seemed as if he were imprisoned—in a bubble. *This may be worse than Hell,* Charles thought. A new idea came to mind.

"Emma," he cried. His voice reverberated until it diminished to a thousand whispers. Maybe this was it for him. Bubbled for eternity. It beat having to deal with damned souls and demons, but then again, he already felt a little claustrophobic.

He took a step back, and the bubble seemed to roll a little. Interestingly, he didn't lose his balance. He grazed his fingers along the surface, and the silvery background shifted as if it were clouds or fog. He did it again, and the bubble hustled forward.

The silvery clouds broke. A golden light shone on him. Shielding his eyes, he saw the bubble was gliding to a place rolling with hills. There were houses scattered about. Off to the left, there seemed to be a town, but the bubble didn't carry him that way. Instead, he was heading toward a small church that sat upon one of the smaller hills.

From the church, a sea of voices sang out. "This little light of mine. I'm going to let it shine."

Children ran beneath him, reaching up to grab the bubble. Worried that they might pop it, he shooed at them, and they waved, smiling as if they knew him.

"No," Charles said, still shooing at them. "I mean go away."

The children kept waving and saying "Hey".

He looked up in time to see the bubble soar over the steps of the church and crash through the door. He yelped and fell back.

"Let it shine. Let it shine. Let it shine."

The pews and choir loft were full, but the pulpit was empty. It grew quiet. There was murmuring among the many faces. They seemed delighted to see him trapped in a bubble. He turned about, not immediately realizing that he was no longer in a bubble. To his dismay, his clothes were sooty. He patted himself off, but the dark mist that bloomed around him didn't make him feel any better.

"Is that you, Chip?" the voice was familiar—almost terrifyingly so.

Overwhelmed with emotion, Charles nearly fell. He grasped the side of a nearby pew. A large man sprang to his feet and helped him into a seat. So many people surrounded him.

"Grandma?" Charles could hardly breathe. "Are you here?"

The smiling faces parted like the Red Sea. Charles's grandmother beamed. Tears ran down her cheeks. "My Chip."

Chapter Twenty-Six

A Dream and a Funeral

Daniel lay in his bed, feeling this past day had been very productive and revealing. Not only had he gone home and spent time with his parents, but he'd also gotten a glimpse of Heaven and discovered that the old man he met on Grandfather Mountain was the archangel, Gabriel. Was that his first time running into an angel? Maybe angels, real angels, went about their day disguised as strangers, giving messages to those who needed them. He'd also rid the world of a few dark spirits with his stone. Then there was Charles, whom he'd spared—for now.

Daniel turned and stared at the wall. He didn't expect to see Charles again. Why would Satan send Charles? He wasn't even an actual demon. He was a man, a disembodied spirit, crafty enough to trick him into going deeper into Hell, but Charles wasn't malevolent—not like real demons. In Hell, Charles had proved to be an ally and even seemed to care about him.

They went through a lot together. He knew that Charles had the capacity to do good. Maybe Satan couldn't see that and had made a mistake sending him.

Daniel rolled to his other side. He took solace in knowing that he had a powerful friend. A friend who he hadn't met yet—as far as he knew, anyway. This friend was his only way out of this mess. Would this friend intervene? What would it take for Him to do so?

Thoughts swirled about as he stilled himself to rest. Images of the damned emerged from the blackness. Evil faces blinked in and out of focus. Figures of triumph drifted from the sky and landed upon monsters. They extended a hand to Daniel as he lay in his bed, watching and wondering if this was his imagination.

Hours into his slumber, Daniel had an interesting dream. While driving north toward Fort Bragg, Daniel saw a man dressed like a magician wearing black. His top hat and cape shined with silk. When he bowed, Daniel saw the cape's inner lining was red. He flourished a short black cane with a white tip.

This strange man had a gaping smile that unsettled Daniel. He was old and spry, with teeth sharpened like stakes. His beady eyes sparkled as if he held many secrets. His gray hair curled below his shoulders at the back of his head.

In the rearview mirror, the magician flicked his cane, and it opened into an umbrella. An unseen wind lifted him into the air, carrying him quickly along the northbound road. Daniel pressed harder on the gas pedal, but the man closed the distance between them. He was flying alongside the car, peering into the window, smiling wickedly. The umbrella spun wildly in his hand.

Let me in, Daniel. His voice was brittle and airy.

Daniel stomped on the brake, and the car skidded to a stop. The man landed in front of the car. He tapped the umbrella to the ground, and it turned back into a cane. He walked in a showy way, bringing his knees up high, spinning the cane in his hand like the leader of a band, making his way to the window. His face blocked out the setting sun. Daniel couldn't look at him. He could hardly breathe.

The magician tapped his cane against the glass to the beat of an old nursery rhyme and spoke with a mocking, singsong voice. "Little Daniel, don't you hide. I have come to help you die. You will be hung within Satan's wall, screaming forever a soundless squall. I know you hear me."

Daniel's thigh tingled with numbness. He gripped it and felt something nestled within his pocket. The keystone. A sense of fear seemed to spill in from the one outside his window.

"That won't help you," the magician growled. "Nothing can."

Daniel took out the translucent blue stone. It glowed in his palm, casting everything in sight with shades of blue. The stranger backed away. Daniel stepped out of the car but wasn't on the highway anymore. He was standing in front of a closed coffin.

He gasped. "Captain Jones?" His former commander's two sons were on either side of him. The youngest took hold of Daniel's hand and looked at him.

"Why do you ruin the best people?" he asked.

Daniel backed away. "It's not my fault."

The oldest one turned. He pointed a gun at Daniel's chest. "You murdered him." He pulled the trigger.

Daniel woke. His room was bathed in dull morning light. A young woman was sitting at the end of his bed. "Good morning, Sunshine."

Daniel jumped from his bed. The stone dropped to the floor.

"I'm Emma." She seemed unfazed, as if she expected Daniel to respond this way. "I'm a friend of Gabriel's. He asked me to come chat with you."

Daniel snatched the stone. "You should knock first."

"Doesn't work." Emma raised a fist and knocked at the wall, but her hand passed through it without making a sound. "But if you prefer, I'll wait in the car, and we can talk on the way."

"Charles mentioned you, but Gabriel never did," Daniel said. "How can I trust you?"

"Well," Emma stood, "if you're willing, throw that stone at me. It won't affect me like it does others."

"You're serious?"

She thought about it. "Usually."

Daniel considered this. She might be bluffing because they were indoors. He wouldn't let her get off that easily. "OK. Give me a minute." He walked by her and opened his window and removed the screen.

"None of that will be necessary," she said.

"Sure, it won't." Daniel stepped back with the stone in hand. "If you're not scared of the stone, stand there and let's see what happens."

Emma sighed and took her place. "All right, hotshot. Let's do this."

Daniel slung the stone, but before it reached Emma, it froze in midair, hovering.

Emma took it and tossed it back to Daniel. "See?"

Daniel nodded. The scent of breakfast was calling him to the kitchen. "I'm relieved."

"Glad to put you at ease."

"So, I *can* trust Charles."

"I think so," Emma said. "Go get some breakfast. You have a busy day. I'll wait in the car."

Daniel joined his parents for breakfast. His father offered him some old dress clothes, since he hadn't packed anything formal enough for a funeral. Luckily, they fit. His mother offered him money, but he refused. Before leaving, he called Kristine, but it went straight to voicemail. He left a brief message saying he'd call when he returned home. Then he gave his mother and father extended hugs and goodbyes before leaving.

Emma sat in the front passenger seat, smiling. Her eyes were vividly blue in the light. "Got quite a day ahead of you, Daniel."

"Tell me about it." Daniel backed down the drive and asked, "So, what's up? Why are you here?"

"I've been asked to stick with you today by a mutual friend," she said.

"Gabriel?"

"No," Emma said, "but I bet you can guess on your next try."

Daniel didn't respond. The funeral would begin in a few hours. In the corner of his vision, he thought he saw a man in black waving a hat. He looked again, but no one was there. Days ago, he would have considered it his imagination, but the memory of the magician, and his horrible song was too fresh in his head. And his days of considering things mere coincidences were over.

"Have you ever heard of an evil spirit that dresses like a magician?" he asked.

"Several," Emma said. "Why?"

Daniel watched the road. "This one is small and had a gray mullet and sharpened teeth. Wears a top hat."

Emma responded instantly. "That's the Nothingness King. Why? Have you seen him?"

Daniel nodded. "I think he's coming after me today."

When Daniel reached the checkpoint to enter Fort Bragg, he was amazed at how different it felt to come onto the base as a civilian. Not much had changed since his departure from the military. The parking lot near his old unit was as rugged as ever. There were plenty of soldiers walking around, but he didn't recognize anyone.

He cut the engine and looked at Emma. "Are you coming with me?"

"I have to check on other things, but I'll be here when you get back."

Daniel pocketed his keys and marched to the CQ office to sign in. He was surprised that Bobby still lived in the barracks. *What kind of staff sergeant does that?* Sergeant Faircloth's room was on the third floor, three doors down on the left. He answered in his dress blues. "What's up, brother?" They slapped hands and patted each other on the back.

"Why are you still in the barracks, Big Sarge?" Daniel said with a hint of laughter.

"You know what you can do with that "Big Sarge" talk." Bobby fumbled with his tie. "Don't come up in here with that." He went back to the mirror. Daniel followed him in. "I'll get out of here before long. I just got promoted. Haven't had time to find a place."

Daniel saw a strange wooden owl perched on top of the wardrobe. There was also a painting of an owl on the nightstand. "What's up with the owls?"

Bobby turned to Daniel, his eyes wide. His smile was contagious. "Whooooo wants to know?"

"The next time I come here, I'm stopping by a taxidermist." Daniel sat down at the desk, where he found two miniature statues of owls. "Seriously? Did you join the Freemasons or something?"

"First off, don't you bring no stuffed owl up in here. Ever. And no, I ain't no Freemason. I like owls. Why? You got a problem with owls?"

Daniel held up his hands in surrender. "OK. You like owls. Must be a new thing."

Once Sergeant Faircloth was satisfied with his uniform, the two left for the funeral in Sergeant Faircloth's car. They had more than enough time to get there, but had been wired to get wherever they needed to be early. Bobby filled Daniel in on who had left the unit in the past year and what was different. Apparently, not much had happened other than Sergeant Faircloth's promotion and the death of Captain Jones.

At the funeral home, Bobby pointed out a couple of soldiers who were chatting under a large oak tree. "Look at these two knuckleheads. They remind me of how we were back in the day, and I'm in charge of 'em. Ain't that some crazy karma?"

Daniel chuckled. "I didn't think you believed in karma."

"I don't." Sergeant Faircloth got out of the car. "It's a figure of speech."

Daniel followed him over and met the two knuckleheads. They weren't knuckleheads at all, actually. Bobby checked their uniforms and Daniel heard someone calling from the parking lot.

"Sergeant Strong."

Daniel turned and smiled. "Sergeant Harris." He walked to his old friend. There were others he recognized, but they were eyeing their phones or heading into the funeral home. "How've you been?"

Sergeant Harris looked solemnly at the funeral home's front door. "Not as good as I'd like, unfortunately." He was close to Captain Jones. They had worked together at company headquarters, at least when Daniel was there. The sergeant turned back to Daniel. "Where are you living now?"

"Boone," Daniel said. "On my second semester at App State."

"Good for you." He patted Daniel's arm. "What do you think about all that mess on Grandfather Mountain?"

Daniel rubbed the back of his head. Kristine had mentioned the lights and the cloud, but he didn't think it was a big deal. Not so big that anyone at Bragg would care. "Are you talkin' about the cloud and the lights?"

Sergeant Harris raised his chin. "You heard anything today?"

"No. Why?"

"The cloud's still there and has grown," Sergeant Harris said. "They shut the park because of a lack of visibility. As for the lights, they were flashing all through the night around the foot of it. Crazy, huh?"

"Goodness." Daniel couldn't believe it. He was tempted to tell Sergeant Harris everything that had happened to him, but thought it best to keep to himself. His heart raced, and he took deep breaths to settle the panic that was rising in his chest. The funeral home doors opened, and many started for the entrance.

Sergeant Harris patted him on the shoulder. "See you inside."

Beside the funeral home, there was a large green lawn with several trees planted along the far side, with benches placed between them. Two young children sat near a bench, playing in the mulch. He had met them once but knew they were Captain Jones's sons.

Something deep within him told him that now was the time to speak with those boys. Daniel peered back at Bobby, who was still chatting with his soldiers, then headed toward the children, feeling a little apprehensive. What should he say?

When he reached them, neither of boys acknowledged him. "Hey guys. What are you up to?"

"Playing," the younger one said matter-of-factly. The older one said nothing.

There was a wooden fence that bordered the funeral home's property. A forest was on the other side of it. Long, skinny fingers with knobby joints reached through the fence. Daniel heard voices speaking from there. *Let us in, little ones. We can eat the pain away. It's burrowed into your bones.* More fingers gripped the edges of the fence. Their voices whispered pleas the boys couldn't hear, not with their ears anyway.

Daniel knelt down and revealed the stone. "Have you guys ever seen a rock like this before?"

"Whoa, that's cool," said the older one. "Where did you find that?"

"I found it glowing in the dark." Daniel flipped it over. "Wanna hold it?"

"Excuse me, children," someone said. Daniel turned. The old man, Gabriel, was behind him. "Mind if I have a seat?"

"That's what benches are for," the little one said, shrugging.

The demons along the fence were gone. Gabriel sat in the grass next to Daniel. "I see you met my friend, Daniel. He's got a neat-looking rock, doesn't he?"

"It's neat all right," the oldest one said. "I bet it's worth a million dollars."

"It may be, but some things are priceless," Gabriel said, "like you."

"What does priceless mean?" the little one said.

"He means we're not worth much money." The older brother frowned at the ground as he dug into the mulch with a stick. "It's why Momma's giving us to Grandma and Grandpa."

"Oh no," Gabriel said. "Priceless means you are far more valuable than money. Someone very special," Gabriel pointed skyward, "told me to let you know He's looking out for you."

"Wow, if I'm worth that much, I'm gonna have a lot of pancakes," the little one said.

Gabriel chuckled. "Indeed, you will."

"What makes us so special?" the older one asked. "Is it because of what our daddy did?"

"Your father..." Gabriel sighed. "I know you miss him, but what makes you special is who you are. Not what he or anybody else did."

The two boys kept quiet. Daniel looked at the funeral home, wondering where their mother was. "It's all right," said the older one, "you don't have to stay. You can go."

"Do you see this?" Gabriel pulled a tiny Godzilla figurine from his pocket.

"That's the littlest monster I've ever seen," said the little one.

"Monsters aren't little," the older one said to his brother. "They're big and scary."

"That's the thing," Gabriel said, kneeling. "Monsters are as big as we let them be. If we're afraid of them, they'll get bigger and scarier, but if we see them for what they truly are, we'll see that they're hardly two inches tall. Here, you keep it."

The little one took it. "Thanks."

The older one stared at Gabriel. He looked to be full of questions, almost as if he understood that he was speaking with an angel rather than an old man. "I remember. You were in my dream with the other man, fighting the monster."

Gabriel shrugged. "I get around. As for you," he pulled an unsharpened pencil from his coat pocket, "my friend enjoyed the letter you wrote Him. He wants you to know that He is with you always." Gabriel leaned forward. "The monsters won't haunt your dreams anymore."

The boy took the pencil from Gabriel. "Promise?"

"I do." Gabriel nodded. "And so does my friend, whose promises are as priceless as you."

"Boys!" an older lady shouted from a doorway at the funeral home. "Get over here. You'd better not be dirty."

"Go to your grandma, children," Gabriel said.

The two boys took off with their new trinkets in hand. Their grandmother gave Daniel a hard look. "Who is that you were sitting with?" she asked as they neared her.

"One is an angel. The other man's name is Daniel."

"There's only one person there," the grandmother said as she closed the door behind them.

Daniel came to his feet. Gabriel stood next to him. "You've pleased the Father, the Son, and the Holy Spirit. Glad to see that you're willing to give up the stone."

Daniel pocketed it. "They need it more than I do."

"What they need is their father." Gabriel started to the front of the funeral home. "Unfortunately, he took that away from them."

"So, what is that little toy and pencil supposed to do when the Devil comes for them?" Daniel asked.

"Nothing," Gabriel said. "The same with your stone."

"My stone gets rid of them," Daniel said. "I've seen it."

Gabriel stopped and looked at Daniel. "Those boys don't need stones. Quite frankly, neither do you."

"Easy for you to say." They walked up the steps.

Gabriel paused at the door. "Their grandmother will recall this day not only as the day her son was buried, but the day her grandchildren claimed an angel visited them. She and those children will remember. Their faith will be their shield and should it ever crumble, I'll be there to take the brunt of Satan's blow, and I do not stand alone. Neither do you."

The intensity in Gabriel's eyes sent an emotional wave through Daniel. All he could do was nod as the angel led the way into the funeral home. He veered to the left as Daniel headed to the pews at the back of the fellowship hall, where he joined Sergeant Faircloth and the two knuckleheads. Once the service was over, Bobby drove Daniel back to his car.

Emma stood beside it, waiting. "I'm afraid I have some troubling news."

Chapter Twenty-Seven

Get to the Pit

Get to the pit.

Kristine struggled to sleep. All she could think about was the pit Daniel had fallen into, and all the strange things that had happened since. The lingering cloud. The smoke. And even the lights that moved about the surface of Grandfather Mountain at night. When she did sleep, she dreamt she was there. Daniel stood at the pit, gazing into it with wonder. Firelight shimmered over his face. "Get to the pit," he said, before dropping in.

She couldn't believe he did that. Why wasn't he afraid? And more importantly, why did he jump? She crept to the edge and peered in. A red glow gave way to explosive red waves of molten rock. There were bodies in it. Arms stretched, dripping with lava. Heads emerged, screaming maniacally. It rose quickly. Kristine ran away and kept hearing the same thing. *Get to the pit.* The ground shook. Murderous heat pushed against her back.

She awoke with a single thought echoing in her head.

Get to the pit.

Why did she feel such a pressing need to go there? She looked up Grandfather Mountain on her laptop and found that the park was closed due to limited visibility. The lenticular cloud had thickened overnight and covered most of the mountain. Traffic would be redirected until conditions improved.

Get to the pit.

"It's closed," Kristine said, shutting her laptop. "They won't let me go up there."

Get to the pit.

What was the harm in trying? More than likely, they'd have her turn around, unless it cleared up before she got there. Maybe if she tried to get there, this craving of hers would be satisfied. "I don't want to go alone, and Daniel won't be back 'til later," she said to herself.

A thought occurred to her. *Mandy will go. Hurry. Get to the pit.*

Kristine checked the time. She needed to be at work within an hour. As much as she hated doing it, she called in sick. It would be slow anyway, and it was the first time she'd ever laid out of work. Next, she dialed up Mandy.

"Hey girl," she said. "Let's go to Grandfather Mountain."

Mandy yawned. "I thought you had to work?"

"I called in sick." She got her jacket on and gathered her keys and purse. "I can pick you up if you wanna come."

Mandy groaned as if she were pulling herself out of bed. "As long as I'm not driving."

Kristine picked Mandy up, and they stopped at a drive-thru diner for lunch. In between bites of a BLT, Mandy asked, "Are you sure you want to head up there now? It's closed."

Kristine set her coffee down. "Remember how I told you about Daniel falling into a hole up there?"

"Yeah," Mandy said, "but that doesn't explain the sudden urgency to get up there when it's closed."

"I don't know how to explain it." Kristine pulled a strand of her hair over her ear. "I feel like I'm supposed to—that I have to try to get to the pit. If we can't get up there, I'll know it's all in my head, but I have this feeling that for whatever reason, we'll get there." She picked up her coffee. "And we'll find out what's really going on."

They got back on the road, and about a half hour later, they came to a line of traffic. Farther up, a police car blocked anyone from taking the left that led to Grandfather Mountain. When Kristine reached the front of the line, the police officer said, "You have to turn right or turn around."

"I'm coming to pick up my father," Kristine lied. "He's a park ranger."

The officer folded his arms and sighed. "Doesn't matter. No one's allowed through."

"Steven?" Mandy leaned over Kristine's lap. "Oh my goodness, it's you!"

"Mandy?" He leaned down and smiled in a goofy way. "What are you doing up here?"

"Kristine asked me to ride with her to pick up her dad," Mandy said. "Why don't I see you around anymore?"

"I've been busy," he said, "but you can call me anytime. It's not like I've left town."

"I've been meaning to," Mandy giggled. It seemed genuine. She liked this guy. "When do you get off work?"

Steven shrugged and looked at the line of cars behind them. "Maybe not until this settles down. Tell ya what. You two go ahead and pick up your dad. Be careful though. The fog gets thicker the higher you go. If I don't see you ride back through here in thirty minutes, I'll—"

"We won't be back this way," Kristine said. "My dad lives farther down the road, but I'll be careful."

"Talk to you later, Steven!" Mandy winked at him.

The two laughed as they went around the police car and onto the road toward Grandfather Mountain. "You'd better call him," Kristine said.

Mandy sighed. "I know, but he's a cop."

"So what? He's nice. Maybe a little gullible, but nice."

"Yeah," Mandy looked back at Steven. "I know."

"Didn't I tell you we'd get up here?" Kristine said with a chuckle. She was giddy with excitement.

The visibility was bad, but Kristine saw well enough to stay on the road. Thick fog clouded the beauty of this place. The entrance to Grandfather Mountain National Park was unoccupied, and the gate was open. In all this gray, Kristine had the feeling that they were being watched by something. She imagined two women with long hair in shadowy dresses standing by the open gate beckoning them to continue. She ignored the impulses that begged her to go back and accelerated uphill.

Winds pushed against the driver's side of the car, letting out a long whistling howl that tested her will to continue the climb. She figured a park ranger, or somebody, would emerge from the gray and have them turn around and leave, but it didn't happen. The park was deserted. Kristine and Mandy had Grandfather Mountain to themselves.

At the summit, the air stilled, but a long roar ripped about the mountain as winds pushed the dark, lingering cloud in a counterclockwise swirl. She parked near the gift shop and smelled smoke when she got out. It felt strange to see the parking lot so empty.

"What now?" Mandy rubbed her arms, although it wasn't cold. In fact, it felt strangely warm and stuffy.

Kristine looked to the Bridge Trail. Again, she imagined two women in dark clothes standing at the start of the trail, waiting for her. She wouldn't let some baseless fear make her turn back after coming so far. Besides, she needed to get to the pit. "Follow me," she said, heading straight to the trail.

It didn't take her long to find the place. She recognized the boulders where she sat, praying for Daniel. She went off the path and climbed the hill to where he fell, the very place where he saw something shimmering in the darkness beneath a dead tree. All that had fallen away. She peered down into the gaping black hole. Mandy stood next to her, gasping.

"Wow," she said. "That looks deep."

A burst of red light flashed from within. It hurt Kristine's eyes. She stumbled. Mandy took her hand, and they both fell back down the hill.

The pain didn't hit her all at once, but Kristine found it hard to move. "Are you OK?"

Mandy massaged her wrist, grimacing. "Let's get out of here."

Kristine came to her knees but felt a presence standing over her. She looked up. Two women dressed in rotted dresses smiled at her. Their eyes were glossy black. They hovered a foot from the ground, their toes pointed downward. Kristine struggled for breath. Was it her imagination? "Mandy? Are you seeing this?"

Mandy looked up and screamed.

That triggered the two floating women to speak. In unison, they chanted. "Into the pit. Into the pit..."

Kristine felt an urgency to head back to the pit and jump in. If she did, they'd spare Mandy. They'd spare Daniel. They'd spare the world if she'd sacrifice herself.

Mandy took her hand and pulled her onto the path. "We've got to go."

That snapped Kristine out of her stupor. They started off but didn't make it far. A group of strange, bare-chested men with decaying skin and horns on their heads blocked their way. The stench of carbon and sulfur wafted into Kristine's face, irritating her eyes. She fell back, coughing and rubbing her eyes. Mandy pulled her behind a boulder. But what good would that do? One of the demons reached for them, but it recoiled as if something hidden had bitten it.

Kristine didn't know what kept it from grabbing her, but she was thankful. The other demons tried to near them but stepped back as well. The land shook and grumbled. One of the hovering women peered into the pit. "It begins."

Chapter Twenty-Eight

Chance and the Demon Horde

It was late in the day. Fewer stones fell from the sky, which still burned red. It was less intense but still hot and suffocating outside the City of Grayton. Within hours, it would grow dark and horribly cold. That wouldn't bother Chance, but his brother, Harrison, would suffer a great deal if he didn't get back to town soon enough.

Demons traveled along the path that led from the city to the Purging Mountains, so Chance and Harrison hiked up the bloody plains toward the judge's quarters, where they could get closer to the entrance into the mountain without being detected. The smoke and steam that crawled through the slimy wasteland provided concealment from wandering eyes.

This wasn't difficult for Chance, but Harrison struggled. He muffled his coughs well enough, but the slick surface caused him to fall hard on his side. Chance helped him up. "Here ya go." He offered his brother a kerchief. "Ain't no shame in holdin' on to me."

Harrison nodded. He looked at his blood-soaked clothes. "This ain't comin' out anytime soon. May as well roll around in it for a while. Make it all match."

Chance winked at the joke and continued trudging uphill. After three miles, another path came into view. Two lines of tired souls marched along it—no demons. One went left toward the judge's quarters carrying stones. The other headed to the Purging Mountains empty-handed.

Harrison smothered a cough and whispered, "What are they doing?"

"Looks like they're taking the rock they've dug out of the mountain to the courtyard. We should head there and jump in the line heading back to the mountain."

"Why not jump in now?" Harrison tied the kerchief over his nose and mouth and cinched it.

Chance looked to the right. Through small breaks in the smoke, he could see the mountain burning. "The valley of death is less than a mile from here. Demons are likely monitoring this road from the mountain. They could spot us jumping in from here, but not from the judge's quarters."

Harrison clutched Chance's arm and grimaced.

"You all right?" Chance asked.

Harrison managed a smile. "Just a bout of pain is all. Come on."

Chance made his way toward the judge's quarters, keeping the trail to his right. The souls were barely visible through the smoke. Harrison's gait and breathing seemed broken and jagged, but he kept up well enough. Chance had in mind to stop and help his brother gather himself, but the day was waning. Too much delay would make things far worse.

Between coughs, Harrison asked. "What's the plan?"

"Find my hat."

"No kidding." Harrison couldn't hide his exasperation. "What if a demon recognizes one of us?"

"They won't recognize you," Chance said. "As for me... If they spot me, you go on back to town. I'll be all right as long as they don't get a hold of you. Whoever's got my hat is inside doin' most of the digging, so

I'll go into their tunnel while you wait outside. If something comes up, give me two long whistles, and then head back to town.

"Goodness, Chance." Harrison struggled through a coughing fit. "You're dead set on gettin' me out of your hair, aren't you?"

Chance turned and faced his brother. "They can't do anything to me, but they can to you. Send you to one of the deeper hells." He continued toward the judge's quarters. "It would take an act of God for me to find you. And on top of that, it's gettin' dark. You may think it gets cold in town, but out here, you'll be frozen 'til mornin'."

Harrison didn't respond. He didn't need for Chance to feel the anger behind him. Chance didn't blame him. The plan was too simplistic, and his brother didn't have anything meaningful to do. Even if he had to whistle, Chance likely wouldn't hear him.

His thoughts turned to his sister, Emma. She wasn't supposed to get mixed up in this war. When he heard she joined the cause on Earth, he had hoped that she'd chosen a passive role: inspiring, comforting, leading humankind to God one way or another. Unfortunately, she chose a role where she'd confront evil head-on. While the armor of God and the light of Heaven were mighty weapons against the forces of darkness, the threat of capture, torture, and imprisonment were real. In time, one could be saved, but scars would remain.

Behind him, Harrison groaned. "Oh no, Chance."

"What?" Chance turned.

His brother fell. "Get back!" He pushed Chance away. "Go on now. Get back." Flames rolled over his pantlegs, over his arms. He went to the ground and rolled, but the bloody plains aggravated the fire. He cried out.

It was the second death. Everyone in Hell suffered it endlessly, and it happened sporadically. Chance gazed at his brother and then at the trail. No one noticed. "Harrison—"

"Just go," Harrison growled. Fire rolled up his neck and set to his face, distorting it. Chance took him by the back of the shirt and dragged him westward. The harvester's shack emerged from the smoke. The judge's quarters would be on the other side of it; the courtyard just beyond that.

The incline wasn't as steep here, but there was a dip in the land that could conceal his brother. Chance pulled him into it. Harrison was covered in fire—fire that did not affect Chance. His brother was a trouper, though. He whimpered and writhed but kept relatively quiet, considering the circumstances. Chance tried to put the fire out, but it was no use.

His brother pushed him away. His face smoked and melted. "Get it done, brother."

Tears fell from Chance's eyes. His lips quivered. He looked about, as if there might be something he could use to heal his brother. Unfortunately, there was nothing. Even if he buried him right there in the ground, Harrison would burn until the second death passed. Later, the cold would heal him with its harsh hands.

"Go," Harrison muttered. He lay back and became motionless—unconscious. He was a charred corpse in a field of smoke and blood. Gone. Chance wished he had left his brother in the rainy city. The rain didn't stop it from happening, but Harrison said it had helped.

Chance remained with his brother and prayed silently. He had died before his brother, but he'd been present the night his brother died. Harrison was asleep when he stretched an arm out and knocked the oil lamp off his bedside table. His rug and bed went up faster than gunpowder. It was painful to witness the first time and painful still.

Chance had longed to reunite with his brother and was ready to present him to the Kingdom of Heaven, but Harrison's soul didn't gravitate to God. He descended. Chance was devastated, which was why he had volunteered for this and never left.

"Move it, maggots!" On the road, Judge Baxter waddled into view. He stopped beside the harvester's shack and placed his hands on his chubby hips, eying the souls who were carrying stones toward the courtyard. "Hurry up."

Chance placed his hand on his brother's charred jaw. "I'll be back for you, little brother." He stood and quietly moved behind the shack. The smoke was thinner, and the sky was blood red. It would soon be dark. He sprinted twenty yards to the rear of the judge's quarters.

Around the side of the dried-out wooden lodge, in a cloud of dust, souls tossed large stones into the pit where the trials took place. They turned on the spot and started back toward the valley of death with their eyes cast downward, bodies bent and sluggish. No demons monitored their activity, which was the small blessing that Chance needed. Judge Baxter wouldn't be a problem. The squat little man was an actor at heart and played his part in self-adulation.

Chance trotted to the line marching back to the mountain, and no one seemed to notice or care as he fell in behind a taller man with torn and bruised arms. Chance bowed his head and mimicked the posture of those around him.

"Move it," Judge Baxter growled absently as Chance slumped by. "Everyone will work overnight inside the tunnel."

Chance gazed ahead to the mountain of fire. It shimmered and flamed like the wick of a giant candle. Its smoke billowed to the sky and escaped through the cracks formed throughout the harsh day. The valley wasn't far, but the souls moved slowly—too slowly. It took all his discipline to refrain from pushing ahead.

He thought about his brother who lay charred in the dip behind the judge's quarters and his sister who had gotten herself into a dangerous position on Earth. About a quarter-mile away from the valley, the path that came from Grayton merged with this one. Demons now lined either side of the path, barking commands and handling weaker souls harshly. Not long after that, Chance came into the valley, where men and women crowded the foot of the mountain.

They had built a long ramp that led to the mouth of a cave. It was where souls entered Hell—the very place where Daniel had entered days earlier. A massive pile of stones sat to the left of it. A man with stained red skin and horns hammered into either side of his head emerged from the dark of the cave, raising his hands.

"Silence! Master Azazel wants to speak."

A boot with metallic claws at the toe cap slammed against the man's back, sending him tumbling down the pile of stones. The giant demon, Azazel, stepped out scowling, daring anyone to show a hint of disrespect. "We suffered for this day." He pointed to the sky. "The day we rise."

The crowd cheered.

Azazel continued. "Our enemy is soft. They've basked in peace as we've grown stronger. Our time of waiting is over!" He raised his arms in victory.

Cheers rose again.

"Quiet!" Azazel's face hardened. A V-shaped vein on his forehead glowed orangish red. "Angels. Although they are cowards, they will try to stop us. Mankind will flee, but we must teach them to suffer as we have so they can be free—like us." Azazel balled a massive fist and squeezed. "Strong like us."

Cheers rose again.

Azazel pulled a sawed-off shotgun from his holster and aimed it at the front of the crowd. It grew silent. "Traitors are already among us, but we will not be deterred. We cannot be stopped. We are united and will stand against the Almighty Oppressor!" Azazel raised his weapon to the sky and fired. "Are you ready for liberation?" He fired again. "Are you?"

Fists punched at the air. The crowd shouted, "Aye!"

"Will you obey your commanders?"

"Aye!"

"Then we will be victorious." Azazel opened his arms. Lightning flashed in the sky. Thunderbolts clashed and created a circle overhead. As it expanded, static energy prickled at Chance. Unwinged demons with dark purple skin dropped from it and into the crowd.

"Behold your commanders!"

These demons were from the Malebolge. Winged demons swooped down from the circle and soared overhead, glaring down at the crowd of damned souls.

"You will obey them! If you hesitate, you are a traitor! Do you understand?"

"Aye!"

Chance looked about the sky. Demons were diving into the crowd and grabbing random souls, lifting them by their throats. He needed to get into that cave before one decided to scoop him up.

"Fall in, you rats," a nearby unwinged demon demanded. Several men lined up shoulder-to-shoulder before the demon and stood like soldiers.

To Chance's right, another demon growled at another group, "Never disobey me."

Bodies pushed against Chance's back. He turned. More demons jabbed spears at a crowd of men, ushering them closer to the cave. He slid between bodies, weaving his way toward the entrance.

"You!" A thick hand took his wrist and yanked. He came nose-to-nose with a larger demon. Bright-green eyes and dark purple skin, no wings. It stunk worse than an outhouse in the middle of summer. "You show no fear," it growled. Its breath was lethal; black plumes trailed its words. "Do you wish to challenge me?" It folded its swollen hands into mallet-sized fists.

Chance averted his gaze. "No, sir." He didn't need a confrontation right now, but it seemed like it would come, regardless. He peeked at the cave, which was twenty feet away.

"Then you are mine," the demon grumbled. "Where I go, you follow. Understand?"

"Aye," Chance said. In all the years he'd roamed Hell, never had he felt so sick, but this wasn't the first time he had to feign subservience. He hoped it would be the last, though.

"Oh, you reek of insubordination." The demon punched Chance on the shoulder. "Bow and kiss my feet!"

All around him, Chance saw grown men and women bowing and kissing the taloned feet of demons. Not Chance. Never. He smiled a wry smile and began to kneel, eying the demon's knobby knees.

Chapter Twenty-Nine
Beau's Demise

Hours after burying Angela next to her mother, young Beau sat alone in his cabin, drowning himself in whiskey. Townsfolk came to pay their condolences, but he never let them in. Eventually, they went on their way. He was through with it all, especially God. If he hadn't been so drunk, he would have found the family Bible and tossed it in the fireplace.

Old Beau sat on the porch next to Ralph, listening to young Beau's wavering sobs that would burst sporadically from the cabin. Something would crash against a wall, and the cries would go from somberness to rage.

"It didn't happen!" drunken Beau screamed raggedly. "It's not real. Nothing is!"

The night would come, and sobs would pierce the silence. The crickets would pause and listen to the wailing. A wolf or a dog would echo the cry, but no help would come for Beau, who grew more deranged and dependent on whiskey. Old Beau didn't say so to Ralph, but he was ready to walk away. He couldn't take much more of this.

It was six days before young Beau stumbled out of the house. He fell off the porch, laughing derisively. A black squid was wrapped around his head. Tentacles hugged his face and neck. "More drink," it shrieked.

He struggled to his feet and let out a long bellowing "Oh!" as if starting a song. "I'm off to get myself a drink!" He stumbled to a fall. "I might have to crawl and might even stink."

The squid tightened its grip. "More drink. More drink."

Young Beau pressed his hands to either side of his head, then pushed himself up. Blinking and rubbing his eyes, he stumbled across the yard toward town.

Ralph looked at the older Beau and patted his knee. "Don't be so upset with yourself. You were in a lot of pain and didn't know what else to do."

"I remember it well." Beau stared between the boards of the porch into the darkness. If he were still a shadow-man, that's where he'd be. Was the Nothingness King down there, watching his younger self fall apart?

"The whiskey did me in." He got up and walked down the steps. A few feet away, an empty bottle lay in the yard. Many more would follow. "All those years I spent as a shadow, I never understood why I felt the way I did about death, while other shadows seemed so indifferent."

Ralph came to his side and massaged Beau's shoulder. "I know this is difficult."

Beau pushed his hand away. "Have you ever lost a wife, a mother, a father, a daughter?" He knew his question was rude but wouldn't apologize. Reliving all this gnawed at him.

"In time, you'll understand why you need to see this, and you are right, Beau. I'm not like you or anyone from the line of Adam and Eve, but I feel your pain. Your tears, even when you're alone, are not in vain."

Beau feared whatever lay ahead. The Nothingness King was coming for him, and his younger self was a hot mess. He headed toward town. "Let's get on with it, then."

Beau put all his frustration into his gait. It didn't take long for him to catch up with young Beau, who had fallen unconscious in the middle of the road. A man who was riding into town woke him up some time later and gave him a ride to town. Beau thanked him and nearly fell out of the wagon when he climbed off. He looked at the general store, but realized his pockets were empty.

The squid squeezed Beau's head. "More drink!"

"I ain't robbing the place," Beau muttered, touching his temple. He winced a smile at a couple of men walking by. "Mornin'."

"Drink now!" the squid demanded.

"They won't do credit, neither." Young Beau looked at the saloon several buildings down. "You know what? Never mind the general store."

Beau tried to hide his drunkenness on his way to the saloon. The wall on his right, and sometimes the rail on his left, proved useful. When he finally pushed through the doors to the saloon, he found the owner behind the bar, taking note of what was in stock.

He glanced up and set his pen down. "Hey there, Beau. Terribly sorry about—well, you know. Angela was a sweet girl."

Young Beau's lips trembled. The squid squeezed. "Now."

"That's mighty kind of you, Mr. Jacobs." He stumbled to the counter. "Um, I'm trying to live with it all. It's been," Beau gazed at the full bottles of whiskey on the shelf behind Mr. Jacobs, "a terrible shock."

"Anything I can do?" Mr. Jacobs said. He sounded sincere.

"Spare me a drink?" Beau asked nervously.

Mr. Jacobs didn't respond immediately. He stared at Beau, almost as if he could see the squid wrapped around his head. "I'll spare you one, but only one."

"Thank you kindly." Beau eyed the piano beside the bar as Mr. Jacobs poured him a glass. "Say, why doesn't anyone ever play on that there piano?"

"Oh, a few people do." Mr. Jacobs slid a small glass of whiskey toward Beau. "Mind you, they aren't as good as you, but every now and then someone will play well enough. Sounds good when they do."

"It would sound better if you didn't park the back toward the wall. The music comes out the back, you know." Beau took a long sip from his glass. "Wait a second. You don't have any musicians to play for ya? No wonder it's always empty in here."

Mr. Jacobs' eyes widened. He sucked in a breath and appeared pained. "It's not always empty." He took a rag and began wiping down a perfectly clean counter. "It's just that this is a small town. Most folks want to ride out a few miles for bigger crowds and looser women."

Beau leaned on the counter and finished his whiskey. "I'm not meaning no disrespect, Mr. Jacobs. This here's a fine establishment. That upright piano is right nice too. What if I played it—in the evenings, as everyone's riding in after work? I'll play Friday and Saturday nights too."

"That's a kind offer, Beau." Mr. Jacobs started cleaning his already clean glasses. "But I can't pay anything."

"You won't have to pay me at all," Beau said. "I'll work for tips."

Mr. Jacobs laughed. "Well, you'll be playing all evening for nothing. Nobody tips around here. Not even their hat."

"Well, if business picks up, would you tip me?" Beau asked.

Mr. Jacobs set the glass down and sighed. "I suppose I could."

"Then let's give it a shot." Beau walked over to the piano and let his fingers rest upon the keys. "Who knows? Maybe people from out of town will start coming here on the weekends, rather than the other way around."

And they did. That evening, and every evening after that, Beau manned the piano, taking requests and playing songs he'd learned over the course of many years. He could read music like a teacher could read a book. Shorter songs that he didn't know, he picked up quickly. He attracted crowds, and in those crowds were other musicians. Some of them were rather good. After a few months of this, Mr. Jacobs' house band was the hottest thing within fifty miles, and sometimes people came from farther than that to hear them play.

Mr. Jacobs' saloon changed a lot. They brought in smaller tables and set them closer to the walls. The poker tables were always busy. The four rooms in the back became permanently occupied by ladies who offered services that had the religious folk in town very upset—at least on Sunday. Beau only cared for the piano and his bottomless whiskey glass that sat on it. He poured all his love and emotion into entertaining the guests. Their joy filled the hole left in his heart for a time.

The customers loved his playing enough to tip him, but few knew that his best music came after most of them were long gone or passed out in the back somewhere. Music had become a prayer for Beau, and late at night, he'd pray before walking home. He'd bow his head and caress the white and black keys with the slightest touch, preparing for the seriousness of the moment. It was a solemn prayer; one that begged the return of his precious wife and daughter.

The music he played would wake those from their stupor. They'd gawk and gather around him, watching his hands and sipping on whatever remained in their glasses. Such spectacular music, passionate and true, would move the scariest of men to tears, but it wouldn't wake the dead.

Beau knew this but refused to give up on the prayer. Every night, he'd stop by their graves and wait. He'd sit there and sip straight from a fine bottle of whiskey. He was past the point of talking to them. The silence and being close to them suited him well enough. It helped him a great deal. If he didn't do this, he was certain that he'd lose himself. After all, they were the only ones in the world who truly understood him.

The pain and sadness that Beau carried lightened over the years. He smiled and laughed more genuinely. He even returned to playing at the church, minding not to drink too much on Saturday night, no matter how much the squid protested. That was until the flood.

Beau didn't think much of the flood at first. He even went fishing in it with Mr. Jacobs. They had a delightful time catching several fish within the span of a couple of hours. They laughed about how their arms were getting tired until they saw wooden caskets bobbing along in the light brown water. It didn't recede for several days, and when it did, Beau found that his wife and child were among the graves that were gone—desecrated by this act of God.

It was as if he'd lost them again. In a fit of rage, he stormed into the church and screamed at the pastor. "I've had it with you, your church, and your God!" He threw a near-empty whiskey bottle through a stained-glass window. "You took everyone from me! I find some peace and you take them away again!"

The pastor tried to calm him. "That isn't what..."

Beau grabbed the pastor and flung him out of the way. "Your God is no god to me." He stormed for the exit but then turned and yelled, "I denounce Him! I loathe Him and all His mysterious ways!" Beau spat a whiskey-laced loogie toward the preacher before kicking the doors open and leaving. Mr. Jacobs wasn't keen on allowing Beau to play the piano much more after that. Most people in town chose not to look his way. Even Mr. Garrison refused to meet his eye during transactions at the general store.

The disdain was mutual, but it pained Beau to feel so alienated among those he'd known all his life. His sadness was so great that he couldn't bear to drink anymore. The squid shrank into nothingness over time. He found the family's Bible and set it on a table beside his chair. Why he let it sit there, he wasn't sure. He regretted what he'd said to the preacher in the church that day many years ago, but still, he no longer prayed and didn't care to open it. He left that to the hypocrites in town, who talked their ways frontwards and backwards about forgiveness yet spared none in practice.

One night, after another lonely dinner, Beau opened that Bible and in it, written in his wife's hand, were the names of their family members, all of them dead—except him. He traced the lines, longing for Evelyn and Angela—all of them. What had happened nearly a decade ago seemed like yesterday. Maybe if he tried hard enough, he could see her writing down these names, smiling under her small spectacles. Maybe she could see him when she gazed up. See him the same as he saw her. She waved and he waved back. Unfortunately, Beau was neither mad nor a fool. It was wishful thinking. His imagination. Evelyn's face looked troubled as he got up from his chair, dropping the Bible back to the table.

On the night that followed, he read the Bible, taking extra time on the passages his wife had underlined and wrote notes in the margins. He often fell asleep with it sitting in his lap. It was all he had left to remember of his family. Well, that—and the forests. After Angela died, he had stopped foraging, but now, after so many years, he returned to it. He felt like a child again and oftentimes came home sore from the walk.

One Saturday night, he cut through town to return home. He had done this several times before without incident and didn't expect any trouble this time, either. Mr. Jacobs' saloon no longer drew the crowds it once had. Of course, everyone blamed him for that. On this night, the saloon was rowdier than usual. The pianist was missing keys and out of time, but no one seemed to notice other than Beau. Several young men were sitting on the porch outside. All of them were laughing until they caught sight of him meandering down the road.

"Hey!" A scrappy young lad leaped from the porch and came alongside Beau. "Ain't you the old piano man? The one who cursed God in the church?"

Beau didn't answer. He kept walking.

"You best hope they got a piano down in Hell for you, Mister."

The slight didn't trouble Beau at all, but it brought back all the memories, reminding him of his many mistakes. He went to the place where his child and wife had once been buried and sat there. Beau hadn't cried in a long time, but this night, he did. He got so worked up that he struggled for breath and couldn't swallow. His sinuses were draining so badly. He ended up coughing. The coughing turned to gagging. He heaved for air, but none came. This was it. His dying day.

The townspeople spoke of it as a ghost tale for many years afterward. How a young Christian boy had begged Beau to repent of his sins or be sent to Hell that very night, and when Beau refused, the punishment was due. The pastor seemed particularly proud of coming up with that line.

Older Beau stood next to Ralph, watching his younger self die. Eventually, he turned his attention to the land where his loved ones were once buried. Ralph leaned close to him. "Beau, you need to see this."

"No, I don't." Beau looked at the starry sky.

"You were murdered."

"No, I wasn't." Beau looked at Ralph. "I couldn't breathe right. Choked on my own tears."

Ralph nodded at young Beau. "Then what is that?"

Beau turned. His face numbed. "The Nothingness King."

On top of his younger self, the Nothingness King sat wearing his signature dark suit and fancy top hat. He scowled at the older Beau and Ralph. His yellow eyes slanted with meanness, as if sensing their presence.

Young Beau lurched, and the Nothingness King turned back to him. "Shh. It's over. The pain. The misery. It's all over." He took young Beau by the hand and pulled him out of his body.

"W-What is this?" young Beau asked, looking about.

"You've died." Over them, a golden light about the size of a seed glowed brightly. Young Beau cringed at it. The Nothingness King whispered in his ear. "You angered the Almighty a great deal when you spoke so hatefully of Him in His own house. He means to send you to Hell personally."

"I didn't mean it," Beau whimpered. "I was angry. I lost my family."

The light intensified, and the king spoke in a hurried and hushed tone. "It was brave what you did. I admire you, Beau. You stood up to a tyrant, and for that, I will help you. I will save you from His wrath. You needn't enter Hell tonight. Pledge your loyalty to me." The king extended his hand. "You'll never suffer again. Kneel. Do it."

Beau took the hand of the Nothingness King and kneeled. "I'm yours."

His spirit drained of color. The light around him dimmed until only a shadow remained. The king and Beau entered the woods, but the golden light remained. From it, his daughter Angela emerged with Evelyn. They looked about, distressed.

"Where's Daddy?" Angela asked.

"He's been deceived," his wife said tearfully.

"Is there anything we can do?"

Evelyn shook her head. "Just pray. Pray for your daddy."

They turned and faded into the light. It diminished and it was dark again. Beau and Ralph were all that remained. Beau stared at his body, eyes fixed on distant stars.

"I was never denied?" Beau asked. "I was deceived?"

Ralph nodded.

Beau peered into the forest, searching for those unnerving yellow eyes. "I didn't remember this until now." He rubbed the back of his head. "That thing... that wasn't Azrael. I thought I was chosen by him to be a shadow."

"The Nothingness King lost you to Azrael, but you feared Heaven's light and had forgotten everything: who you were, who you loved. That's why Azrael allowed you to become a shadow-man. He made sure that you remembered your name, knowing that it would help you someday. That day has come, Beau."

"This is it?" Realizing it was over, the fears were gone, but for some reason, something wasn't settling for him. "What's come of the Nothingness King?"

"He reigns in outer darkness, making deals with desperate souls on behalf of Satan." Ralph flourished his hand, and images of the Nothingness King beckoning this soul and that soul cascaded across the sky. He turned back to Beau. "In exchange, he gains strength in this world. Satan has offered him twice as much if he can broker a deal with your friend, Daniel Strong."

"That won't happen," Beau said. "Daniel walked away from Satan. The Nothingness King won't faze him."

"That may be true." Ralph sighed and folded his arms. "But his trial isn't over. Yours is, though." A golden seed lit up in front of them. "Your family has waited a long time for this."

The light bore a hole through the darkness and in that light came his daughter, his wife, his parents, and hers. Angela jumped into his arms. She smelled like a warm spring breeze. His wife extended her hand, and he took it. The rest of their family gathered around them.

The old world was gone. Heaven surrounded him. Angels trumpeted from the sky. Scores of people, some he recognized but many he didn't, swarmed around him singing a welcome song.

His two girls held him tight. The wrinkles in his hands faded. His clothes became clean. "Why aren't you grown up?" Beau asked Angela.

"Because..." she stuck out a finger. A butterfly that left trails of rainbow in its wake landed on it. "I was waiting for you."

Beau was overwhelmed. The sky cascaded with color. A deep green forest and river sat in a valley to his left. Castles were sprinkled along the water's edge. The air smelled like honey. His wife whispered, "I can't wait to take you foraging."

Beau smiled and ran his fingers through his daughter's hair. "We will." Tears ran down his cheeks. All this joy and glory. He loved it and needed it so much, but—Daniel was in danger. All around him, flowers vibrated; sprinkles of light leaped from their petals and leaves. The grass was as gentle as a blanket on his feet. He touched his wife's and daughter's cheeks. "I love you so much. But there is something I must do." He looked at Ralph. "I need to help Daniel."

Chapter Thirty

A Short Walk with Grandma

Impossible. Although Charles had died and abided in Hell for around seventy years, he walked about Heaven with his sweet grandmother latched to his arm. Everyone kept their distance, not out of judgment, but respect. They waved and smiled, happy for his dear grandmother, who quietly led him up a hill that rose to a horizon glistening with dozens of stars dancing about the sky. Like miniature suns, they shone with various colors of light. When comets darted by, the stars chased after them.

"Our Father," Granny said, "is such an artist. Nothing pleases Him more than to dazzle us with His wonders." She snuggled against Charles.

"It's beautiful," Charles said. They stopped at the summit. A massive castle sat in a lower valley. Its walls, towers and parapets looked to be made of platinum; windows shimmered yellow. Light from the playful suns scattered about the land, as if day and night were partaking in a whimsical dance, and beyond all this was a forest of gigantic trees that stretched over thousands of homes.

His grandmother said, "This is God's gift to all of us. We ask much of His wonder and are given that and more." She sighed. "But tonight, the sky is for you alone, Chip. He told me so."

"God told you?" Charles struggled to believe this. Although it must have been possible, considering this was Heaven. God must be around here somewhere. He looked about the hilltops and along the horizon, almost expecting to see Him. "How could He possibly make time for only one person?"

"Oh," his grandmother patted his arm, "He does that from time to time. Had tea with me this morning." Her eyes sparkled. "He said to me, 'Candice, tonight I have something special planned for you.'" She nodded. "My first thought was that cherubim were going to serenade me. He knew my thoughts, so we both laughed about that."

Charles shifted uncomfortably. "With all the troubles in the world, shouldn't He be focused on the bigger picture? Healing the sick? Helping those in need?" Charles shook his head. He felt as if he were being disrespectful. "I'm sorry. I'm glad He spent time with you, but the world needs Him now."

"It's OK, Chip." His grandmother massaged the tightness from his shoulders. "God is great, not only because He is the Most High. He's also the most humble, not because He wants to fulfill a requirement or earn points. It's just who He is. God loves us all. He makes time for each of us, even you."

Charles watched the stars play along like children on a playground and said, "But I'm not on his side. I'm doing what the Devil's told me."

"Are you?" his grandmother asked. "You didn't betray Emma, and you saved a young girl's life."

Charles rubbed his forehead. "How do you know about that?"

"God told me you would." She squeezed his arm. "You wouldn't have been able to make it here otherwise."

Charles gazed into a valley where a crowd danced and clapped to a merry tune. "Well, tell Him I said thank you the next time you see Him."

"He already knows you're thankful." His grandmother swayed side to side. "But He did tell me once that it's still nice to hear it spoken from time to time, so I *will* tell Him."

They contemplated the valley below. The greenery sparkled as if it were littered with diamonds. Charles saw a small girl straddling the shoulders of a lion. She pointed beyond a river to the forest, and the lion seemed to speak to her. Such a relationship seemed impossible.

He looked at his grandmother and said, "You know, I doubt He would ever spend time with me after all I've done."

She peered at him and smiled. "You'd be surprised. When you entered Hell, I grieved so terribly." She stared intently ahead at the forests and castles. "I locked myself in my room and prayed for days. Friends and family went to His throne and pleaded for you. None of us knew it, but He was already answering my prayers. Do you know of a young man by the name of Chance?"

Charles wasn't good with names. He didn't care to know anyone in Hell. He shook his head.

"He infiltrated demonic ranks to pull you out of the Malebolge and got you as close to Heaven as possible in that place. We expected you to take the bus any ol' time. I'm surprised you never did."

Charles removed his hat and rubbed his head. He'd had no idea. All this time, he thought the demons had chosen him for his talents. "This Chance guy—he's in Hell saving one person at a time?"

"He's part of a missionary team, but they can't force anyone to leave Hell. Everyone must decide for themselves to come to His Kingdom or not."

Charles thought about his mother and though it pained him, his father came to mind as well. Would Chance help them? Would God let that happen? Can any soul be saved from eternal damnation?

His grandmother knew him well enough to understand what he was thinking. "I've prayed for your mother and, although less often—your father as well. Chance reached your mother, but she fled. I asked him not to bother with your father until you and your mother were safe. While prayer does help, it is still their choice to stay or not."

Charles wiped his eyes and sniffed. Thinking of his mother and father made him wonder about Daniel and Kristine. What were they doing? Were they safe? What about the mountain? "I need to speak with God." Charles noticed a change. The air felt more brisk. A haze swept over the land and through the sky. He took his grandmother's hands. "Tell Him we need His help."

A wind pressed into his face. Everything blurred and swirled into prisms of light. When it stopped, he was dizzy, and lying face down in the hall outside of Kristine's room. Why was he here? He didn't think of this place. Maybe God kicked him out of Heaven or sent him where he was most needed.

He put his ear to Kristine's door. Nothing. If the twin overseers were here, they were quiet. Charles stepped through the door and into Kristine's room. No one was inside, not even a spirit. He went to the window. It was daytime. How long had he been gone? It seemed like only a few minutes, but judging by the light in the sky, hours had passed.

A gravelly voice spoke from behind him. "You not tell me when Karen wakey wakes. Bad minion."

Great. It was Iffy, the most annoying creature on the face of the earth. "Where's—Karen?" Charles asked.

Iffy, the furry monster with the golf ball-shaped eyes and long, oddball nose dropped its jaw, exposing its huge mouth. It slapped its hands to its head. "You lost Karen? You let mean girls take my Karen?" It folded its arms. "You are not my minion anymore."

"Mean girls?" Charles planted his hands on top of his hat. "What happened?"

"Mean girls drop many yummy demons. Very slippery, but I catch them. I come back, and Karen and mean girls are all gone."

"Do you have any idea where they went?"

"I do." Iffy turned its gaze away snobbishly. "They went outside."

"You don't say." Iffy was the densest thing that Charles had ever dealt with. He rubbed his face harshly. "Was Karen listening to them?"

"Maybe. Mean girls talk, talk, talk, talk, talk." Iffy flapped his hands to indicate talking. "Never stop. Must be tired of talking so much. Keep saying same thing. I'll never forget." It brought its hand to its chin. "Hmm, I forgot."

Charles brought his hands over his face.

"Wait! I have idea," Iffy said. "I ask one of their yummies."

"What?"

Iffy opened its cartoonishly large mouth, casually reached its furry arm deep inside, and pulled out a small shadowy demon by the scruff of its neck. It looked absolutely incensed. It swung its tiny fists and bit at the air. Iffy flicked its head with a finger, causing it to spin. "Bad yummy."

"We will set you free if you answer a question for me," Charles said. Iffy gave a disapproving look. "Deal with it. You forgot what they kept saying over and over."

"Fine," Iffy said, frowning. "Hurry up. I'm getting hungry."

Charles got eye-level with the miniature demon. "Where did your masters take the girl?"

The demon grinned and pointed a skinny finger skyward. "Get to the pit."

"On the mountain?" Charles asked, standing straight.

The demon threw punches back at Iffy. "Set me free, furball."

"No," Iffy said. "You are mine—not Mr. Hat's."

The demon threw a tantrum as Iffy swallowed it whole. "Mmm, delicious." It stared at Charles, twisting its mouth as if it regretted something. "If he behaves, I make him my minion. Now go find my Karen."

Charles was no longer concerned with Iffy or the tiny demon it held captive in its mouth. He turned his focus to Daniel and closed his eyes. The air changed.

"What are you doing?" Daniel said. "Sit down."

Charles opened his eyes. He was crouched in the backseat. The clock on the dash read 5:30. He sat. Daniel was driving. Emma looked back at him, smiling. "Hi Charles. Where have you been?" She sounded as if she was well aware of his brief trip to Heaven.

"Is it really 5:30?" Charles shifted to the driver's side of the car.

"Yep," Emma said, "and we still have a lot of road ahead of us."

Charles looked out the window. Billboards and trees came and went. "Two of the overseers talked Kristine into going onto the mountain."

"We know," Daniel said.

"We're heading there now." Emma turned to Charles. "How did you find out?"

Charles pushed his bowler hat farther back on his head. "There's an annoying thing that stays with Kristine. He calls himself—"

"Iffy told you!" Emma turned to Daniel with a huge smile on her face. "Iffy is Kristine's childhood imaginary friend, who eats demons for breakfast. Helped her get over her nightmares and fear of the dark." She turned to Charles. "He's usually very shy. He must like you."

"Imaginary friend?" Charles scratched his head. "Kind of makes sense now. Why does he call her Karen?"

"Because she grew up and started acting more like her mom, whose name *is* Karen." Emma looked at Daniel. "I'm going to peek in on Kristine real quick. You two be nice."

She disappeared. Charles sat back in his seat. "Would it hurt you to clean the windows or wipe off all the dust in here? My goodness, Daniel."

"You want to lecture me about cleanliness right now?" Daniel eased the car into the left lane to pass another.

"Not really." Charles brushed off the shoulder of his jacket. "But I've sat in several vehicles now, and this is more comparable to a dumpster than anything." He sniffed the air and cringed. "I can't believe you're making Emma, an angel, sit in this."

Emma reappeared in the front seat. She was flushed, rubbing her forehead. "Kristine and Mandy are at the pit on Grandfather Mountain as I had expected, but they're surrounded by demons." She looked at Daniel. "They're already in the living world. Physically here."

"Oh, man." Daniel gripped the steering wheel tightly and accelerated. "Why did they go up there in the first place?"

"It's not their fault," Emma said. "If it's anyone's fault, it's mine. I knew the twin overseers would talk them into heading up there, but didn't think demons would breach until nightfall."

Charles leaned over the console. "Shouldn't they be all right? The Holy Spirit is with them."

"It's with Kristine, and yes, it'll hold them off for a time." Emma looked at Daniel. "But if they lose faith, the enemy will get to them. Pray she keeps her faith strong."

"If they're surrounded by demons, where're all the angels?" Daniel asked.

"They're preparing for battle." Emma looked at the sky. "I don't know when the attack is. Let's hope we're not too late."

"Can you stay with them until we get there?" Daniel passed a string of cars.

"The way you're driving, I'll have to stay here," Emma said. "But if you slowed down..."

"Not a chance." Daniel peeked down at the clock on his dashboard and sped up. "If you're staying here, I'm cutting our travel time in half."

"How long will it take?" Charles asked.

Daniel gripped the steering wheel. "Thirty minutes if I don't crash or get pulled over."

"I'll take care of that." Emma turned to Charles. "You handle the stoplights."

It was the longest thirty minutes Charles had ever experienced. Every time he looked at the clock on the dash, it seemed to remain the same, or incremented by a single minute. When they neared Boone, every stoplight had a demon on it. Charles jumped to them and swatted them off the line to make sure the light changed for Daniel.

He turned on a road that seemed to head uphill. They passed a sign indicating that Grandfather Mountain was five miles away. The cars ahead pressed their brakes and slowed to a crawl.

Daniel sent a hand through his hair. "All that just to run into this."

Emma disappeared and reappeared. "There's a police officer at the intersection ahead. He's blocking the road with his patrol car and making everyone turn right."

"Is there room for me to get around it?" Daniel asked.

"Yes," Emma said. "You'll have to drive off the road, though."

"That won't be a problem."

The sky was dark now. But to their left, a long band of shimmering redness marked where the pit lay. Time was running out for Kristine and Mandy—for the world. The flashing lights of the police car emerged.

The officer stood next to it, giving directions to a driver who had stopped.

"Time to get moving." Daniel went into the oncoming lane. Tires squealed. The officer looked up, his eyes widened. Charles smiled as Daniel swerved off the road and into a patch of dirt to get around the police car. The dumbstruck look on the officer's blood-drained face brought a laugh out of Charles. His experience with law enforcement hadn't been the best, considering it was an officer who had originally killed him. Not to mention all the years he was locked up.

Dirt and gravel flew up behind them. They came onto the blocked road with a series of bumps. He looked out the back window. Darkness and distance obscured the officer's slack-jawed face.

Daniel adjusted the rearview mirror. "I guess we'll have the police helping us out pretty soon."

"He'll call it in, but no one will hear the transmission," Emma said. She looked back at Charles. "We're on our own."

Her eyes didn't display the confidence that Charles had grown accustomed to. Was she afraid? They entered a fog that diffused fiery red light. The watch in his pocket began to knock against his ribs.

Chapter Thirty-One

If the Hat Fits ...

C hance would be the first to tell anyone that he wasn't perfect. Sure, he made the cut to get into Heaven, but thankfully, only God knew how much of a heathen he truly was. The day he knelt before God and asked to be a missionary in Hell, he was surprised the Almighty didn't hesitate or question his motive. The response was simple.

"Go in peace and know that I am with you."

Chance thought he was being dismissed until Michael the Archangel handed him a hat. "What's this for?" he asked.

Michael's amber eyes glinted, and a rueful smile stretched beneath them. "Godspeed."

Not getting the hint because he wasn't familiar with Michael's sense of humor at the time, Chance took the hat and started to leave. "Thank you."

Michael called after him. "Why don't you see if it fits?"

Chance turned. Michael didn't seem like much. Yes, he was fit, but there was nothing imposing about him. He always had a look on his face, as if he had the funniest thought running through his mind.

"Don't tell me you don't want to put it on." Michael swaggered toward Chance with a quirked lip. "It matches what you wore back in nineteenth-century Texas."

Chance looked at the hat for the first time. "By golly, it does." He flipped the hat around. It was a fine hat. Sturdy too. "If it wasn't so nice, I'd say it's the very hat I wore."

"Maybe it is," Michael shrugged, "with some minor enhancements. Either way, it'll serve you well in Hell, friend."

That was when Chance knew for sure that God had given him the job. He bowed and placed the hat on his head. It was snug and felt right. Energy surged through him. So much so that he didn't know what to do other than run. He zipped through the heavens, across vast lands. He entered a city and ran up the side of a tall building, then leaped into the sky. He cut through the air as if it were water. When he hit the ground, he sprinted on and might have run for eternity if Michael hadn't caught up and stripped the hat from his head.

Chance stumbled to the ground, out of breath. He peered up at the captain of the archangels. "How far did I run?" he asked.

Michael peered over his shoulder. He turned back with that big ol' smile of his. "I'd say far enough for now." He helped Chance to his feet. "You'll need to control it, or it'll be no use to you."

Chance bent over, panting. "How do I do that?"

"Take a deep breath." Michael demonstrated and exhaled. "Settle yourself." He placed the hat against Chance's chest. "You wear the hat. The hat doesn't wear you. Got it?"

"Not really." Chance looked at the hat. "But here goes nothing."

The hat had remained with him since until he was tricked into handing it over. Now, without it, he knelt before a demon—to pledge loyalty to it? *Never.* God would forgive him if he pledged false allegiance to a demon, but Chance was too proud of who he was and how unwavering God was toward him to do so. They could tie him down and cut him to bits a million times over and still he'd pledge nothing.

"Do it, maggot," the demon growled.

Chance chuckled. "Well, I would, but I don't know what to call you."

"Fool!" The demon shook with anger. "You call me Master."

"Very well." Although Chance was without his hat, he was still fast and strong. These particular demons from the Malebolge were weaker than they seemed. They looked mean and could put a hurting on those forced to suffer in their realm, but that wasn't Chance. So when he slammed his elbow against the side of the demon's knee, that demon didn't only fall—its leg snapped like a brittle branch. It toppled to its side, screeching like a banshee.

Chance weaved his way through the crowd toward the tunnel. Everyone around him was frail and could be easily pushed aside, but he moved about carefully, not wanting to hurt the damned or draw any more unwanted attention to himself. It was hot and dark in the cave. Damned souls stood along the walls holding torches. Their arms quivered with fatigue. Demons shouted at their subordinates and struck them if they didn't comply quickly enough.

Chance moved forward while everyone else seemed hesitant. He came into a large, stony chamber with torches the size of men lined along the walls. More torches shimmered overhead in the darkness. Dust drizzled like rain, and a ramp spiraled upward along the wall. A dark blur shot down the ramp and stopped a few stories up. It was a demon, and it pressed a hand to the wall to stay afoot.

"It's finished. Ground troops first. Demons only for now." This was a high-ranking demon called Malecoda. It wore Chance's hat but used a rope to keep it on its head. Even with that, the hat was slipping. "Humans can't be trusted in the battle that's sure to come." Malecoda took a seat and pulled the hat off his head. "Get moving."

The damned seemed relieved by this news. Chance pushed his way to the first bend in the ramp. Malecoda was not a pushover, but it wasn't the smartest demon in Hell either. What it lacked in brains, however, it made up for in brawn. Chance could take it, but if a few other demons got involved, they'd overpower him. If he got to the hat, however, he'd be too fast for any of them to catch him, or even see him.

"Hey!" a voice boomed from the cave's entrance. Chance knew better than to turn around. Unfortunately, that didn't help him because everyone else did.

He huffed through his nose and turned. It was the demon with a broken leg, along with several of its ugly comrades. "Howdy. Long time no see."

The demon hobbled forward and pointed. "Grab him!"

Those surrounding Chance seemed too confused to follow through on those orders. They did, however, issue him looks as if to say, "You sure messed up big time, buddy."

"Grab him now!" the demon screamed raggedly.

A few tried to take hold of Chance's wrists, but he nudged them off and started up the spiraling ramp. His eyes darted to Malecoda, who glared back but seemed confused about the situation.

The broken demon said, "If any of you let him pass, we'll rip your heads from your necks and toss your worthless bodies into the valley."

That got their attention. A gaggle of men and women pressed against him. Chance could have easily forced his way past them but didn't want to harm anyone. Hell was burden enough for these folks. He turned and faced the small band of demons that pursued him. There were six of them. None of them had wings, and all appeared to be from the Malebolge.

The hopper pointed. "He broke my leg with a single stroke."

Chance looked to Malecoda, who held his hat in its claws precariously. A slight breeze could cause the hat to drop, but unfortunately, the air was still in here.

A demon neared him but stopped short of kicking distance, looking him up and down. Reeking of mold and sulfur, it turned to its hobbling comrade. "This man hurt you?" It broke into fits of laughter. "You let a wretched imbecile such as this shatter your knee?"

"Wait! I know this man." Malecoda dropped from the higher ledge, expanding its wings to slow its descent. It landed between Chance and the other demons. Chance's hat still hung loosely from its claws. "Yes, I know this one." It lashed out. Claws raked across Chance's face. He went to his knees, gripping his face, pretending that it hurt while focusing on the hat.

"Who is he?" another demon asked.

"He is not supposed to be here," Malecoda said. "Azazel sent him to Lust."

The demons glared at him as if confused. One asked, "Are you saying he escaped the Second Hell?"

"Only to be caught again," Malecoda said, switching the hat to its other claw. "Bind him and take him deeper. Chain him in a pit in the heretic's yard."

"Who do you think you are, ordering me around?" The demon punched Malecoda in the shoulder.

"Yeah," another demon added. "Why don't you go chain him?"

The hat was straining to escape Malecoda's grip. Chance inched closer while the argument escalated. With a flash of speed, he twitched his arm, grabbed the brim of the hat and yanked it away from Malecoda, who didn't notice. In fact, they were so engaged with each other, Chance could've simply walked out completely unobserved, but he knew better than to test such a theory.

He slapped the hat onto his head, and the world slowed. He darted through the crowd. Bodies flew left and right as a mighty force plowed the path ahead of him. He exited the cave and was standing over Harrison's burned body soon after. The sky had darkened to purple, and the cold would be here soon, but not soon enough. Too much was happening. Chance needed divine intervention. He took his brother's crumpled hand and began to pray.

Chapter Thirty-Two
A Long Way to the Top

Daniel sped through dense fog up the curvy road that led to Grandfather Mountain National Park. Emma and Charles might have protested if they weren't spirits. Even if they had, he likely wouldn't have slowed too much. He needed to get to Kristine.

He drove through the entrance and went up the steep ascent. The fog thinned the higher they went. They'd be at the summit within minutes.

Charles cleared his throat. "We may have an angel in the car, but I don't think she can help much if you send us flying over a cliff."

He had a point. Daniel decelerated but kept a brisk pace, hugging turns and accelerating on short straightaways. "When we reach the summit, I'll park near the trail. It should take us straight to where I fell into Hell."

"It's not going to be easy," Emma said. "We'll likely have to fight our way in and back out."

"Don't worry. I have a stone that will send anything that gets in our way back to Hell," Daniel said, turning the car sharply.

"Your stone won't do much against hundreds, if not thousands, of demons," Emma said.

Charles slapped his forehead. "I forgot. I still have that meeting to go to."

Emma looked back at him. "You may want to skip that."

Charles shifted in his seat. "If the twins are here, it means that Rogknot is there. I think I can pit them against each other. They're not on good terms. You worry about what you have to do. I'll be fine."

Charles disappeared.

Emma sat back in her seat and shook her head. "That man isn't as smart as he thinks he is."

"Ha, tell me about it," Daniel said.

A rock slammed against the driver's side of the car. Daniel accelerated through a blanket of earth. The car skidded as he whipped the wheel around a 180-degree turn. He slammed on the brakes as more rocks fell ahead.

"I've got this." Emma pulled herself through the windshield onto the hood. "Floor it!"

Daniel did. Boulders rolled behind the car. Emma held her hands to the higher elevations, as if she were holding up the sky. After several boulders went over them, she lowered her hands and leaped through the windshield into her seat.

"We're good now," Emma said. She closed her eyes and vanished for a few seconds. "Kristine and Mandy are still surrounded. The demons have grown in numbers, but they're still keeping their distance from Kristine and Mandy."

"At least we have that going for us."

They passed the museum and the overflow parking lot. A horrible stench lingered in the air. It smelled like burning rot. Daniel brought his hand over his nose. "This isn't good."

"It's going to be ugly." Emma tied her hair back, staring ahead like a boxer waiting on the next round. "No matter what happens, don't lose hope. Keep fighting."

They came to the top parking lot. Red light shimmered from the Bridge Trail. Flecks of fire rose and disappeared into the reddish underbelly of the cloud overhead. Kristine's car was parked near the trail, but no one was in it. Daniel parked beside it.

Emma stepped through the door. "Let's go."

Daniel unfastened his seatbelt and hurried after her. When he got to his feet, lightheadedness made the world seem dreamlike. He held onto the car to keep from falling. There was a thud behind him. He turned. Emma was gone. He was alone. Feeling faint, he looked to the ground. His body lay there motionless, eyes glazed over, staring at his front tire.

A voice spoke from behind. "Welcome home, Danny."

Daniel turned. It was the magician from his dream. It was the Nothingness King.

Chapter Thirty-Three

When Things Don't Go According to Plan

Charles passed through the transparent tunnel, keeping his eyes on the other end. As he expected, Rogknot was alone on the rooftop. Charles was confident that once he heard what the twins were up to, he'd be enraged, and the three overseers would be at war with each other. After all, a house divided will not stand.

He landed a few feet from Rogknot, who was pacing about. His face was red, and he gritted his teeth. "You're late again."

Charles didn't acknowledge the accusation. "I told you the other two were up to something."

"What do you mean?" Rogknot stopped and turned. "What's going on?"

Perfect, Charles thought. He maintained a serious expression. "The other two overseers are gathering a force of demons to take away your territory."

Rogknot looked westward and seemed pensive, which must've been a real struggle considering his perpetual anger. "My sisters *have* been preoccupied with things that don't concern us lately."

"See?" Charles neared him. "It's because they've been planning a massive invasion tonight."

"They wouldn't betray me," he glared at Charles, "but you would."

Charles straightened his back and gripped his lapels. "If you don't believe me, go have a look. They're on Grandfather Mountain."

The overseer snatched Charles by the necktie and pulled him close. "You're coming with me." The world blurred as they zipped through it.

Jumping with Rogknot wasn't ideal. He wanted to get back to Daniel and Emma, but his plan seemed to be working. When Rogknot found out what the twins were doing and how they had given up his name, the overseers would be at war with each other.

His necktie nearly strangled him as they flew through the transparent tunnel. They entered the shimmering red haze. The air was hot where they landed. Rogknot tossed him to the ground. Kristine and Mandy were huddled behind a large boulder. Demons surrounded them, taunting but not attacking. The Holy Spirit was shielding them. The twins stood on either side of the pit, breathing in smoke. Their bellies filled, and they exhaled blackish eel-like demons into the sky.

"What is this?" Rogknot hissed.

Mandy and Kristine looked right at Charles. Their eyes widened. Their breathing was quick and shallow. They saw him. He wanted to warn them, tell them to run while the demons were still hesitant to attack, but the demons were watching him. He looked back at the twins.

"We're doing what we must," one said. She and her sister glided to Rogknot. "Charles must return to Hell. He is not loyal to us."

"He reeks of Heaven," the other growled.

Rogknot looked back at him, as did the demons surrounding Kristine and Mandy.

Charles laughed nervously. "Come on. This is ridiculous."

Rogknot marched toward him and yanked him toward the pit. "You've been a thorn in my side since you've been here."

Charles looked up at the angry overseer, nursing his wrist. "You think I'm the traitor?" He pointed at the twins. "Your two idiot girlfriends told me your name, Rogknot. Now, who's the traitor?"

Rogknot smiled. "That is a false name."

"Who's the idiot again?" one of the twins asked.

Charles felt foolish and didn't have a clever retort. His pocket watch was vibrating so much that his jacket shook. He got to his feet, swatting dirt from his pants, and smiled with as much false confidence as he could muster. "You three are so predictable." He walked away from Rogknot, who steadily approached him. "You're so easily deceived, and I get it. You've been on Earth too long, and therefore, haven't the slightest idea how the ancient ones think, or what their intentions are tonight."

A voice rattled in his ear. "What are our intentions, Heartless?"

Hot breath singed the side of his face. Charles turned. Two ancient demons, Abaddon, along with Azazel, stood before him, with legions of demons behind them. Not an angel in sight. Charles's breath caught in his throat. "There you are." He couldn't help that his voice rose several octaves. *My, how horribly wrong things have gone.* "I've no need to speak for you. I'll let you speak for yourself." Charles bowed slightly, but reached into his pocket and took hold of his extremely jumpy timepiece. It was a struggle to keep a hold of it.

"Drop whatever that is." Abaddon twirled a massive hammer in his hand and pushed Charles back with it.

Charles held out his hand, gripping the out-of-control timepiece as best he could. It shook his arm about, as if he were erasing imaginary words written all over an imaginary chalkboard. "I'm afraid that if I do…" His voice had a vibrato. He lost his balance and nearly fell. "Something terrible will happen." He wasn't bluffing.

"Something terrible will happen if you don't." Abaddon smashed a boulder with his hammer, reducing it to rubble.

"Oh, well. Here you go." Charles depressed the crown of his watch and tossed it toward Abaddon. It was a simple nonchalant toss that anyone could catch, but Charles knew there would be no catching this. What occurred was something he hadn't quite expected, either. Given the levity of the situation, it seemed to happen in slow motion.

Bright yellow light expanded from within the watch. Light blue bolts of electricity escaped and entered the eye sockets of every demon Charles could see. They covered their eyes, seemingly blinded and pained by the shocking experience. A deafening noise followed it. Charles sprinted to Kristine and Mandy, taking each of their hands. He thought of Daniel, but he couldn't leap—not with Kristine and Mandy, most likely because they weren't a part of the spirit world.

"Run," he muttered.

They started to, but what they saw coming down the trail dashed their will. Kristine sank to her knees, covering her mouth with her hands. Mandy hugged her, burying her face into Kristine's shoulder. They sobbed, and Charles felt tears welling in his eyes.

The Nothingness King had emerged from the crowd. Daniel's body was draped over his shoulder. His arms dangled limply.

A massive weight smashed against Charles's back and head, driving him unnaturally fast and hard to the ground. His feet dangled over his head for a few seconds before they returned to the soil. He caught a glimpse of Abaddon resting his weapon on his shoulder.

He wanted to call for Emma. Where was she, anyway? He was too dazed and couldn't recall her name. Kristine and Mandy sat in the middle of this crowd of demons like mice in a pit full of vipers. The vipers were still too afraid of them to strike, but they were closer. Fear had grown while the girls' spirits had diminished.

The Nothingness King casually walked to the pit and dropped into Hell with Daniel. What was the name Charles wanted to say? He wracked his brain, trying to remember. *What was it? Oh yes, a name.*

"Grandma!" He cried out so loudly that Kristine and Mandy jumped. The mutterings of demons went silent. Charles shouted again, "Grandma!" His head felt heavy, so he rested it on the dirt and managed one more word. "Help."

CHAPTER THIRTY-FOUR

DANIEL AND THE NOTHINGNESS KING

Dread consumed Daniel. He held onto his car door, looking into the pale eyes of the Nothingness King. His hideous smile reached into Daniel's lungs and squeezed out all the oxygen, all the life. He looked back down at his feet, where his body lay like a corpse.

"Daniel," the Nothingness King said harshly. "It's time to go home. Enough of this."

"You're not real." Daniel pushed from the car and stumbled away from the Nothingness King. He fell to his knees and crawled toward the Bridge Trail, feeling certain that he was in as much trouble as Kristine and Mandy—maybe more.

The Nothingness King followed after him. "You can't speak me out of existence, Daniel." He pushed the end of his cane into Daniel's back. It touched a nerve that stole all his strength, pinning him to the ground. The king kicked Daniel over and looked into his eyes. "I'm not without mercy, my boy. I'll allow you to see your friend, Kristine, one more time. Would you like that?"

Daniel didn't want to play this game, but he needed time to breathe. Time to recover his depleted strength. "Where is she?"

The Nothingness King tucked his cane under his arm and walked closer to the beginning of the trail. "I'll show you."

Daniel shook as he came to his feet and followed the king. His fear gave way to anger, and it flowed through him like a river swelled by a storm. It felt good to feel rage. It fed his confidence. "What did you do to her?"

The Nothingness King stopped and turned. "I gave her a simple suggestion, and she took to it like a moth to flame. Behold, the woman you destroyed." He pointed his cane toward the Swinging Bridge. From it hung a lifeless body. The wind blew her red hair, revealing her face.

"No." The grief that tolled in his heart sent him back to the ground. He closed his eyes, shaking his head. "That's not real. She's alive."

"But she's dangling there," the Nothingness King neared him and whispered in his ear. "A brilliant girl is dead, because you're too selfish to give up. The only reason we're here is because of you. What I did for her was a mercy."

Daniel lunged at the Nothingness King's legs and brought him to the ground. The old magician opened his arms, laughing, feeding Daniel's wrath. He mounted the king and dropped elbows, forearms and fists upon the king's head and neck until the laughter ended. The Nothingness King lay motionless in a bloodied heap.

Gasping for breath, Daniel sat atop the Nothingness King. Blood oozed down the asphalt. It was over. He looked at the bridge. Kristine wasn't there. "Oh no. Look at the mess you've made," a raspy voice said.

He looked down. Daniel wasn't on top of the Nothingness King. He was on Kristine. He did this to her. The only person he truly loved. He brought her into his arms, squeezing her tight. Her body was limp and heavy. He cried.

"This can't be happening."

"Oh, you foul man," the Nothingness King sneered from behind. "So typical. A beautiful woman murdered by a jealous boyfriend."

Daniel was speechless. How was this possible? He lay her body on the asphalt. She took a heaving breath and coughed.

"Why did you hurt me?" Her eyes were wide with fear. "Please, don't kill me. I won't tell anybody what you did. I promise."

"I didn't do this." He looked to the Nothingness King. "You did."

"Enough!" The Nothingness King grimaced. "Do you want your girl to live or die?"

"Live!"

"Then come with me." The Nothingness King extended a gloved hand. "I'll spare your girl."

Something about all this didn't seem real. Daniel looked at Kristine. Her eyes were wrong. The expression on her face was wrong. It wasn't her. He reached into his pocket for the stone. It wasn't there.

"Looking for this?" The Nothingness King held it up. Its blue glow seemed almost white in this darkness. "It would do nothing to me. I'm beyond its power, and I'm beyond my capacity for patience."

The Nothingness King threw the stone. It smashed into Daniel's chest. He fell back onto the pavement. The Nothingness King stepped over him. "No one escapes Hell." Above him, the cloud seemed to coil downward like a giant shadowy serpent. It opened its massive mouth and devoured Daniel.

He woke to intense coldness. The Nothingness King had him by the neck, pressing him to an ice-cold wall. Daniel recognized this place. It was the tunnel that led to the bottommost chamber in Hell, Satan's lair. Across from him, distorted images of people submerged in ice gawked at him.

"Welcome home, traitor." The Nothingness King gave him a push, and Daniel's body drifted deeper into the ice. He fought against it, but his movements weakened until he froze in place. This was it. His eternal home.

He stared back at the Nothingness King, who watched him from the tunnel. A gloved hand rested on his chin, like an artist trying to determine what was missing from his masterpiece. Footsteps echoed from the left. Satan emerged and stood beside him. His golden hair shined with beads of light. "While I do love your work," he said, "this one doesn't hit the mark."

The Nothingness King nodded. "I agree."

Satan knocked on the ice. The reverberations blared in Daniel's head. His body stung and ached.

Satan turned to the Nothingness King. "This isn't the Daniel I want to see each time I walk along my hall." He sighed. "I have to go. Finish this." Satan spread his wings and took off in a blur.

The Nothingness King rubbed a finger along his lips. The ice distorted his face. It looked to be melting. It suddenly released Daniel, and he was underwater flailing. Air bubbles trailed behind him—toward the surface. He turned and saw light beaming in a blue sky. He swam toward it. His lungs burned for air.

The Nothingness King walked along the surface of the water, peering down at him with a net in his hands. He dropped it in. Dark iron weights tied its edges. It fell over Daniel, pulling him deeper.

He couldn't wait any longer. He inhaled water.

At the surface, the Nothingness King kneeled. "I am a fisher of men. Dead men."

Daniel realized he was gripping the net and wondered why. It was futile. He was a plaything in a demon's dream and had no control. God couldn't hear him from such a place, trapped in the mind of this evil entity. How did this come to pass? How did he escape last time? He had made things right with his parents, hadn't he? He had spoken with angels, yet here he was.

He sank deeper into darker waters. The pressure ceased. The cold no longer troubled him. He was free, finally. Out in the darkness, he found something peculiar, somewhat familiar. A dark black sphere. A thin, jagged line stretched from it. When it reached him, he heard a voice. *I'm coming, Daniel.*

Daniel spoke. His words traveled in the form of waves. "Who is this?"

The line zipped back. "Beau." Something was sucking him back toward the surface. The darkness faded to light. The water returned to ice. Daniel smashed through it and fell into the hall. The Nothingness King grabbed his arm, and Daniel swatted him away. A whirling noise grew in strength from behind him. Daniel turned and saw green bolts tear past him. They struck the Nothingness King.

Ice exploded from everywhere. There was nowhere to run. He shut his eyes and waited for the furious pain. It never came. A strong hand took him by the shoulder. Beau looked young and fierce. They were back on the mountain, surrounded by angry jeering demons.

CHAPTER THIRTY-FIVE

GRANDMA STOPS BY

Charles was once damned to Hell and given a demonic position. He had thought that demons had chosen him to join their ranks, but the truth was that an angel named Chance had done it for his grandmother. How did he miss that? It would've been helpful if he'd known. Perhaps he wouldn't have tricked himself into thinking he was something he wasn't—a demon. As horrible as his afterlife had been up to this point, it did have its perks. For example, Abaddon had clobbered him with a massive hammer, and while it did hurt badly, he was conscious. However, he was exhausted and worthless in trying to defend Kristine or Mandy, whose spirits had weakened considerably.

He heard something different. A number of demons cried out and went splat nearby, as if someone had tossed them from the cliff above him. That got Charles moving. He crawled closer to Kristine and Mandy, who were still crouched behind the boulder. A demon pulled at his feet, but Kristine and Mandy took his arms and helped him get free.

"Thank you," he said. "I'm a friend of Daniel's."

Kristine and Mandy seemed as frightened of him as the demons surrounding them, but at least they had the wherewithal to know he was an ally. Sure, he likely looked like a walking corpse to them, but his high level of sophistication and uncanny ability to anger powerful demons must've won them over.

Abaddon's voice boomed from the crowd. "You bunch of empty-headed oafs. Somebody get up there and find that girl."

"No need." Emma came to the ledge and peered down at them with her hands on her hips. She looked quite pleased with that smile of hers. Didn't she understand that they were surrounded by thousands of demons?

Obviously not, she casually dropped down to him and the girls. With her came an air of new hope, at least for Charles. She took Mandy's and Kristine's hands and said, "Don't worry. A friend has gone after Daniel. When he gets back, we'll work on getting you out of here. OK?"

A demon surged in toward them, but once it was within a few feet, it fell over and seemed to sleep. Kristine and Mandy stepped back, but Emma calmed them. "They can't handle getting too close. The Holy Spirit is present, but your fear will strengthen them. Bow your head. Pray. Do whatever you have to do to stay brave."

Kristine said nothing. She stared at the demon as if it were a giant insect filled with nastier little insects. The presence of the Holy Spirit didn't deter the demons. Another rushed them, and Emma swatted it away. More demons dropped from the cliff, landing all around them.

Kristine and Mandy were rigid and pale. The demons grew in numbers, crowding the surrounding area. Emma pulled the girls closer to the rock wall and stood guard over them. She glared at Charles as if he had wronged her.

"What?" he asked.

She rolled her eyes. Demons surged toward her, but she recovered and fended them off. That's when he figured out what he did—or rather, what he wasn't doing.

"I'm sorry," he said, "but I'm not much of a fighter. I did get hit by a giant hammer."

Emma was too busy to respond, but Charles knew what she was thinking. He was lazy, or likely a coward. That got him to his feet, which wasn't a great idea, since four demons jumped on him. Unfortunately, his presence didn't put them to sleep, nor was he as graceful as a particular female warrior angel, but he *did* have them occupied four to one. Not bad, in his estimation.

"Drop him in the pit!" Abaddon pointed his hammer at Charles and marched toward Emma as she fought off a half-dozen others. Charles forced himself up under the weight of the four demons and charged at Abaddon.

This was it. She would see his worth. Not only was he cunning, but fit to defend her against the greatest of Satan's generals. Abaddon backhanded him and his trajectory went in the opposite direction that he'd intended. While Charles was grateful it wasn't the hammer, he couldn't help but feel a little more useless now that he wasn't occupying the attention of any demons.

Emma was surrounded. Abaddon headed toward her, cutting through the crowd of demons. More demons dropped from the cliff. One slammed upon Charles. He thought he'd rather get struck by Abaddon again as he pushed the demon off.

Emma screamed. Charles jolted to his feet. Abaddon had her by the hair and was ready to strike when bright white lightning flashed from the sky. A thunderbolt shot into the pit. Demons dropped all around, hiding their eyes. Those who didn't fell limp to the ground.

While the demons were down, Charles hurried to Emma and pulled her closer to Kristine and Mandy. Everything seemed to stop. Something touched his shoulder and he screamed. When he turned, he found his grandmother was with him.

He covered his face, remembering how he had called for her. He could've called for anybody, but no, he had to drag her into this mess. "What are you doing here?"

"You called for me, Chip, and I'll stay as long as I can." She nodded for emphasis.

Demons were beginning to wake. Charles had no idea how many there were, but they outnumbered the trees, and more still rose from the pit.

His grandmother stepped toward the demons, and they cowered back. The slower ones collapsed and fell asleep. A few proved to be thumb-suckers, too. She turned to him and said, "They smell awful." She winced. "I think I'll need to sit for a moment."

"Ms. Thorne?" Emma helped her over to the rock wall and sat her beside Kristine and Mandy. She gave Charles a hard look. "Didn't know Charles would bring you into this."

"I was hit with a hammer." Charles was a little tired of having to explain this. "It may not seem like much to you, but he caught me unawares. I tried calling you, but—oh, never mind."

"Don't you worry, Chip," Grandma said tiredly. "It'll be all right."

Charles felt a little humbled in that moment, but what could he say with Emma staring daggers through him? Although his grandma had saved their hides, the situation wasn't much better. Thousands of tall, muscular demons surrounded them. They didn't come too close, though, likely fearing whatever power his grandmother possessed. Those who tried fell asleep and had to be pulled away and beaten awake.

His grandmother seemed to be losing whatever strength she brought with her. He gazed in the direction of the pit and met Abaddon's eyes. He pointed his weapon at Charles. "Finish them!"

Another thick bolt of lightning shot from the sky and into the pit, scattering demons like cockroaches in sudden light and electrifying those who were too close. Static electricity fluttered over his skin. A succession of flashes and loud bangs shook the earth. Charles lost his balance and fell. A dark silhouette ran straight at him. It was Beau, but he looked younger and stronger. He carried Daniel as if he were carrying a child.

Beau sat him next to Kristine. Daniel seemed exhausted. Kristine took his hand. The demons let out a massive roar. Daniel's smile waned when he looked at the pit. Charles turned. Satan had emerged.

CHAPTER THIRTY-SIX

HELL UNLEASHED

Daniel knew where he was, but nothing looked or felt right. Fiery sparks disappeared into smoke that curled overhead like a snake preparing to strike, and everything was covered in shimmering shades of red. Their fear must've outweighed their faith, because Satan's forces were moving in on him, Kristine, and Mandy. If not for Emma and Beau, they would've been tossed into the pit by now, but their strength was fleeting.

Charles struggled to his feet. He looked at his grandmother. "Stay near the girls." He straightened his coat and turned to Daniel. "They're gonna need our help."

Daniel nodded. It was a hopeless situation, and he felt great shame. All of this was because of him. Maybe the Nothingness King was right. Maybe he should've stayed in Hell. Every living soul would suffer if he didn't do something about it.

He reached into his pocket and felt the keystone. All he needed to do was sling it at the head of the snake. Behind the mob, Satan and his generals were huddled. They seemed content and confident, but they didn't know what Daniel held in his fist. He squeezed the stone and came to his feet.

Upon seeing this, Satan addressed his army. "Why haven't you thrown them in the pit already? Attack! I want them out of here now!"

The weight of the crowd forced Beau and Emma back. The demons at the front fell to the ground and slept. Those behind them fell on top of them, crawling until they succumbed to sleep. Others dropped from the ledge overhead. Beau and Emma were strong enough to hold them off. Charles kicked and slapped at the crowd from behind them, but still the demons kept coming. There was soon a wall of sleeping demons, and the demons behind them pushed them closer. Emma and Beau were forced back again. There was little room to move, and the sleepers began to stir.

"All of us need to fight," Emma said, gasping. "We have to hold them off a little longer."

"Seven against thousands?" Charles said incredulously. His face was torn and cracked; his shoulder looked to be out of socket. "If your friends don't get off their harps soon, we're taking the plunge no matter how hard we fight."

His grandmother took his hand and patted it. "You must have faith. Faith is the key to defeating them."

"I've got a plan that might end this." Daniel uncapped his fist so they could see the stone. Its pale blue light cast awkward shadows on their faces. "Get me a clear shot at Satan."

Beau squinted at him. "Is that the keystone?"

Daniel nodded. "It'll send them back to Hell."

"If we had a gazillion of them, I bet we'd have a chance," Charles said, jerking his arm out of a demon's grip.

"I only need to hit the one that matters." Daniel gripped the stone. "All I need is to see him."

"What if you miss?" Charles asked.

Daniel glared at him. "I won't." Missing wasn't an option.

"It's worth a shot." Emma pushed back a mass of lethargic demons. Her eyes darted to Charles and Beau. "Come on."

The three of them plowed a narrow path through the mob, tossing sleepy demons left and right. Daniel felt a hand touch his back. It was Kristine. She looked as if she had been lost in the wilderness for days. Mandy sat with Charles's grandmother, who hugged her and said, "...Every day there is a banquet and merrymaking. Earlier today, I woke to..."

Kristine squeezed his shoulder. "You can do this," she whispered.

Daniel nodded, but deep down, he wasn't sure. Gabriel had mentioned that he shouldn't put too much faith in the stone, but maybe that was because it was out of his hands once he'd thrown it. If he hit his mark, it would be a major win for them, regardless.

The path was nearly complete. Daniel locked eyes with Azazel, one of Satan's most powerful generals. A shiver coursed through him. His hand shook. Satan edged into view. His pale moon eyes cut into Daniel's heart. Satan seemed confident, which meant that he didn't know what was coming.

Daniel gathered his strength and slung the keystone hard. The trajectory was dead on, darting straight at Satan's chest. A demon reached out to catch it, but it passed through its palm as if it were air, and that demon turned to smoke and sank to the ground. The nightmare would be over soon. Daniel straightened his back and exhaled, feeling pride in his delivery.

Satan brought his hand up. His lip quirked. The stone struck his palm and stopped. He glanced at it, then back at Daniel. Raising his fist, light traveled down his arm to the rest of him. A blast of energy sent Daniel back into Kristine, against the rock face, then to the ground.

The demons all woke. They grew raucous. Charles, Beau, and Emma had fallen back as well. They got to their feet and tried to fight back. A demon grabbed Charles by the coat and pulled him into the crowd.

"I've got him." Beau started to leave.

"No." Daniel gripped Beau's shirt and turned him around. "We can't lose you too."

Beau smiled. "This is part of the plan, Daniel." Electric light flashed in Beau's eyes. Daniel let him go. "We'll be back."

Beau lunged into the crowd. Lightning flashed and demons cried out. The pressure from the crowd relented. Daniel turned to Kristine. She and Mandy lay on either side of Charles's grandmother.

"They'll be OK," she said.

Behind him, Emma shouted. "Chance! Get up here. We need you."

The crowd was pushing in on them again. She was losing ground. Daniel went to her aid, kicking, pushing, punching, and pulling himself from the grips of demons.

From the masses, Azazel emerged. The giant demon's grin sent a dagger of fear into Daniel. He fell back, staring up at the ancient demon. There was no fight left in him. He crawled until his back was to the wall. Emma was swarmed. This was the end. Whatever plan Beau alluded to had gone wrong.

"Chance!" Emma's fever-pitched scream did little to assuage Daniel's growing fear as Azazel approached, relishing the fear that emanated from Daniel.

CHAPTER THIRTY-SEVEN

"CHANCE"

C hance muttered his prayers. His brother's charred hand felt hot, rugged, and brittle. The sky was dark purple, and only a few wisps of smoke rolled along the hard, red ground. Harrison's skin frosted over as frigid air moved in. It didn't affect Chance, however. He didn't belong here, but his brother did.

Harrison gasped. His grip tightened. The whites of his eyes were in stark contrast to his charred body. He let out a raspy groan. "Chance?"

Chance used his forearm to smear away tears. "I got the hat." He touched his brother's chest. "I'll get you into the city soon. You need to heal a little more, so you don't fall apart on me when I take you."

"It hurts," Harrison rasped. His rugged hand prickled against Chance's palm. The chill of the night whipped about them, slicing like a samurai's blade.

"It'll be all right." Chance knew his words weren't much comfort. Comforting was never his strong suit. "It's warmer in town."

Harrison stretched and screamed while brushing layers of frost and charred skin from his arms. He was healing a great deal now, but the cold was tearing into him.

"Let's go." Chance pried his stiff brother from the ground and held him like a small child.

Chance! Get up here. We need you.

He turned toward the mountain. That was Emma. It was the first time he had ever heard her call for him. Considering the state of things, he wasn't surprised. "Emma's calling. I'll have to leave you at the bus stop." He darted toward Grayton.

The cloud insulated the town from the extreme cold. The rain was cool, but warm enough to thaw Harrison. The streets were empty, but his old crew was loitering around the reinstituted bus stop.

Chance eyed them suspiciously. "Have you had any trouble?"

Jethro spotted him first. "None."

Miguel stepped closer. "The demons were called to the mountain, so the bus stop is back in business."

"Those demons will be back sooner or later," Chance said.

"We're not going anywhere." Miguel looked at the others. "Are we fellas?"

Marlin said, "That's right."

Chance nodded. He wasn't sure if he trusted them, but Emma needed him, which meant the world did as well. He prayed silently to God that his old team would do the right thing and set Harrison on the curb. "Will you see that my brother gets on the next bus?"

"If that's what he wants," Miguel said.

Chance! Emma's voice sounded more desperate.

He turned to the mountain but wasn't quite finished with his brother. Was there anything else he should say?

Harrison grabbed Chance's pant leg. "Go. Save our sister."

Chance pulled his brother from the ground and hugged him for the first time in a long time. He'd bring him along if he knew it wasn't dangerous. "See you on the other side, little brother."

"Who you callin' little?" Harrison managed a smile as he dropped to the curb. "Get on now."

Chance dashed to the Purging Mountain. The portal in the sky was larger now. Demons poured through it and headed straight into the tunnel. The air in front of Chance sent them against the walls as he zipped through. Countless fell as he sprinted up the shaft, where lines of demons coiled up toward the surface.

Emma shouted again, sounding more desperate. He couldn't go any faster. When he breached the ground and came upon the surface of the earth, he felt as if he had just woken from death. The burdens of Hell were behind him. The strength of the Holy Spirit invigorated him. He inhaled, but the air felt sick. Hell was strangling it with smoke and fire.

Demons were piled around his sister and others. Azazel was thrusting a fist at Daniel. It would land a harsh blow that would likely kill the man. Chance smashed into a boulder that projected toward Azazel and crushed him against the cliff face. Everyone looked about, stunned.

He freed his sister and pulled her back. He moved so quickly that no one could see him. All they saw was a wall of light shielding Emma, Daniel, and the others from the demons.

Chapter Thirty-Eight

Charles and Beau

Two strong taloned hands gripped Charles by the arms and pulled him through the angry crowd toward the pit. Those nearby treated him to a hard stomp or a sharp kick. They preferred the head. Charles felt like the hammer was still worse, but his suit was likely in ruins now.

Although Charles jerked and fought the best he could, the demons got him to the edge of the pit, regardless. They were about to pitch him in when electric, thorny vines wrapped about his captors. They dropped Charles and shook rigidly before collapsing. Those nearby hid their eyes from the light.

Beau pulled Charles to his feet. "Follow me."

Charles didn't have time to question him. Demons were recovering. Beau extended his arm. Lightning bolts jumped from his fingertips and zapped a gang of demons that tried to head them off. Beau knocked them aside and bounded down a steep embankment.

Charles shouted, "That's the wrong way!" A flood of demons pursued him, so he sprinted after Beau. Trees littered the embankment. While Beau moved gracefully, gripping one tree after the other on his descent, Charles lost his footing and went tumbling. He smacked into a few trees before rolling to a stop on a somewhat flat strip of land.

Beau pulled him to his feet.

"Gotta keep moving."

Charles heaved a breath and glanced uphill. They were getting closer. They started off again.

"Where are we going?"

"To the foot of the mountain," Beau said breathlessly. "No time. Just move."

The forest around them was catching fire. It lit up the night enough that Charles could see a massive wall of smoke swirling ahead before entering it. The jeers and shouts of demons were close behind.

They broke through the smoke and came into a dense and dark forest. "We shouldn't get too far from Daniel," Charles said, panting. His legs were heavy and hot with fatigue.

"We're drawing them away. To an ambush. It's part of the plan." Beau hurdled a boulder and tumbled down another steep embankment. Charles was certain that wasn't part of the plan. He tried sliding down, but to his dismay, roots and rocks tore at his pants and legs. He tried to get up and run and started tumbling again.

Charles knocked against a tree, whirled around, and smacked to a stop against Beau. They both struggled to get up. Beau got there first and began dragging Charles by the collar. It was a good thing, too, because the demons were handling the fall much better than they were. Many of them had spread their wings and were gliding after them.

One snatched at Charles and barely missed. Beau grunted and pulled Charles from the ground.

They went airborne over another drop. The wingless demons fell straight down, while Charles and Beau glided farther away somehow. Beau was beside him, gripping his coat like a cat carries its young. Trees passed beneath them.

"We're flying!" Charles looked at Beau. "Wait! Where are your wings?"

"I have to focus." They dipped a little when Beau spoke.

Charles looked back toward the cliff. The winged demons were feet away. He saw their harsh, spiky teeth glistening with saliva. "Go faster."

Beau looked over his shoulder. They dipped again. Treetops smacked against Charles's feet. He turned in time to see himself and Beau smash through a line of trees. They toppled to the forest floor. The land was entirely dark. All around them, demons landed and sniffed the air, searching.

Charles went to all fours and whispered, "Beau?"

"Can't hide." Beau sounded breathless. He pulled Charles to his feet. "They'll find us. We must move."

They dashed through darkness. The foliage was thick. Charles's tattered clothes ripped as he bounded through thick briar patches. He turned, and a demon smacked him with a branch. His momentum sent him rolling against Beau's legs, who went tumbling forward.

Beau sent bolts of lightning back at the demon. The lights from his fingertips were dim. Whatever power he possessed had been depleted. The demons flanked them, and the clubbing began. Abaddon dropped from the sky with his hammer. "Restrain them. I need four wingers to take them back to the pit. The rest of you start forming a perimeter around the mountain. Hurry up. Spread the word."

"That means we made it," Charles said aloud, which was a mistake. Although they were at the foot of the mountain, there was no one there, and he had captured the attention of a powerful, ancient demon who likely despised him more than anything in existence.

Abaddon's dark red eyes met Charles's, then smashed his war hammer against Charles's head—again—but at least this time, his face sank into soft dirt. Every bit of him hurt, especially his head, but the dirt felt nice.

The demons used vines to bind him and Beau. It took six of them to subdue him. Another phenomenal whack struck Charles.

"I'm not even fighting back," he growled. Another whack. Maybe he best keep quiet.

He faced away from the mountain. The area seemed a little brighter, as if moonlight was cutting through the trees, but no moon shone this night. The light intensified and expanded along the ridge.

Abaddon stepped toward the light and commanded his troops. "This is it. No mercy."

The light went out. Over the sound of his breathing, Charles heard leaves rustling, limbs breaking, and demons growling.

There was a thud. A dark body was propelled back. Lights soared down from the sky. Nearby, demons went skyward. An angel in golden armor dropped onto the back of a winged demon, a spear in his hand. A wall of light flashed from the south. Demons jetted toward it, screaming. Small comets zipped through the air and smacked several demonic heads and continued uphill.

Downhill, Charles heard the battle. Demonic silhouettes swung weapons, but there was no angel in sight that he could tell. The light diminished. A flurry of demons fell from the sky. Others took flight. The chaos subsided. Demons marched triumphantly uphill from where the battle took place, cheering.

One shouted, "The first battle is ours, Master!"

"We captured a little birdie," another announced.

Sure enough, demons were dragging a net that contained a man, who glowed dimly. This angel didn't wear armor or have wings. It coughed and retched, likely due to the foul stench of the demons.

Charles lay his head on the ground. The angelic army was a bunch of cowards, fleeing while one of their own was captured. *Too much time in Paradise*, he guessed. How could this night get any worse? At this rate, the entire world would be living a real nightmare come morning.

"Bring it to me," Abaddon commanded.

The angel was draped in a dark mesh net. His hands and feet were bound as well. He fought back with tired, listless movements. His captors threw him at the feet of Abaddon. The angel seemed too exhausted to struggle any further. He lay there, groaning.

Abaddon glared at the angel. "Your ambush failed. Your brothers abandoned you." He gripped the angel's short hair through the netting and yanked his head back. "Denounce your God. Hail Satan. Join us."

"W-what if I don't?" The angel's voice was childlike and terrified.

"I'll smash you until every piece of you passes through that net. We'll scoop you up in buckets." He shoved the angel's head toward the ground and stood straight. "Have you retrained in the hottest pit in Hell."

The angel began to sob. The demons surrounding them laughed and jeered. Charles looked at Beau, who dropped his gaze in shame. "We've got to do something," he whispered.

Beau shook his head. "What?"

The angel sobbed. "I don't know." It was a pitiful sight and pitiful to hear.

Abaddon raised his war hammer, twirling it threateningly. "Do it now," he growled.

"If that's the case, then—" The sobs became hysterical. It sounded like laughter—almost maniacal. The angel glowed brighter—dangerously bright. The flesh of nearby demons sizzled and smoked. They backed away. "I think," the angel leveled his gaze with Abaddon, his eyes glowing amber, "never."

Abaddon grew rigid. "Michael!" He swung his weapon, but it never reached its target. In fact, he and Michael were gone. All that remained was a burning net and a broken hammer. Thunder rolled overhead.

The demons looked about frantically, questioning each other. Their movements and posture were hesitant and twitchy.

A distant cry descended from the sky. Charles tried to wriggle out of his restraints. A heavy foot came down on his back. "Stop moving."

A demon pointed overhead. "Look out."

A large body, Abaddon, sped down from the sky like a rocket. The ground exploded. Dirt rained. Trees fell. Angels swept down, snatching demons and flying off.

Another light, shining with all the colors of the rainbow, came over and untwisted the vines that bound Charles and Beau.

"Ralph? Is that you?" Beau stood up, rubbing his wrists.

"Or if you prefer, Raphael. Hello, Charles." The angel pulled Charles to his feet, eying his head seriously. "Hold still." He placed his hand over Charles's ear. A pleasant fluttering sound rushed through him. When Raphael removed his hand, Charles sank to the ground.

"Wow! I didn't realize how much my head hurt." He came back to his feet, looking at his tattered outfit. "Do you think you could do anything about my clothes?"

Beau showed no interest in Charles's miraculous recovery. He gazed at Raphael. "You're different than you were."

"This isn't over," Raphael said. "Get back to the others and get them out of here. Leave the devils to us." He leaped into the sky, leaving a trail of rainbow light behind him.

Charles took Beau by the hand, closed his eyes, and jumped to Daniel. The air was hot. Fire glowed vibrantly orange. They were backed against the rock wall. Mandy and Kristine had succumbed to the smoke. His grandmother sat between the girls, fanning them. Two demons had a hold on Daniel. Beau took one off him. Charles grabbed the other and got swatted. Daniel returned the favor with a hard right hook. While the demon was dazed, Beau pulled him off and tossed him aside.

A mass of demons had Emma surrounded. She fought hard but was pushed back to the wall. A blurry line of light cut through the crowd, giving her relief. A man in a cowboy hat appeared. He spoke to Emma. Something seemed familiar about him. *Chance, perhaps?* They were surrounded again, but from the lower elevations, a light emerged from behind the demonic army.

Chapter Thirty-Nine

The Battle

Things weren't going well, but Daniel was relieved when Charles and Beau had returned. It gave him hope. The man in the cowboy hat, Chance, had come back too, after a gang of winged demons carried him off. Daniel dropped to a knee beside Kristine and Mandy, who were still unconscious. He imagined he'd be out too if the air didn't improve soon. Charles's grandmother smiled at him.

"It's almost over," she said.

"Yeah?" Daniel looked about. Demons were everywhere, and the world seemed more like Hell now. He came to his feet, feeling fatigued.

Emma came over and spoke to Charles's grandmother. "It's time to take you home." She looked up at Daniel. "My brother's going to keep them back as long as he can, so you guys can get out of here."

"Your brother got caught once already. If it happens again—"

"The best warriors in Heaven have arrived. These demons can't worry about you and them at the same time." She leaned over and blew upon Kristine and Mandy. The air freshened, and they slowly woke. "Get to your cars." Emma took Charles's grandmother's hands, and they disappeared.

Chance slowed beside them. "Get moving. I got you covered."

Kristine and Mandy got to their feet, and the three of them started toward the parking lot. Beau and Charles were close behind.

Daniel peeked over his shoulder. Demons had turned their attention to a wall of golden light. Overhead, the dark spiraling cloud of smoke writhed and let out a screaming roar. It was so massive, and so unearthly, that Daniel and the girls came to a stop. The cloud unfurled into a giant snake and dropped down on top of them, engulfing them in smoke. Daniel fell and struggled for breath. Kristine was gagging and coughing ahead of him. He couldn't see or breathe. There was no escaping this.

A beam of light cut through the smoke. The smoke-snake jerked away. Its deep guttural cry shook the ground. It reformed into a hulking dragon with deep, black eyes. An angel in bright white clothing and no weapons or armor pulled Daniel off his feet and carried him down the trail. Two other angels had Kristine and Mandy. But where were Beau, Charles, and Chance?

The angel seemed to know his thoughts. "Your friends will be fine."

The smoke-dragon lunged after them. The angel set Daniel to his feet and flung what looked like glowing ninja stars at the giant beast. They exploded, and a great wind blew it apart. It began to reshape. Demons dropped from the ledge and attacked.

The angel pulled Daniel along the trail toward the demons. Spears flew at them. There was a flash of light, and the spears were gone. Angels dipped from the sky and carried the demons back toward the pit. Daniel and the angel continued. The parking lot wasn't far now. Another group of demons rushed at them from their eleven o'clock position. A line of armored angels dropped from the sky and fought them back.

Daniel nearly fell when his feet slapped onto the asphalt. Never had he been so thankful to be in a parking lot. Several angels were guarding Kristine and Mandy as they got in her car. His angel patted him on the shoulder. "Godspeed."

Kristine and Mandy got out of her car and went for Daniel's.

"What's wrong?" Daniel's throat felt ragged.

"It won't start!" Kristine shouted. She and Mandy piled into his car. He wished he had cleaned his car out now.

An explosion went off behind him and sent him sprawling beside his car. A wall of fire stretched along the horizon and from there, Satan emerged. He still glowed with golden light. His hand still clutched the keystone. Rows upon rows of demons followed after him. Behind them, the smoke-dragon filled the sky. Daniel got to his feet and reached for the car door handle but couldn't find it.

Beside him, the angel said, "Still your soul, Daniel, and move along." He stared at Satan and all the demons with him. He lifted his hand in the air and hundreds of angels dropped from the sky.

Kristine opened the car door from the inside. "Get in!"

Demons sprinted toward them, and the angels went to meet them. Everyone around his car was brawling, except Daniel's angel and Satan, who eyed each other with bad intentions.

Satan spoke first. "Let me have the boy and we'll leave, Michael. Deal?"

Daniel leaped in and fumbled for his keys. Mandy was in the back seat, panting. "Go. Go. Go."

"No kidding." Daniel ripped his keys from his pocket. They slipped from his hand and fell in the parking lot. Satan rose into the air. Michael leaped after him, grabbing his ankle and jerking him down. Satan rebounded and smashed into Michael. The two jetted into the sky, disappearing into the darkness.

Daniel got his keys, and despite shaking, inserted them into the ignition, but the car wouldn't start.

"Look out!" Kristine cried.

Satan pulled his car door off and slung it back. Michael dropped from the sky, took Satan by a wing, and pulled him away. Winds picked up again, and Satan leaped at Michael. They disappeared into the sky again.

"We've got to go," Kristine said.

Daniel tried again, but the car still wouldn't start. "The battery's dead or something. We're stuck."

There was a thud and the car jostled. They all screamed. Michael was on the hood. He bent down and asked, "Car trouble?"

"It won't start," Daniel said.

"It's why I prefer to fly." Michael leveled his gaze at Satan, who stood about thirty feet away. Angels and demons remained engaged in hand-to-hand combat. Azazel came alongside Satan, nursing a wound on his chest with one hand, and gripping his shotgun with the other. The smoke-dragon bit at glowing beads of light that zipped about its head like a swarm of bees. Michael snapped his fingers. "There. Try it now."

The car started. Demons jumped onto the hood and roof. Angels jumped on them. Demons tried to subdue Michael, but when they touched him, they passed out. Michael hopped beside the car. "You don't need an invitation to leave this party, Daniel."

"I don't want to run over any of you."

"It wouldn't faze us," Michael said. "Go."

Daniel pressed on the gas, but the car tilted forward. Angels and demons rolled off. In the rearview mirror, Daniel saw that the smoke-dragon had the rear end of his car clamped in its mouth. They were stuck. Behind it, an angel in a black shawl that sparkled like stars struck the beast with a scythe. It was Azrael. The smoke-dragon released the car but ripped the rear axle off in the process.

Azrael joined Michael, whispering something.

"Why fight me, Michael?" Satan asked. He still glowed with the keystone clutched in his fist. "It's pointless. You can't destroy us. We're here to stay unless you hand over that man-child."

Azazel pulled his shotgun out and aimed it at Azrael. "Move and I'll blast you back to Heaven."

Michael raised his voice and spoke to Satan. "Have you not grown tired of your delusions, brother? Because I have."

"I'm delusional? You gave up your freedom to Him." He stabbed a finger skyward, then down at Michael. "That's delusional. We will forever stand against His tyranny!"

Azazel whooped and fired his weapon at the sky. What demons remained cheered and banged their chests.

"You're a spoiled child in desperate need of discipline," Michael said, moving toward Satan.

A hot wind swept dust into a swirl. Azazel roared. His body, bones, and muscles inflated. Long, fiery horns cut through his head and pricked at the darkness. Azrael flew like a missile, right at its head. Azazel leveled his shotgun and fired. The shots missed, but Azrael did not. He cut through Azazel with his scythe. The smoke-dragon dropped from the sky and landed on him.

Satan extended his arm to Michael, and fire burst from his hand. Michael rolled under it and swatted the keystone out of Satan's palm. Satan lunged after it, but Michael took him to the ground, and they wrestled.

Behind them from the fire, the Nothingness King sauntered out, grinning hideously. Michael was too preoccupied to see him coming up on the keystone, and it was too far away for Daniel to do anything.

As the Nothingness King stooped for the stone, Gabriel appeared and kicked the stone toward Daniel's car. The Nothingness King flung his cane at Gabriel, but the angel disappeared. So many emotions rolled through Daniel as he leaped from his car for the keystone. So many emotions that he could hardly control his movements. Ahead of him, the Nothingness King sprinted toward him, but he'd be too late. The keystone was right there, within his reach, when a sandaled foot crushed it.

All things fell silent, even the wind. The chaos? The fire, the darkness, the fighting? It was all gone. Everything was gone.

"Kristine?" Daniel turned. She, Mandy, the car, and the parking lot were gone. Actually, he was gone. This wasn't Grandfather Mountain, but a mountain of golden sand and silvery boulders. Castles pierced through clouds that swirled across the sky. Towers extended beyond the stars. There was so much to see that he didn't realize who was standing beside him.

"Why do you crawl on your hands and knees to a stone?"

A strange kind of fatherly fear washed over Daniel. He kneeled and stared at the holes in the feet of the sandaled man. "The stone..." He shook his head. "I was going to send Satan back with it."

The King of Heaven opened his hand. There were bits of rock in it. "This is what remains of that stone. Can you see there is nothing within it?" He closed his fist and pointed at Daniel's chest. "But there is so much more within you, Daniel Strong." He helped him to his feet. "What do you think gives the stone its strength?"

Daniel shook his head. "You?"

He smiled. "I place no value in stones." He placed His hand on Daniel's shoulder. "I give all that I have for you."

"What does that mean?" Daniel said. "Are you saying I have to fight Satan? What could I possibly do against him? Your best angels are fighting him and he's not going anywhere. We need you. The world needs you. Everything's messed up. Will you help us? Please?"

Jesus gazed at the distant sky castles. His brown eyes sparkled with compassion. "Do you know that I have never left you? Even when you walked away, I was there."

Daniel dropped his head. He wasn't sure why he felt so ashamed. The words weren't spoken in a hurtful way. "I'm trying. I promise I am."

"Son—" A beautiful woman with dark black hair came to Jesus's side and took His hand. "This boy is weary. He's gone through so much. Would you ease his burden?"

Jesus chuckled. "Woman, it isn't time, but through faith, this boy can do anything. I am with him." He turned to Daniel. "I am with you, always."

The woman lay her head on Jesus's shoulder. Her gentle eyes went to Daniel, and she smiled.

There was a flash, and Daniel was back on Grandfather Mountain, kneeling before a crumpled stone. There was no magical light within it. Satan and Michael sparred several yards away. Azrael kept the giant smoke-monster occupied, while Raphael and Gabriel fought Azazel. The Nothingness King darted to Daniel but stopped when he saw the stone was crushed. He shook with rage.

He raised his cane to strike.

Daniel brought up his arms to block it, but the cane never struck. The Nothingness King leaped back with a yelp. Jesus snapped the cane with His thumb. Darkness lifted from the earth like a veil from a bride. Michael pushed Satan aside and walked off, nodding at the King of Kings. Satan looked dumbfounded, like a child who knew he was guilty but was thinking up a lie.

"It's not time for you!" Satan glared at Daniel. "That boy is a nuisance. He belongs to me. He came to me and only righted himself out of fear. He doesn't love you. He doesn't know love. He's—"

"Enough," Jesus said. "You will leave. Return to the house you built." He pointed down the trail toward the pit. The fires died. The land became lush and green. Trees lifted back to the sky. Flowers with golden petals sprouted to life. The smoke-dragon dropped to the earth and sank into the ground.

Satan grimaced. His arms strained, and he looked on the verge of exploding. His army stood silent. He exhaled, and to Daniel's surprise, started for the pit. Daniel expected a glare, but Satan never turned. He addressed the demons.

"Come," he said. "We've had our fun." He looked at Jesus. "And I promise, there'll be more."

The angels were gone. The demons too. The dark of night returned, but the sky remained clear. Jesus touched Daniel's shoulder. "Do not forget what I said."

Chapter Forty

The Next Day

The world was calm, quiet, and dark again. The foul stench of Hell was replaced by the scent of nature. The winds returned and chilled Daniel, letting him know it was a good idea to head home.

Kristine's car started this time, and she headed off the mountain with Mandy. No doubt, they had a lot to talk about on the way back to Boone. Daniel's car door and rear axle were fixed, and even the gas was topped off. However, whoever fixed it left the cleaning for him. He followed Kristine and Mandy back to town. The police checkpoint was gone, and despite all that had happened, there wasn't any traffic on the way home.

It was 1 am when he reached his apartment. He turned on the television, but there wasn't any talk about what had occurred on the mountain. He opened his laptop and searched the web, and still nothing.

He awoke the next day, sitting on his couch with the laptop sitting slightly askew on his thighs. He set it aside and turned on the news. After a few minutes of commercials and a weather report, a news reporter said that Grandfather Mountain was reopened, and never-before-seen flowers were in bloom. Local botanists weren't sure how they got there, but they believed they were a new species of flower that hadn't been named yet. The newscaster offered a suggestion: Grandfather Goldens.

The doorbell rang. Kristine's voice called to him. "Are you up?"

She was up before him? He looked at the clock on the microwave. It read 7:14. Daniel answered the door. "Good morning." They hugged before she came in. "Do you remember anything about last night?"

"You mean demons and angels?" Kristine shook her head as she came in. "Nothing. Not even a giant dragon made of smoke."

Daniel chuckled and closed the door. "And it's like the world doesn't even know."

"I know, right?"

"How's Mandy?"

"We talked earlier. She's fine." She walked into the kitchen and looked in the fridge, which was empty.

"Sorry about that," Daniel said. "I haven't been to the store."

Kristine smiled. "I can see that." She spotted the ring on the counter and picked it up. "What's this? Oh!"

An invisible weight pressed on Daniel's chest and throat. "Um..." He wasn't ready. He hadn't figured out what he would say.

Little lights zipped in from the vents and spun around Kristine. The joyous little fairies were not helping him come up with anything useful. "I can explain."

Orna sat on Kristine's shoulder. Her little band of fairies danced through the air, cheering. Tears were in Kristine's eyes. "Um. What on earth are these things?"

"Never mind us, dear," Orna said brightly. "Daniel has something he'd like to say."

"Right." Daniel clapped his hands together and rubbed the back of his neck. This wasn't what he had planned at all. "Oh!" He jogged over to Kristine and kneeled. "I'm afraid I'll need that back for a moment, if you don't mind."

Kristine gave it back, and fairies were zipping all around them both now. "You didn't mean to do this now, did you?"

"What better time than now?" He took her hands. "Ms. Kristine Groves, will you marry me?"

Orna whispered in her ear, "It's your turn, deary."

The fairies paused. It was quiet—too quiet.

"I can't believe this," Kristine said. "Yes. I will. I'll marry you."

The fairies went nuts. If they'd been physically of this world, they would've broken everything that Daniel owned. He and Kristine held on to each other in the middle of it all.

There was a sound from his bedroom. He turned. At the end of the hall, he saw that his mirror had been repaired. Beau came out of Daniel's bedroom with a young girl and a woman. They were all carrying baskets full of fruit.

"Good morning," he said. "Thought you might be hungry."

Daniel touched Beau's face as he came into the kitchen. "Are you actually here—in the flesh?"

"We are," Beau said, eying the fairies with a bit of suspicion, "but we can't stay long, I'm afraid."

Kristine turned. "You were there last night."

"That's right." Beau sat his basket on the counter and gestured to the ladies who were with him. "I'd like y'all to meet my wife, Evelyn, and daughter, Angela."

They greeted each other. When Beau got to Daniel, they hugged like lifelong friends. "I hope you like berries." He looked about the house. "Where's your table?"

Another thing Daniel needed to correct. He motioned to the living room. "Please, have a seat."

Evelyn and Angela set their baskets on the counter next to Beau's. Daniel grabbed a handful of blueberries and joined them, sitting next to Kristine. "These berries are from Heaven?"

"I grew it all myself," Angela said. "Hope you like it."

"I'm sure we will," Kristine said.

Beau was all smiles and looked much younger than he had days ago. He and his wife were cheery and bumped shoulders playfully. It was nice to see him so happy as they talked.

"Do you know what happened to everybody else?" Daniel asked.

They all turned to Beau.

"That's another reason we came," he said. "To tell you what happened. Emma and Charles's grandmother made it home with no trouble. Charles, however, got pulled into the pit. Chance and I went after him." He looked at Daniel. "You were in good hands, obviously—but Charles," he shook his head, "not so much. Turns out that I got myself caught trying to save him. The good thing about that is I found Charles first, before the professional, mind you."

"Oh, stop it," Evelyn said. "You sound prideful."

"But it's true, Mama," Angela said.

"Either way," Beau continued, "because I was with Charles, Chance found us pretty quickly. From there, we went to the bus stop. I met Chance's and Emma's brother, along with three other fellas. When Ralph showed up, Emma was with him. She said she was taking over as lead missionary, and that compelled Chance and Charles to stay."

"So, is Charles a part of Heaven's Army now?" Daniel asked.

Beau shrugged. "Hard to say for sure, but I think so." He must've seen the concern on Daniel's face. "Don't worry. They'll be OK. I heard that much from an excellent source."

Malecoda entered the Malebolge and leaped from the cliff over legions of returning demons. He drifted to the second trench and landed next to three demons who stood on the ledge, admiring the brawl below. "Get me Elaine Love Thorne now!" He shoved them over the ledge. "Hurry up!"

The souls at the bottom were covered in mush, fighting viciously, as they always did. The three he pushed worked their way through the crowd, but at their pace, it would be days before they'd find her. He dropped from the ledge and glided over the mob, identifying everyone until he found her. He smashed his shoulder into her, and she went sprawling. Four demons leaped to defend him while he stood over Charles's mother.

"Your little Chip has gone too far, which means," he took her up by the throat, "you're on the fast track to demonic transition, sister."

Elaine gripped his forearm, gasping for breath. Something fell from the sky and plopped into the mud beside him. It was ticking and shaking in the mud. A golden chain was attached to it. He dropped Elaine to the ground. "Watch her," he commanded the nearby demons.

He picked up the chain. A jittery pocket watch was attached to it. He clicked it open, and it exploded. He fell back, blinded. Something tore across his back. He screamed, and a fleshy wing was crammed into his mouth. He spat it out and got to his feet.

"Let's go, Charles!" a woman called from overhead.

Charles? Malecoda forced his eyes open and looked about. Everyone was still lying on the floor of the trench, weakly trying to get to their feet. The demons who had been guarding him were asleep, but the most infuriating thing was that Elaine was gone.

Malecoda looked up. Charles was holding his watch. His clothes were clean. His skin glowed. His smile was content. He tipped his bowler hat. "Did it taste like crow?" he asked, then vanished from sight.

THE END

Acknowledgements

When I finished Infernal Fall, I knew there was more to this story but wasn't sure where it would go. This happens. We graduate school and look on to the next chapter. We may leave one career for another. Maybe we defeat a disease and find a life full of possibilities that days ago seemed impossible.

Sometimes the past finds its way into our thoughts, and sometimes it hurts. I wrote this book to give those who are struggling with the past hope for tomorrow. The sins of yesterday do not define us. We were made to shine. We were made for many things. Sins may dirty up our spirits, but they can be washed away, which means that we are not our sins. We are more than the evils that can pollute our hearts for a time.

While I look forward to Jesus's return, I know that He wants us to shine and to help others shine with us. Many people help me shine every day. This book wouldn't be what it is without others. I'd like to thank Jamie Chavez for her help with the developmental edit. Dawn Carter for the line edit. Descendant Publishing for the production of this book. The Kindlers, my wonderful critique group at Realm Makers, and my friends at Word Weavers.

All my friends and family are in my words. I look back on my many experiences to help bring stories to life. Don't fear the things in the past, but look to them and learn. Thank you for reading.

Sincerely,
Bryan

THANKS FOR READING

If you want to be one of the first to know about new releases and updates, sign up for our mailing list by visiting **www.descendantpublishing.com**. Scroll to the bottom of the page and fill out the form with your name and email.

Please leave a review for ***Almost Paradise***. Reviews go a long way in helping the authors you love get noticed by other readers. So if you enjoyed *Almost Paradise* please leave leave a review on Amazon and recommend it to friends and family. YOU are our greatest asset for spreading the word about EPIC stories!

ABOUT THE AUTHOR

Bryan Mitchell lives in Archdale, North Carolina with his wife and children. He is an Army Veteran and has a master's degree in computer science and a bachelor's degree in English. His debut novel, Infernal Fall, won the Realm Award for Best Horror. He is a member of Realm Makers and Word Weavers, which are Christian writer communities. Beyond higher education, he enhanced his storytelling abilities by attending Realm Makers conferences and the Novel Writing Intensive headed by Stephen James and Robert Dugoni. You can learn more about Bryan at www.bryantimothymitchell.com.

More from the Publisher

Continue your EPIC journey with more great reads...

Drafted

Book 1 in the Drafted Series

By: Tommie Michele

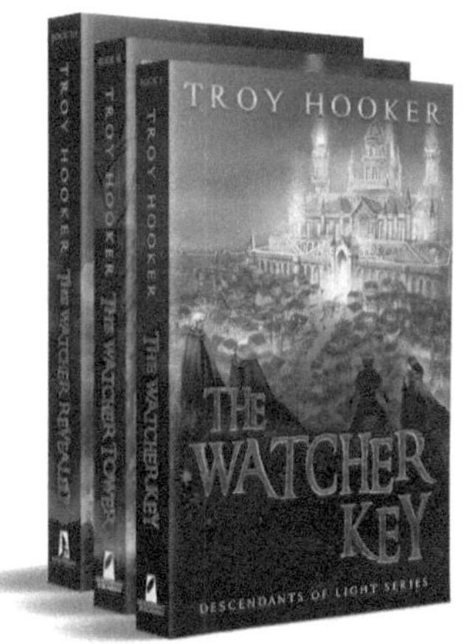

Descendants of Light Series

By: Troy Hooker

Book 1: The Watcher Key

Book 2: The Water Tower

Book 3: The Watcher Revealed

Look for more EPIC stories at:
www.descendantpublishing.com